THE CASCADE FACTOR

Hope you enjoy
Best Wish —
Bob Zen

The Cascade Factor

A Novel

Robert Zeisler

iUniverse, Inc.
New York Lincoln Shanghai

The Cascade Factor
A Novel

iUniverse, Inc.

For information address:
iUniverse, Inc.
2021 Pine Lake Road, Suite 100
Lincoln, NE 68512
www.iuniverse.com

ISBN: 0-595-29953-9 (pbk)
ISBN: 0-595-66086-X (cloth)

Printed in the United States of America

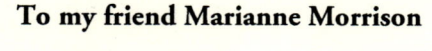
To my friend Marianne Morrison

Acknowledgments

Writing fiction means winding one's way through a labyrinth of characters' traits and motivations, locales and setting, dangerous circumstances and devious plot twists. The process often proves challenging, and I want to thank the many people who helped me navigate through the morass:

My top-flight "sounding board team" of Lisa Richards and Paul Sorensen who listened to endless ideas and patiently kept me on track and encouraged me when the maze proved frustrating.

Two "plot-gurus," Steven Feiger and Dr. Steven Fox, who suggested dramatic twists that streamlined the story and ratcheted up the suspense.

Diane O'Connell whose editorial skills transformed a manuscript into a novel. I couldn't have done it without her.

Many supportive readers—too many to mention individually—who offered their time to read drafts, highlight problems and share suggestions to make the book more compelling.

Thank you, all.

PROLOGUE

▼

CHICAGO. AUGUST 1968

"The whole world is watching"

The tension hovered over Grant Park, an ominous storm cloud inviting the first spark of lightning. This was the third straight night of demonstrations, each more violent than the previous. This is what he'd come for.

K.P. Forsythe and his friend Matthew McCalley had hitchhiked to Chicago to join the YIPPIES, the SDS, and thousands more protesting the Vietnam War at the Democratic Convention. One look at K.P.'s ratty clothes and long hair and the cops would label him a "peacenik" or a "flower child," but K.P. was neither. Younger and more radical than Matthew, he prided himself on a growing list of arrests. His arrests began almost three years earlier in December, 1964 at a Berkeley free-speech sit-in, when he was a just a freshman, and an aggressive cop roughed him up. From that point on, he adopted increasingly harsh anti-establishment views, a dogged resolve to stop the War, and an enmity towards those in power.

Matthew, on the other hand, presented a different picture, an idealistic single father with Marly, a six-year-old daughter, back home. The two men, however, shared strong views of the immorality of the Vietnam War and believed the brassy old bastards who supported it had to go—just like Lyndon Johnson.

K.P. and Matthew joined the protest and found themselves in the largest and most confrontational crowd yet. The violence came quickly. K.P.'s heart pounded as a bearded demonstrator in a tie-dyed shirt and threadbare jeans tore down the American flag, and the city's top cop ordered riot-control forces to clear the area. Commands blared from bullhorns as Grant Park turned into a battle zone. Twenty-five thousand police and National Guard troops marched solidly from three sides, cramming the protestors together—the fourth side being the Lake. K.P. had never seen that many pigs in one place, and all with anger flaming on their faces.

When the demonstrators resisted, police squadron leaders howled, "Grab your clubs and clear them out!" The police and National Guard troops, their arms whipping in huge arcs, attacked the protestors. Vicious blows crunched against flesh and bone alike, buckling knees and bloodying faces.

Anchored atop TV news trucks, glaring lights and live cameras captured the blows as angry cops pummeled the demonstrators. Meanwhile, behind the cameras, media-savvy young demonstrators waved signs and taunted the beleaguered police.

Determined to disperse the crowd, the cops charged K.P. and Matthew's group. The protestors screamed in agony as the police clubbed and shoved them. Explosive pops ricocheted off nearby skyscrapers, twice and three times, as teargas cylinders were fired and spewed clouds of choking gas.

Matthew grabbed K.P. by the arm. "Let's get the hell out of here," he yelled.

K.P. jerked back his arm, his eyes flashing, "No, No. Don't you get it?" he screamed. "The whole world is watching! We've got the pigs right where we want them."

Their discussion and delay proved costly. Two policemen knocked them to the ground. One impaled Matthew with his baton, driving it deep into his gut, yelling, "Get your punk ass out of Chicago." Matthew gasped for breath and spit up blood as K.P. crawled to him.

A few yards away, a TV truck became the center of a group of demonstrators endlessly chanting, "The whole world is watching. The whole world is watching."

K.P. assisted Matthew as they struggled to stand; their eyes wet and burning from swirls of tear gas. A National Guard squad, intent on stopping the TV images, closed in, joined by a pair of Chicago policemen wielding their riot batons like baseball bats.

K.P., red with anger, screamed in the cops' faces, "You're all fucking pigs!" The police responded. K.P. watched the policeman cock his arm and saw the roundhouse swing in time to dive out of the way. Matthew, beside him, did not.

With the benefit of velocity, the black oak struck Matthew's temple, first with the sound of cracking orange crates, then a soft tissue squish like thick mud yielding underfoot. The fracture traveled neck to forehead, opening a ragged fissure and oozing gray matter. Without brains to control them, limbs and joints buckled, and Matthew folded to the pavement, a scarecrow unhinged from its stake. A nearby TV camera recorded the brutal scene.

All three networks broadcast live from the protest. In California, a six-year-old girl named Marly played with her favorite "Dolly" in front of the television and idly scratched her hair just above the right ear. Then, when the noise and violence erupted, she turned to the TV and her childish face turned first confused, then horrified as she stared unblinking at the screen. She ran from the room hysterical and screaming, "Daddy! Daddy!"

CHAPTER 1

---▼---

CHICAGO. TUESDAY, OCTOBER 16, 2001. MIDNIGHT

Marly lay nude across the well-worked bed; her floral comforter wedged against the brass footboard, the crumpled sheets obscured by matching pillows. The musky perfume of sex filled her bedroom. Absently, she scratched at the hair over her right ear and stared at the ceiling, then mused about the evening, her fingers toying with a pair of purple silk scarves.

It had been a lust-filled night. She'd enticed Zack into acting out her fantasy; his role was an intruder, tying her up, threatening to ravish her, and forcing her into oral sex. Marly enjoyed experimenting. More than that, she adored Zack and sought to please him with ever more creative experiences. He'd left just minutes ago, but she missed him already, his scent and his sex, the security of his body next to hers.

A soft knock at the door interrupted her thoughts. He must have forgotten something, or better yet, returned for more. Her body tingled. She donned the purple scarves, positioning them to hang enticingly over her bare breasts.

"Encore?" she cooed as she swept open the door. Startled, seeing the twisted face that greeted her, she moved to cover her nudity, but was shoved backwards into the apartment. The offender grabbed her, holding her from behind. She struggled in vain. She tried to scream, but gagged when her attacker shoved a wadded handkerchief into her mouth. Her assailant used the scarves to tie her hands and feet so tightly the blood flow stopped.

Confused and terrified, her eyes cried, *Why?* Tears streamed down her face. She had to free her hands or feet, someway to escape, but the scarves were much too tight; her attacker saw to that. Already, her hands were blue and turning numb.

Please don't, she begged with her eyes. Panic surged through Marly, pouring adrenaline into her system. Her skin burned, her temples throbbed and her mind raced through endless, futile options. Kick! Scratch! She ordered her body, though she was unable to move her feet and barely able to wiggle her wrists. All the while, she wailed and screamed, yet knew no one would hear.

She felt the hands lifting her, her feet losing the floor. What is happening? Her fear soared. The balcony! *Oh, no. Oh, please no. Please no!*

Her assailant pushed open the balcony door, and yanked aside the sheer curtains.

Oh my God! Oh my God!

Marly twisted and squirmed, struggling for anything to scratch, grab, or poke. Her efforts were futile save a tiny piece of latex glove that lodged beneath a fingernail.

The cold October air burned her bare skin. "Help! Help! Please somebody help," she yelled, but no one could hear the muffled cries.

A hand reached for her face, and snagged loose the gag. A deadly kiss touched her cheek.

"Please…" a single word, a final plea.

The weightless, tumbling sensation consumed her. In slow motion she watched windows and walls somersault past and sensed the air being sucked from her lungs. If only her arms were free, she thought, she could deploy them as wings and glide gently to earth.

First, came an incredible, crushing impact—then, only black.

The murderer did not wait for the results, and raced to the stairwell, descended the twenty stories and escaped through the back door.

Meanwhile, a loud and chaotic crowd gathered around the broken body.

The assassin pulled the watch cap lower and with the back of a hand wiped away a flood of tears.

CHAPTER 2

▼

CHICAGO. WEDNESDAY, OCTOBER 17, 2001. 12:30 A.M.

What a night. Zack Dreyben had left Marly's chic, high-rise apartment just before midnight. As he often did, he'd brought along his devoted companion, Katie—a fluffy-tailed, brown and white mongrel with a princess attitude. Fortunately for Zack, Marly lived a mile and a half away, close enough to be convenient, but not so close as to prompt unexpected visits. He and Katie enjoyed the crisp mid-October air, as they strolled towards the Lake and home. Zack liked walking in the City at night. Noisy and snarled in daylight, Armitage Avenue, became a peaceful pathway at night lined with inviting, boutique windows. On their walk home, he and Katie took a brief detour to "the hill" behind the High School where dogs were allowed off their leashes to play and attend to nature's demands.

Ironically, Zack wasn't tired. In fact, he actually felt energized after making love to Marly. She was his best lover ever, always creative, but tonight, inspired. Smugly, he smiled as his hand went to two tiny scratches on his neck, and he allowed himself the pleasure of mentally replaying the night. Marly, eager for sex, wanted to leave the restaurant even before they'd finished their appetizers. When they returned to her apartment, she excused herself while Zack responded to Katie's usual tail-wagging welcome. Marly reappeared, clad only in a coy smile and two long, silk scarves draped around her neck and hanging enticingly over her breasts. She removed the scarves and teasingly wrapped them around him. He knew she enjoyed innovative sex. Tonight, she'd delighted in silky bondage.

A Chicago patrol car and EMS ambulance, lights flashing, sirens wailing, screamed past and jolted him back to the present. His curiosity piqued, he turned to watch. Before long they screeched to a stop somewhere up the street. He stared for a moment, hesitated, and then decided to follow the action.

He and Katie hustled, but it still took fifteen minutes to retrace their steps. When he joined the rapidly growing crowd, he found Marly's building the focal point of activity. Zack, enveloped by curiosity seekers and peering over shorter heads, saw a scarlet EMS blanket covering a body, and assumed it the victim of some foul play. He looked up to see Marly's apartment. The lights were on. The balcony doors were open, the sheer curtains floating in the wind.

Something was wrong, very wrong. Marly would never leave the door open and the curtains flailing about, too finicky for that. He thought he might edge through the crowd to the entrance and grab an elevator to the twentieth floor. However, two iron-faced cops had secured the double glass doors preventing anyone from entering or leaving unless they presented identification proving they were residents.

Now what? *Use the cell phone you moron*, and immediately punched the "mem" key and "2" to dial the number.

A nasally voice answered, "Harrison."

"Who?" Zack asked.

"Detective Harrison, Chicago PD. Who's this?"

"My name is Zack Dreyben. I'm calling my girlfriend, Marly McCalley," confident his memory-dialed call reached the correct number. Even as he talked, he felt his lungs tighten and his breathing become shallow. "I'm downstairs. What the hell is going on?"

"You'd better come up to 2015, right now. I'll clear it with the guys on the door. You tell 'em Harrison told you to come up."

Zack's heart exploded. "No, No, Oh, goddamn it, no," he mumbled. Dragging Katie by the leash, he muscled his way through the crowd to the door and the two cops.

"Harrison said to tell you it's OK," Zack blurted to the patrolman at the door.

"Yeah, OK. Go on up," the cop said, a wearisome "I wish I was anywhere but here" look in his eyes.

He and Katie dashed across the lobby past the first set of elevators to the second bank marked "15-25." He knew the rules. He should be using the freight elevator because he had Katie with him, but right now, he couldn't care less. He pressed the round plastic button, and heard the soft ding as the polished brass doors parted. Inside, he punched "20" without looking and waited impatiently for the doors to close. *Damned slow elevator.*

When the doors finally opened, he noticed the police had taped yellow crime-scene banners across Marly's doorway. Two men with badges looped over their belts approached him in the hallway. The gray-haired one wore a skintight polo and formed a stop-sign with a massive right hand. His face held scars, faded by a few decades; perhaps the signs of growing up Irish in a tough south side neighborhood.

"Name?" he asked.

"Zack Dreyben."

The man pointed a finger toward apartment 2015. "You know the woman that lives here?"

Zack recognized the voice from the phone, and figured this must be Detective Harrison, and probably the guy in charge. "Yeah, she's my girlfriend."

The Detective stared over half-glasses perched dangerously on a brawler's nose that must have caught its share of left-hooks. "Well, we have some questions for you."

"What the hell happened?" Zack asked.

"A woman fell. We think from this apartment. Can't tell ya' nuthin' more at this point."

"It wasn't Marly, was it?"

"McCalley? Not sure, but could be," the Detective said. "You know if she's got any family here?"

"No, I'm probably closer to her than anyone," his voice more steady than he felt.

"Think you can ID the body?"

Zack cringed at the nonchalant manner. He took a deep breath and for that moment it helped clear his head. "Yeah," he finally managed.

"We'll do that at the morgue later," the second detective added sidling closer to the conversation.

"Right now, we got a couple more questions," Harrison said. "When was the last time you saw her?"

"Just a little while ago. We went out for dinner, then came back here."

The other Detective frowned and glanced down at Katie. "Dinner with the dog?" This second cop was shorter and darker than his partner—Italian, or maybe Greek—and his coarse face carried a heavy five o'clock shadow. Both detectives wore casual clothes, but his were different—expensive, designer stuff. Zack saw the jacket logo and wondered, how the hell does a cop afford Yves Saint Laurent? And, he wore a jangling, gold Rolex, suspended by a gold band several links too long; he kept running his finger around and under the band.

"No, we left her here. She's fine here. We do that a lot."

"What time did ya' leave here?" Harrison asked.

"A little before midnight, I think."

The second Detective pulled his hand from his watchband and pointed to the fresh marks on Zack's neck. "How'd you get those scratches?"

Zack tensed. He felt the Detective's suspicion, but answered truthfully. "Marly and I were fooling around a little."

"Fooling around? What does that mean *exactly*? Sex? Any more scratches?"

"Maybe, I'm not sure," Zack said, and glared at his questioner. He didn't like this guy. Zack wanted to know how the accident happened. How and when did Marly fall? And, he wasn't learning any of that. He figured this overdressed cop must be one of those self-important pricks the Chicago PD was famous for.

"Where did you go to dinner?"

"*Glow*, the new Asian joint down the street about four blocks."

"Did the two of you fight tonight?"

"No, hell no," Zack answered, unable to hide his irritation. He remembered the small disagreement with Marly at dinner. It wasn't a big deal, and he let it go.

"You say you can identify the body?" Detective Harrison asked.

"Yeah OK, but I have to drop my dog off."

"OK, work with Stockano here," he said, at last identifying his partner. "No hurry though. It takes a while for the M.E. to finish up."

"M.E.?" Zack asked.

"Medical   Examiner...the   Coroner...the   morgue," Stockano quickly explained.

Harrison aimed a penetrating stare at Stockano, "OK. OK." Zack could see an uneasy tension between the two. Harrison reset his glasses with a hefty index finger, then faced Zack and said, "Oh, and by the way, I assume you'll be staying around...I mean not leaving town."

"Yeah, sure." Zack didn't think much about it. Understandably, there would be more questions.

Zack turned to leave, but Harrison stopped him with a firm hand on his arm. "One last thing, we need to get those clothes you're wearing for some tests, and, oh yeah, a blood sample. Stockano here will go with you."

"What? What the hell are you talking about?"

"Homicide forensics," Stockano answered, his finger again hooked under the Rolex.

Zack, his adrenalin pumping, finally comprehended. The questions...where they had dinner; when he left Marly's...Holy shit! They were lining him up as a suspect! His mind raced; he had to be careful. The cops would be watching for clues. How should he act? What would they be looking for? Sweat dripped from his forehead. He had just been tagged as a possible murderer! Fuck, what do they think they know?

CHAPTER 3

▼

CHICAGO. WEDNESDAY, OCTOBER 17, 2001. 2:30 A.M.

Zack dreaded this. He didn't trust Detective Stockano, and worse, he wasn't sure he could identify Marly's body and maintain his composure. He just wanted this over with. The morgue. The word sent shivers through him. He'd never been through anything so wrenching.

As Stockano settled behind the wheel of the unmarked sedan, Zack patted the vinyl seat urging Katie to jump in next to him. At Zack's condo, Stockano stared like a restless watchdog as Zack undressed and put his black turtleneck and pants in separate evidence bags. He wanted to shower, but Stockano demanded he wait, explaining it was official procedure. Zack dressed quickly in faded jeans, a checked shirt, and navy crewneck.

During the thirty-minute ride to the Coroner's facility, Stockano tried to engage Zack in more dialogue about what had occurred earlier in the evening. Zack, losing a struggle with his emotions, tuned out the Detective. He caught himself imagining what happened to Marly, the horror she must have experienced. His eyes filled, but he resisted sobbing. He forced the image from his mind, and steeled himself for the ordeal.

Stockano made a right turn into a driveway, past a cement pedestal with large blue letters identifying the "Cook County Medical Examiner's Facility" up to a new, single story building with an austere stucco exterior. High-intensity, sodium lights cast a ghoulish yellow glow over the empty parking lot. He parked in a visitor's slot near the door. The Detective pressed the buzzer and they waited only a minute for a uniformed county deputy to admit them. Stockano muttered something in the ear of the deputy who then quickly disappeared. They passed through the dark, unoccupied lobby to a beige door bearing a brown plastic sign identifying this as "Viewing Room A." Zack wondered if there could possibly be a "B" and even a "C?" Stockano went first and flipped a switch for the overhead light. The room, a white box the size of a large closet, reeked of chemicals, and Zack, afraid to touch anything, pushed his hands deep into his pockets. Stockano closed the door and motioned for Zack to step to a large window with drawn curtains.

The Detective coarsely explained. "This new facility is much better. It used to be you'd go into the autopsy room wrapped up in surgical garb and they'd pull the stiff out of the fridge and have you identify the corpse. A lot of folks, you know, just couldn't take that. Now, you stay in here; they bring the body over to the window and we open the curtains. You got as much time as you need. Make sure you're certain."

Stockano dimmed the lights in the viewing room and opened the curtains. On the other side of the window was a brightly lit, wholly white room with a variety of stainless steel sinks, cabinets, and medical equipment. An attendant wearing a lab coat, latex gloves and surgical mask rolled the specially designed, tray-like gurney to the window. A white sheet covered the cadaver except for the feet, an unreadable tag secured to the left big toe. The attendant pulled back the sheet exposing a chalky white torso. Zack couldn't handle it, the colorless, expressionless face; the eyes open and unseeing. He began perspiring. His throat tightened and he tried hard to swallow. The many broken bones mangled and contorted the image, but still he recognized her face. A sour taste backed up in his throat; he ran from the room and vomited.

When he returned, he confirmed the identification signing the form Stockano presented him. Zack, anxious to leave, returned to the Detective's car. Thankful to be outside, he inhaled fully, then exhaled driving the bitter air from his lungs, trying to erase the awful vision in his brain.

As they drove, Stockano resumed his questions focusing on the time Zack left Marly's apartment and probing for a possible reason for her murder. "Tell me again what time you say you left McCalley's apartment?"

Zack found the last-name-only reference irritating and irreverent. "Like I said before, just a little before midnight, I think."

"You're not sure?"

"Well, not exactly, but pretty close. I didn't check a clock if that's what you mean."

"So, it could have been later?"

"A few minutes, give or take, I guess, yeah. What the fuck are you getting at?" He'd been fighting tears for hours, pushing down the hollow pain inside. What did Stockano want from him? He was exhausted and emotionally drained, and

Stockano kept peppering him with questions. Why wouldn't this asshole leave it alone?

The Detective took his eyes from the road and glared at Zack. His expression hardened. "Just answer my questions. How long have the two of you been going together?"

"About three years or so. We started seeing each other in the summer of '98."

"How did you meet?"

"We both work at Magnicin, Inc. It's a computer company here in Chicago." He considered explaining more about the company, but he doubted Stockano really cared. Zack figured he was right before—just a prick cop, trying to prove he's a hard ass.

Stockano continued to look at Zack, dangerously ignoring the road. "What do you do there?" Their car wandered into the next lane cutting off the vehicle behind them. The driver flashed his lights and blasted the horn. Stockano flipped him off without a comment.

"I'm the V.P. of Sales and Marketing."

"And McCalley?"

"Director of Systems Development."

"Did dating someone at work cause problems?"

"We kept it quiet. We thought it better that everyone didn't know. Besides, it was none of their business."

"So you guys kept this a big secret?"

"Pretty much. I mean a couple of people knew like my neighbor Terry. And I think Marly told Lynne, one of the women who worked for her. But, that's about all."

"I thought you said no one at work knew?"

"Generally, yes, but Lynne and Marly were pretty good friends."

"What about McCalley's other friends?"

"Marly didn't really have many friends. She tended to keep to herself a lot."

"What about her family?"

"I don't think she has any family. At least, none that I know of. She once told me her mother died when she was just an infant, and Marly never knew her. I think she said her father died when she was really young, maybe six or seven, and her uncle Kevin raised her. But I haven't heard her talk about him for a long time either, so my guess is that he's probably dead, too. But, you guys can check that."

"No brothers or sisters—you're sure?"

He shook his head; he was sure. He and Marly were both alone. His Dad had sold life insurance, coached his peewee football team, and told Zack he dreamed of him winning a football scholarship. Unfortunately, a drunk crossed the median and ended their relationship. His mother, always unstable, regressed to her own childhood, and died within a year.

Difficult times like tonight revived the bad memories. Back then, a school counselor worked with him and he had the process down—it gave him distance from the pain. He mentally pushed the hurt into the box and visualized closing the door and locking it, suppressing the feelings. But the pain eventually returned. Even now, the emotions remained difficult and the recollections bitter-sweet. He swallowed hard.

He heard Stockano asking him a question, "Who would want to kill her?"

"I…have…no…fucking…idea!"

"No enemies? No one at work that didn't like her? No guy that she'd rejected?"

"Not that I know of."

"Tell me again about those scratches on your neck?" Stockano asked.

"I told you before, we were fooling around."

"Having sex?"

"Yes, damn it, having sex," Zack answered, wondering why the Detective was so fixated on sex? Did Stockano get some perverse kick from listening about other folks sex lives?

"Did you do that a lot?"

Zack took a deep breath. "Not that it's any of your damn business, but yeah we did."

"Did this sex get kinky?"

"What do you mean?"

"Did you ever tie her up?"

Zack flinched. What is with this guy? He remembered the silk scarves and how tonight Marly did want to be tied up. A bolt of lightning shot through his body. Oh fuck, of course, the cops found the silk scarves. But kinky sex? What do I tell him? If I admit that yes, tonight I did tie her up, what can he do about it? Anyway, why does it matter?

"Yeah. We tried for it for the first time tonight," Zack said. "She liked to try new things. When we were done, I untied her, and left for my place around midnight, like I said."

"What did you use to tie her up?"

"She had some purple scarves. I know it sounds weird, but it's really not all that strange," he said, trying hard not to sound defensive.

"I want to get this straight. You're saying you untied her. Is that right? Is that what you're telling me?"

"Damn it, Stockano. That's what I said, isn't it?"

Stockano's eyes widened and his right fist banged the steering wheel. "Bullshit! I don't think so. You know, she was found nude? She didn't jump off that balcony; she was pushed! Even more interesting, her ankles and wrists were tied— get this, with purple scarves, silk purple scarves. No sign of any struggle in her apartment, so she knew her killer well, very well, comfortable enough to be naked with him."

"Tell you what, smart guy," he continued. "We'll examine these with a microscope," he said jerking a thumb toward the back seat and the plastic bags with Zack's clothes. "My guess is we'll find purple silk threads on them, which means while she was naked, you were fully clothed. So much for your story about sexy bondage games; that story only washes if you're both involved, not if you're fully clothed and on your way out the door. Finally, I'm betting we'll find your DNA under her nails. She scratched you trying to save her own life, as you're tossing her over that balcony. So you put all this altogether. I'll tell you what I think. I think you're some kind of sexual sicko, getting your jollies by tying up the girl, fucking her brains out and then tossing her out twenty stories up. That's what I think. Go on pretty boy, guess who my number one candidate is."

CHAPTER 4

_____ ▼ _____

CHICAGO. WEDNESDAY, OCTOBER 17, 2001. 3:24 AM

Stockano pulled the Crown Vic' off Lake Shore Drive at the LaSalle exit and cut around the Park, barely slowing at three red lights and completely ignoring stop signs. Only a cop…Zack thought, but he wasn't complaining; the sooner he got home the better. He lowered his window for some fresh air. His energy and emotions were both past empty, and he felt a gob of hot coals lodge in his gut as Stockano grilled him during the confrontational drive back. Now, close to home, he fisted the door handle, his knuckles white, while he seethed at this fop's accusations. *Just get me the hell home.*

The detective pulled up and double parked in front of Zack's Lincoln Park condo. *Finally.* Zack wanted no parting pleasantries and immediately opened the car door, eager to escape Stockano.

The Detective, however, had words for Zack. "Listen Dreyben, don't even think about leaving the City. Just so you know, I'm not buying any of your horseshit. You and I both know you're up to your ass in this. It may take a couple days, but I'll get enough to make sure you get the needle. Understand? I'm sick and tired of you pretty, Lincoln Park perps thinking you can get away with shit just 'cause you got money. But, get this, I'm onto you! Get it?"

Zack, not trusting his emotions, turned and walked away. Twice now, Stockano had called him a "pretty boy," which struck Zack as odd because Stockano was wearing the designer labels and sporting the gold Rolex. Zack wondered if the attitude came with the badge, or was something else going on? He wanted to think more about that—tomorrow.

Zack unlocked and opened his townhouse door where Katie waited to welcome him. Exhausted and glad to be home, he sat on the hallway rug and hugged her, grateful for her tail-wagging love and affection. "Hi Katie. How's my Katie?"

She wiggled and squirmed her response. He kissed her head, and the tears rushed from his eyes, a tide of emotions unleashed. His wanted to call Marly for solace, but of course, he knew Marly was gone. He'd fought the tears for hours; now waves of loss, frustration, and anger swept over him. Katie instinctively cuddled close as he wept, his face buried in the comfort of her soft fur.

Zack wiped his hand across his face in a weak attempt to dry his eyes. An emotional night for a man not comfortable with emotion, whose sensitive moments seemed too often vicarious experiences, created from a poignant song or an Oscar-winning performance.

Marly, he was learning, had changed his life. Before Marly, he had separated his personal life from work. He met her his first day at Magnicin, and it surprised him when she took no overt note of him. Females did strange things around Zack. They would stare at his Latin color and riddling blue eyes, as if they could "wish" him over to them. Others would feign some lame excuse to speak to him. Marly did none of those things.

Attractive, but not eye-popping, she stood half a foot shorter than Zack, and trim, not wafer-thin. Her auburn hair curled forward and accented earthy eyes, traced by tiny lines from a quick-smile perkiness, suggestive of a morning news anchor. A desk nameplate said "Marilyn McCalley" and offered Zack an opportunity to ask how Marilyn became Marly.

Marly scratched over her right ear, smiled and explained, "When I was a toddler, friends would ask my name. I tried to say 'Marilyn,' but I couldn't get it right. It just came out 'Marly.' And, it stuck. So, now I go by Marly. But, it's cool. I like being different, you know?"

Until he met Marly, Zack had remained quite unattached, and happily so. Over the years, he'd had more than his share of relationships, but none approached a level he'd consider making permanent. Finding women had never been an issue; his captivating good looks and unpretentious charm saw to that. Cities seemed to produce an unending supply of "35ish" good-looking, horny women. However, after a few months they would tire of his inability to commit to a permanent arrangement and move on. Zack never grasped the importance of this permanent pairing ritual to the women he slept with. They would renounce the "June and Ward Cleaver" lifestyle, but seemed to long for just that. Of course, he knew all about the ticking biological clock, but the need to reproduce seemed an anachronism, a relic of the sixties—like Ward and June.

This pattern had one clear advantage. Zack didn't have to end any of the relationships; the women always did. Without fail, they would depart, lamenting that although he seemed bright, had great looks, performed ably in bed, and generally treated them well he "just doesn't get it." Zack would graciously accept the rebuke, and soon have a promising new relationship to enjoy.

At first, Zack resisted his romantic interest in Marly, but he instinctively sensed the chemistry. He believed all the old admonitions like "don't dip your pen in company ink" and more. This situation, though, seemed different.

Zack never dated women with Marly's brain power, and "smarts" didn't hit his list of required attributes. Marly had both undergrad and graduate degrees from Stanford, the computer geek's college. She'd earned a reputation in Silicon Valley for expertise in integrating computer circuits into industrial controls before moving to Chicago to take the job of Director of Systems Development for Magnicin.

From a business angle, Zack understood Magnicin needed top-notch technical talent to deliver on major contracts, and if Magnicin's growth strategy was to become reality, there had to be close cooperation between Marly's technical resources and his marketing team. Furthermore, Zack knew Marly wanted her first management role to be successful. So oddly enough, the traditional adversaries of sales and development commenced an unlikely partnership.

CHICAGO. SUMMER, 1998

July turned to August and the sensual chemistry continued growing between Marly and Zack, but their relationship remained business-like. The quick-hit success Zack expected had not materialized, and for the first time he began to have doubts. He rehashed each opportunity to find the key that would lock in the deal for Magnicin. Every night he watched the business news, so often dominated by two main subjects, the incredible rise in the NASDAQ market, and the growing concern about the year 2000 problem or Y2K for short.

He spotted Marly in the hallway outside his office. Today's eye-catching outfit was a coral-red suit, appealingly snug, with a pink blouse. "Hey Marly, come here," he called. "I've been thinking about something."

"Wow, that's pretty dangerous," she said with a devilish grin. Her heels were silent on the thick carpet as she strolled over and leaned a hip against his VP-sized desk.

"No damn it, I'm serious," he said.

"*OK, what?*"

"Tell me what you know about this Y2K stuff?"

She stood up straight, and her face turned thoughtful. "What do you want to know?"

"How big a deal is it?" he asked.

"Depends on who you talk to."

"Come on, what does that mean?"

"Well, some people believe everything will stop working at midnight the last day of 1999 because most of the computers in the world will be clueless when '99 becomes 2000. Other people think it won't be so bad. No one knows for sure."

"No, I mean how big a *business* deal is it?"

"I don't know. That's your area, *Mr. Vice President*," she teased. Zack never put much stock in titles, especially his own. "But, I do know that a lot of work is being done to check all the hardware and software to find any problems and fix 'em before then."

"How many computers are we talking about?" he asked.

"Thousands and thousands, at least. Again, it depends on what all has to be checked. The government and Wall Street are both pretty worried, though."

"Wall Street and the government?"

"Oh, yeah. I know the Street's analysts were on our CEO about Magnicin's Y2K readiness, because I got called into a meeting to discuss it. But, we're cool because we started updating our software over a year ago. I wasn't here then, but they got a good start, so we should be OK."

"And the government?"

"Empty suits…like they would know software from pig shit."

"What about our clients? How ready are they?"

"Hell, Zack, I don't know. What clients are you talking about?"

"Well, let's start with our best."

"Our best or our biggest?" she asked. They were the same to Zack, but apparently not to Marly.

"Who's the most vulnerable and needs the most help?"

"I'm not sure, give me a second." She scratched her head, squinted and stared at the ceiling. "My guess is the electric utility companies, and the Independent Operators that control electricity transmission across the country."

"Because?"

"A couple of reasons. One, nobody knows how bad their situation is. The North American electric power grid is just a jumble of interconnected companies. A lot of people think the grid was laid out logically. Duh! I mean, no way. It just grew. Now, it's a mess of wires, cables, transformers, sub-stations, and a bunch of generators. No one has a real top-down view and no one knows how big the problems are for sure. And, besides that, their computer staffs suck. Think about it. This is 1998. If you're a hotshot computer science grad are you going to work for a utility when you can sign up with a dot-com and maybe score millions on your options?"

"I see what you mean," he said.

"We do a lot of work for the utilities today, and it's heavy stuff. I'm not sure anyone on their side even gets it. They haven't been able to attract any talent in years. Hell, that's the reason they're our clients now."

He brightened. "So they need us. Need translates to business."

"I guess so, yeah, but how the hell would we even begin?" Marly worried.

"As you would say, that's more your area, *Ms. Systems Director*. Tell you what; meet me after work at Barney's? I'll buy you a drink. We can chat more about this. This could be the key I've been looking for."

Marly nodded her acceptance, waved, and continued down the hall. Zack's index finger tapped his chin, while his mind assessed the situation. What a perfect opportunity. Magnicin could serve existing clients who required a lot of technical resources; did not have the necessary expertise; had a small window of time; and best of all, money could not be a "stopper." After all, the electricity system for the country could be at stake.

*   *   *   *

In a city known for good restaurants, Barney's held its own as a trendy, upscale place in the financial district just a block north of the Board of Trade. Because of their location, they focused on lunch, but enjoyed a reasonable cocktail hour and filled about half their dinner tables on weeknights. The digital clock behind the bar showed six-even when Marly arrived. Zack had just finished his first Guinness. "What would you like?" he asked as he pulled another wooden stool away from the bar for Marly.

"A margarita sounds good."

"On the rocks or frozen? With or without salt?" the bartender asked.

"Rocks, with."

She turned to Zack, "Is this a planning meeting or a celebration?"

"Maybe both. I want to know more about the electricity grid situation. The way you described it, it sounded a little scary, like it's kind of fragile."

The bartender returned with a margarita on the rocks, sea salt clinging to the glass' rim and another pint of dark beer topped with the traditional thick head.

"Cheers," she offered and raised her glass to touch his. "Maybe I made it sound a little dramatic, but controlling the grid is tough enough without a complicating factor like this Y2K crap. Think about this. Thirty years ago, a blackout hit the northeast, affected 30 million people and resulted in a $100 million in losses—today that number would be in the billions. Of course, everyone got in an uproar, and the politicians—those worthless bastards—forced the utilities to get their shit together. All that led to NERC, the North American Electric Reliability Council whose job it is to ensure the reliability of the grid. Well, you know how well that's worked! We continue to have outages and each time there is a new explanation about how the power grid wasn't designed to prevent that particular type of problem. So, yeah, it is fragile. But, no one's got the balls to admit that."

Zack raised his hand, palm up. "So what about the Y2K problem?"

"Like I said, just one more complicating factor. Maybe I can explain it this way." She borrowed a pen from Zack's pocket, unfolded a cocktail napkin and sketched an outline.

"This is the grid," she said pointing to her diagram. "Activity on the grid is controlled through switches that engage or disengage portions of the grid, substations, transformers, etc."

Placing a number of "X's" on the outline she continued, "Look, the new generations of switches are controlled by integrated circuits so that monitoring and control can be done remotely. They're called PLCs or Programmable Logic Controllers. I worked on PLCs when I got out of grad school. The problem is that each of the computer circuits has to be verified as Y2K compliant—meaning the change from 1999 to 2000 won't cause it to malfunction."

She paused as her hand absently scratched her hair. "Checking any one PLC is not too big a deal. The problem comes from the fact that there are thousands and thousands of these controls scattered throughout the transmission facilities, control points, substations, and so on. No one organization is responsible for them, and as far as I know, there is no unified list. Just identifying and locating all the PLCs is a ton of frickin' work, and then every one has to be checked for Y2K compliance."

"So the challenge is more than just the technical issues, it's also a huge project management problem?"

"Yeeeaahhh."

"But, isn't that what we do?" Zack asked.

"Not on this scale."

"But, we're as prepared to attack a technical and project management job as anyone in the business."

"But like…"

"If Magnicin with all our resources doesn't solve the problem, who will? You've already told me they're not competent to pull it off themselves."

She sipped her margarita. "You *are* persuasive. I guess that's why you have the job you have."

"Then you'll help me put together a plan to go after this?"

"Yeah, sure." She flashed a devious smile. "Why not? If we pull this off, it's a full employment program until January, 2000."

He beamed with enthusiasm. "Good, we start the planning tomorrow. Let's finish this drink here at the bar, then I'll buy you dinner."

"Yeah, OK. Cool. I'm starving."

They were seated in a booth along the right wall and across the room from the closest occupants. A starchy, white tablecloth dressed the table, and linen napkins adorned decorative china plates.

Nearly deserted, the spacious room was unnervingly quiet until their waiter approached with long menus, and described the house favorites, tonight's specials and suggested wines. He gave them a few minutes to decide.

The silence resumed. Zack noticed Marly, her hand buried in her hair, seemingly deep in thought and asked, "What are you thinking about?"

"Oh nothing, just some stuff I have to do, that's all," she said. The waiter returned saving her any further explanation.

Zack deferred to her and she selected a Caesar salad and grilled sea bass. His choice was tonight's special; a cracked-pepper encrusted filet mignon, medium rare, with fresh asparagus. He also chose a Sonoma Valley Chardonnay, with a buttery flavor appropriate for her seafood selection.

Over dinner and wine they chatted effortlessly. Marly surprised Zack, explaining the phrase "Windy City" originated as a reference to the locals bragging about their City and not the breezy weather. While the conversation remained light, the intensity heightened. Several times one of them would look up, only to find the other staring back. Their eyes would catch before one would quickly look aside.

When they finished their dinners, Marly admitted an obsession for dark chocolate convincing Zack to share the house signature dessert "Sweet Ecstasy." Both ordered coffee—she cappuccino and he decaf.

Until now Zack had resisted his romantic interest in Marly. Her fingers were rimming the cup when he reached over and touched her hand. "Tell me more about Marly."

She looked at his hand on hers. "There isn't much interesting to tell."

"What do you think about? What are you passionate about?"

Marly paused, then said, "Let's just enjoy tonight. It looks like we're going to have lots of time together." Then she whispered, "It'll be fun."

"OK. We'll concentrate on tonight." He gazed at her as his hand, still on hers, began probing, exploring, his fingers entwining with hers. Their eyes locked, and the words ceased, but an unspoken communication continued. They had crossed a threshold.

CHAPTER 5

––––––––––– ▼ –––––––––––

CHICAGO. WEDNESDAY, OCTOBER 17, 2001. 12:00 P.M.

Lynne Rydahl tucked the blonde wisp back behind her left ear. Cautious by nature—even more so since her divorce from a too-early marriage and a wandering husband—she wore only a trace of lip gloss, though her complexion, natural and clear, would benefit from color. She slumped in the high-back, desk chair, her model's body half-hidden by stacks of clutter, while the aroma of strong coffee wafted from an insulated cup buried in the muddle. Her hand unconsciously occupied the left side of her face, the thumb under her jaw and the middle two fingers slowly massaging in front of her ear. She began to feel nauseous and folded her slender arms over her stomach thinking it might help her feel better. For a while this morning, she'd debated staying home, but thought she should be seen around the office, and so had come to work.

The morning dragged with endless conversation and fruitless speculation. Left to their collective imaginations, the hallway gossip bugs were rehashing old rumors and generating new ones. Lynne checked to make sure the police had released nothing new. The morning reports all said the same thing: "A north side woman fell to her death just after midnight. Her death is listed as suspicious, but no details are yet available."

An unexpected knock startled her and she straightened. Two men, strikingly different in appearance, stood in the open doorway. The older, taller one in a traditional shirt and tie had a wrinkled navy sport coat with gray slacks. His left hand repeatedly rescued the tiny wire glasses perched precariously at the end of a bumpy nose. His third finger wore a braided gold band. The younger man, with the dark complexion, dressed like a *GQ* model in a camel, suede blazer, dark brown patterned trousers and a silk dress shirt with two buttons open. His right index finger relentlessly polished the band on a conspicuous gold Rolex.

"Miss Rydahl?" the older man asked. "I'm Detective Harrison and this is Detective Stockano. Do you have a minute? We'd like to ask you a few questions."

"OK," she agreed, but inside hoped this wouldn't take long. The last people she wished to talk to were the police. Her idle left hand reclaimed her face, the two middle fingers stroking her cheek.

"We'd like to ask you about Marly McCalley," he said. "You worked for her here at Magnicin, correct?"

"Yes."

"Can you describe your relationship with Ms. McCalley?"

"She was my boss." The less she volunteered, the better, she decided. Let them ask if they wanted more.

"How long did you know her?"

"Since she joined the Company in '98."

"What can you tell me about her?"

She shifted in her chair, then placed her hands together on the desk. "Hard worker, very conscientious, dependable."

"Did you spend time with her socially?" he asked.

"Sometimes. We'd meet for drinks on a Friday night or go to a movie or something."

"Did she have lots of friends?"

"Not really. She mostly kept to herself. It took a while to get close to Marly. Once you knew her, though, she was a good friend, and fun to hang out with."

"In what way?"

"She had a good sense of humor."

"What makes you say that?"

"She'd tease people, give 'em gag gifts. You know, as a joke."

"Who did she give these gifts to?" Stockano asked.

"Members of the staff and sometimes Zack Dreyben, our Marketing V.P."

Stockano's eyebrows lifted. "Really? How often?"

"Usually at office parties, celebrations, things like that."

"Can you give us an example?" Stockano pressed.

"Let me think." She paused for a moment. "She liked to kid Dreyben about his limited technical skill. I remember one time; he had just won a big contract with one of the electric utility companies. Marly handed out some gag gifts, and she had this giant switch with two big arrows on it, pointing in opposite directions. One said 'ON' and the other 'OFF.' Marly explained to everyone that she created it especially for Zack so he could understand the technical details of the client's business."

"How did he take that?"

"OK…I guess. We laughed. You know, just Marly's way of poking fun."

"She was brought in as your boss?" Detective Harrison asked.

"Yes. Marly was the Director of Systems Development. I am a Major Projects, Team Manager."

"You were working here before she came?"

Lynne knew exactly where Harrison was going. She took a sip of coffee and quickly replied, "Early on, we were competitive. Although we each played it close to the vest for a couple months, we worked through it. Marly and I were professionals. We had some initial friction, but I never had a smarter, more even-handed boss than Marly. I'm going to miss her. And, yes, before you ask, we *were* friends."

"Who will get her position now?"

She pushed her hair from her face. "I have no idea."

"Would you be a candidate?"

"Yeah, I should be."

Stockano asked the next question. "You mentioned Zack Dreyben before, what can you tell us about him?"

Lynne eyed the second Detective with aversion. It was the second time she'd caught him staring at her chest. "Detective, my face is up here," she said evenly, and then continued. "Dreyben's OK. He's a salesman. You know the type, smooth talker, good looks. He says he's a 'simple marketing guy.' That's probably as good a description as any."

Stockano frowned and stared at Lynne. He leaned forward in his chair, elbows on knees. She thought that maybe she'd been too blunt. "What can you tell us about Dreyben's relationship with McCalley?" he asked.

"They were dating," she answered cautiously.

"We understand that it was more than just dating."

"OK," she replied, and watched for the detectives' reaction to see where this was going.

"Miss Rydahl, we need your cooperation," Harrison said. "Please tell us what you know about their relationship."

"They have been seeing each other for a long time, maybe two or three years."

"Did they have an intimate affair?" Stockano asked.

Lynne grew weary. "They were dating for over two years. What do you think?"

"Could you please answer the question?"

"From what Marly told me, they had a very healthy sex life."

"Just a few more questions," Harrison said. "Do you know anyone who might have a grudge against Ms. McCalley, or have a reason to harm her?"

"Nope, not a soul. Anyone who knew Marly liked her. That's about all I know."

Harrison picked up on Lynne's dismissive tone and took the glasses from his nose, "Anything else you can tell us?"

"I don't think so."

Harrison reached in his pocket. "Here's my card. Please call us if you think of something. It's important. We haven't released any details about McCalley's death, but you've probably guessed. She didn't just fall from that balcony. Right now, no one is above suspicion and no one is safe."

Lynne froze. Those words…"No one is above suspicion and no one is safe." What did he mean?

Lynne showed the Detectives to the door agreeing to call them if anything came to mind. She was shaking when she sat back down.

CHAPTER 6

---▼---

CHICAGO. TUESDAY, OCTOBER 18, 2001. 11:00 A.M.

Detective Jimmy Stockano paced in front of Rob Harrison's embattled old desk at the Eighteenth District. "I say bring him in," Stockano said. "Hell, this gives us everything we need," he said, waving the freshly faxed autopsy report. "It's all here in this fax." When Stockano got excited, he had that irritating habit of saying things twice.

"Jimmy, I don't agree. We have to make sure." As the Chicago PD Detective in charge of the investigation, Rob would make the call. "I know we have opportunity and means, but damn it, we got no motive."

"I tell you, Rob, the guy's a sicko. He got his kinky jollies from tying up the broad, screwing her silly, and then snuffing her out. He just picked a new way, the balcony. You know tying her up and tossing her over."

"But, we got nuthin' to prove that."

Stockano stopped pacing and turned to Rob, "OK, let's go over what we got. One, the forensics guys found fibers matching the silk scarves on his clothes. His story that she wanted to be tied up doesn't hold water because he still had his clothes on. Maybe, maybe, I could buy his story if they were both naked, but not when he's still in street clothes. Then we got this autopsy saying she died from the fall, not something that happened in the apartment, and nothing was messed up in there, no struggle at all. Who else could get her butt naked and tie her up if it wasn't her boyfriend? Besides, they found his DNA under her fingernails. And on of top of all that, his semen in her throat and stomach that had not reacted with digestive acids. That means she blew him within the last few minutes before she fell. That's a mighty small window of time. Who else could have been there within that short of time frame? It don't add up. It just don't add up."

Rob nodded that he understood, but he hadn't changed his mind.

Stockano pressed his case, "OK, let's take his side," he said, waving his arm. "Say they had sex just like he says. I'll give him a break and say maybe he's even telling the truth about her and those scarves. But, that's where his story falls apart. Remember, he said he untied her before he left? Well, if we buy that, then we have to also believe that from the time they had sex until she died—just a couple of minutes—someone else got into her place; convinced her to let him tie her up—remember no struggle—and tossed her over the balcony; and then left; all within a couple of minutes. And, there is no trace of anyone else's DNA under her nails. Rob, it don't make sense. I mean no way does it make sense."

Harrison rolled back from the desk, the sticky old casters howling unhappily. "I hear ya', but it's all circumstantial. You still got no motive. Why the hell did he want to kill her? There's no money issue that we've come up with. There's no jealousy or anything else like that that we know about. There's no indication of a fight. Hell, the people near them in the restaurant hardly noticed them. If they were having a fight serious enough to make the guy kill her, I think that would be a pretty noticeable fight. And you said it yourself, there was no sign of struggle in her apartment—nothing knocked over or even pushed aside. As to your idea that he is just some sicko, we got no evidence of that. He's got no record of any kind of deviant behavior. We checked his place, no sex toys, not even any porno. Hell, if this guy's a sicko, he's the goddamn cleanest sicko I ever seen."

Rob Harrison wanted to end this debate. He had made his decision and they had more work to do. "But, you know what Jimmy? What bothers me the most is the tiny trace of latex they found under her nails. I don't know what it means, but I can't get it out of my mind. Anyway, before we charge him, I want a motive. Let's talk to him again. If we can come up with a motive, believe me, I'll be the first to run his ass in."

*   *   *   *

Rob felt the tension twisting his neck and shoulders. The tabloid nature of the woman's death had ratcheted up the media, and in turn, public opinion. The papers were calling for an immediate arrest. Satellite trucks and reporters were literally following him, but Rob wanted clear evidence before arresting anyone. If he made a mistake and fingered the wrong man, that man would forever wear the stigma of a sexual predator, and Rob refused to do that; he had to be sure. He had always been a careful cop, and he couldn't help but wonder what his Dad would do. Rob's father retired from the police force in 1988. Rob Senior's proudest and darkest moments as a cop both came in 1968. He'd donned riot gear, carried his nightstick and marched with his buddies into Grant Park to break up the hippie protests at the Democratic Convention. He'd dodged nail-spiked tennis balls and piles of human waste the punks threw at him, while the TV cameras only showed one side—the police beating the demonstrators. Worst of all, the city administration left the cops holding the bag, claiming they'd acted without orders.

Rob Senior had thirty honest years of service; he'd done his job and kept his nose clean. Young Rob, as far back as he could recall, wanted to follow his Dad and be a Chicago cop. He figured it was in his blood. Dad, however, demanded he get an education. Rob Junior even remembered once, his Dad getting his Irish up and saying, "I don't care. I didn't have a choice. You do. You can be a cop or anything else you want, *after* you go to college. But, you *are* going to college if I have to kick your butt all the way to the schoolhouse door." Rob remembered worrying at the time because money was tight and no way a cop's salary could support the family *and* send him to school. However, as the family's faith would have it, Rob Jr. became a gifted athlete and eventually earned a full-ride at, of all places, Notre Dame—an Irish kid's dream.

Rob resolved that regardless of the media attention, he would handle this investigation fairly, no easy answers. He also knew the pressure would only increase until he'd made an arrest. He and Stockano had to work fast. Unfortunately, Rob felt the growing tension with Stockano. Jimmy seemed too ready to reach a conclusion and then force the facts to fit that conclusion. Rob decided he'd have to keep a tight rein on Stockano as they stepped next door to the interview room to question Zack Dreyben again.

*   *   *   *

Zack was pacing the perimeter of the tiny room. A steel rectangular table and four folding chairs added to the starkness of cement block walls and gray vinyl flooring. Frosted windows and plastic mini-blinds, extended down one wall, and an industrial-style fluorescent light buzzed overhead. In the center of the table, a fat cigar butt leaned against the side of a plastic ash tray.

Rob motioned for him to take a seat and watched with a detective's eye. Zack's tie was loose, the collar of his blue shirt dark with sweat. His eyes flashed around the room. He sat erect, and nervously jiggled one leg making the metal chair squeak.

Rob decided to push. Details, details. Sometimes the smartest perp would give himself away because he couldn't keep his lies straight.

"OK, let's go over the facts again," Rob began. "What time did you go to dinner?"

"Like I said before," Zack said, "I think we left Marly's place about nine o'clock."

"And, where did you go to eat?"

"*Glow*, an Asian place three or four blocks from her place. We both liked Chinese."

"What did you have?"

"Give me a second to remember," he said. "We split an order of egg rolls. She ordered lemon chicken and I had Szechwan shrimp."

"How long were you there?" Rob quickly continued.

"Hell, I don't know for sure, maybe an hour. We were talking and it's tough to remember exactly."

"Then what?"

"We went back to her place."

"Tell me again about what happened when you went back there."

"OK, one more time. When we walked in, I got down on the floor to say hi to Katie, my dog, while Marly went to the bathroom. Next thing I know, Marly is standing in front of me wearing nothing but those two purple scarves, draped around her neck, you know?"

"Keep going," Rob urged.

"Well, she asked me if I liked what I saw, and of course, I said hell yeah! Then she kind of sexy like, slipped the scarves off, rubbed them on her boobs and then wiped them on my chest."

Rob's suspicion-radar went off. Dreyben's story sounded cold and remote like a *Penthouse* letter, not like someone whose lover was murdered.

"OK, then what?"

"Then she asked if I would like to try something new."

"What does that mean?"

"Well, I wasn't sure at that point, but she said it might be fun to try a little mild bondage, and what did I think."

"What did you say?"

"To be honest, I thought it sounded kind of sexy. We'd never done anything like that, so yeah, I said sure, thinking, why not."

"Go on."

"Could I get some coffee or water or something?" Zack asked.

"In a minute. Keep going." Rob didn't want to give him time to think.

"OK, so after I said yeah, she started undressing me because she said I had way too many clothes on. Then when I was naked too, we went into the bedroom."

"So all this happened in the front hallway?"

"Yes, like I said, I just walked in the door and got on the floor to see Katie."

"OK, so then what happened?"

"We were playing around on the bed and she asked if I'd like to tie her up."

"OK. Keep going."

"So I did. We agreed that if she really didn't like it, she'd just say 'enough' and we'd stop. But, she never said it. She wanted her arms tied to the headboard, her legs spread-eagled, and feet tied at the bottom of the bed."

"Then what?" Rob asked.

"Well, it got pretty wild. You gotta remember, Marly was a sexy woman. In fact, our best times were in bed."

Stockano interrupted, "What exactly did you do?"

"You mean sex wise? Is it really important to go over that?" Zack stared at the two cops and asked, "Why are you so interested in the sex details?"

Stockano returned the stare and said, "Just answer the questions."

"OK, but talking about it, is really weird, you know, especially now. Since she was tied up, I tried to tease her to get her excited, you know? So, I tickled her a little and then I started kissing her all over—if you know what I mean."

"No, tell me," Stockano ordered.

"I went down on her, OK?" Zack said edgily.

"You performed oral sex on her?" Rob clarified.

"Yeah."

"OK, then what?"

Zack shifted his eyes toward the table, away from Rob. "Well, I climbed on top and had intercourse with her."

"She's still tied up?" Stockano asked, sounding disgusted.

"Yeah."

"What then?"

"I untied her and we cuddled for a while and then she went down on me."

"She performed oral sex on you?" Rob again verified.

"Yeah."

"Did you climax from both intercourse and oral sex?" Stockano asked.

Zack paused for a moment and glared at the Detective. "Yeah. Marly could always make me come a couple of times."

"Yeah, sure, sure," Stockano said.

Rob decided to take over the questions. "Then what?"

"It was getting late, so I said I had to go."

"What time was that?"

"Eleven-thirty or so."

"Keep going. What happened?"

"She asked me to stay a little longer, which I did until about eleven-forty-five or thereabouts."

"OK."

"Then I kissed her and got up and got dressed."

"What about her? Did she get dressed?"

"Nope, but that wasn't surprising because she slept in the nude."

"Then what?"

"I kissed her goodbye, put Katie on the leash and let myself out."

"What time again?"

"Shit, for the umpteenth time, a little before midnight as best I can remember!"

"She never got out of bed?"

"No, she just kissed me goodbye and told me to lock the door."

"Did you?"

"Actually, it locks itself. I didn't double lock it because I didn't have a key."

"You don't have a key to her place?" Stockano asked.

Zack turned toward Stockano. "I have one at my place for emergencies, but I don't carry it around."

"OK, what then?" Rob asked.

"I walked with Katie to the back section where the freight elevator is because dogs aren't allowed on the regular elevators.

"So you didn't take one of the passenger elevators?"

"No, like I said I had Katie."

"Keep going."

"There isn't much more. We took the elevator to the ground floor and then went out the side exit cause they don't like dogs in the lobby and started walking home. We were twenty minutes or so down the street when I heard all the commotion and I decided to walk back and see what was going on. That's when I called Marly's place on my cell phone and you answered," he said to Rob.

"What time was all this?"

"Well, I left just before midnight. We walked for maybe twenty minutes or so, but we stopped at "the hill" behind the high school for Katie to pee. So it probably took half an hour, I'd guess."

Rob's finger edged his half-glasses back over the hump on his nose, "So, your story is that you left before midnight and didn't come back until you called me on the cell phone?"

"That's right," Zack answered.

"Did the two of you have a fight?"

"No, not really. We had a minor disagreement at dinner, that's all."

"What about?"

"Marly seemed particularly horny and wanted to leave the restaurant early. She said she had a special plan for the night, but I wanted to finish dinner. That's all, no big thing."

"Did you guys ever fight about other men or other women?" Rob asked, searching for a motive.

"Nope. We were starting to get serious about each other. You know it started out as just great sex, but the last couple of months we were getting a lot closer. Neither of us wanted to see anybody else."

One thing bothered Rob about Zack's story. He didn't mention how he got the scratches on his neck and chest. Rob knew McCalley had Dreyben's DNA under her nails, and the question remained, how and when did she scratch him.

"One last item, what about those scratches? You didn't mention them. Tell us again how that happened? Didn't you tell us that the *first* thing you did was tie her up?" The apparent breach in Zack's story could support Stockano's conclusions.

Zack shifted uneasily on the metal chair. "OK, OK, but you gotta understand we were play-acting. Being tied up was only one part of her idea. Her fantasy included seeing a stranger who had broken into her apartment, planning to attack her. So before I tied her up she kind of wriggled and tussled and begged me to please stop—all make believe, all part of her fantasy for the night. I told you before about Marly's creativity in the sex games department. Anyway, that's when she scratched me."

Stockano sighed. "Your story just gets better and better."

Rob shot a piercing look at Stockano.

"It's the truth. She liked to play make believe sex games. I've said that from the start."

Rob removed and folded his glasses. "All right. Here's where we are. You're the last person to see her alive, as best we know—nobody else around. You admit to tying her up and having sex with her, and we know she died shortly after she performed oral sex on you. We have traces of the silk scarves on your clothing. There's no indication of struggle in her apartment meaning she knew her killer.

But right now, that's all circumstantial and we don't have a motive, so we're not going to formally charge you...yet. Don't try to leave the city unless we tell you it's okay. I'll be honest; right now, you're the number one suspect. If you have any clue as to who did this you had better tell us damn quick, because the way this is going, you're facing first degree murder!"

CHAPTER 7

$$\blacktriangledown$$

CHICAGO, SEPTEMBER 1998

Marly was running late. Zack waited by reading the plaque on the door of the "Theseus" conference room—cleverly named conference rooms being one of those things big companies do to deliver subliminal messages. The plaque explained the mythical hero Theseus possessed exceptional skill and wisdom, and solved the riddle of the labyrinth.

Zack glanced around. The perfectly square room had the latest electronic glitz including a wall-mounted plasma display for executive presentations. Too bad Theseus' wisdom didn't rub off on the folks who sat here in meetings. A round oak table focused a half dozen leather chairs, each with laptop connections that allowed meeting participants to log-on, or tune-out, during meetings. Zack re-checked the clock, 9:15. Where the hell was Marly?

He heard her voice from the hallway. "I know, I know. I'm late. I'm sorry. I got caught in a crisis. Our frickin' intranet went down, but everything's back now." She walked in looking a little disheveled—unusual for Marly. She wore an expensive, business-like navy suit; white silk blouse and a provocatively short skirt.

Zack didn't understand about their intranet, but nodded his acceptance, as he sat in one of the leather chairs and motioned for Marly to do the same. He expected an update on the Y2K plans and he wanted to get on with it. "I need to understand exactly what we can commit to before we engage the customers."

"Good idea, and a nice departure from the usual sales approach."

Zack smiled but suspected Marly intended the jibe to send him a message that their's was a partnership, not a typical business relationship. "Do we need anyone else to sit in?" he asked.

"I don't think so, at least not yet. When we get to how we're actually going to do the work, I'll probably ask Lynne Rydahl to join us. This is going to be a huge frickin' project and we'll need our best talent."

"OK, that's obviously your call, but I'm surprised. I thought you'd said there was some tension between you two."

Marly shifted uneasily in her chair and fussed with her hair. "You're right. It's like there's something going on, you know? She thinks she should have gotten my job, but she's a good techie."

"Like I said…that's your decision. Let's talk about what you've learned about the power grid and what the problems are."

"Are you sure you're ready for this?" Marly asked.

"Why, what's up? If there's a problem, let's hear it. The only way we're going to win this Y2K business is by demonstrating our expertise in generation and transmission. I'm assuming we can do that." He intended to send his own message. This wouldn't be a project where the techies sat back and waited for the marketing guys. They were in this together. "I'll get the clients into the room, but you've got to wow 'em."

"OK, here's the straight shit. We're in trouble. It's already September '98. That gives us just over a year. It's simply not enough time. Besides, we don't even have a contract yet. I've been working my ass off learning as much as possible, but we can't do shit until the clients give us a go ahead."

"Tell you what, let me worry about getting the clients lined up." He knew the deals were close. Didn't she have enough to worry about with the technical stuff? Why do techies always get into shit that doesn't concern them? "I'm close to signing a couple deals right now. The good news is the top management in the utilities is feeling the heat from the media. They'll have to make decisions soon."

"OK, but I have a suggestion. I think you should try to leverage NERC, the North American Electric Reliability Council. You know how I hate government councils and bureaucrats, but NERC's sole mission is the reliability of the grid. The best people from the utilities and transmission companies staff NERC's committees. If you can get them committed, you'll have the whole industry lining up. Otherwise, you'll be spinning your wheels working one company at a time."

Marly was right. "Good idea. I'll contact them today, but I still need an update on what you've learned before I talk to them."

"I've done a ton of work on their Y2K situation. We have a lot to go over, but if I'm going to cover all this, I should have Lynne sit in. Otherwise, I'll have to do it twice. I'll call her." She pushed the speaker button on the conference room phone, waited for the dial tone, and punched in Lynne's extension.

"Lynne Rydahl," the voice answered.

"Lynne, this is Marly. Zack Dreyben and I are in the Theseus conference room. Can you come down and join us?"

"Sure, I'll be there in just a minute."

Her office nearby, she arrived quickly, nodding to them as she slid into a chair next to Zack. In contrast to Marly's business suit, Lynne's loose sweater-and-slacks look seemed more "assembled" than "coordinated" and kept secret any feminine shape. Minimal makeup and unstyled blonde hair failed to highlight her high cheekbones and steely blue-gray eyes.

Zack started, "We're looking at a huge opportunity, and probably the most important project Magnicin has ever worked on."

"OK. What's the deal?" Lynne asked.

Marly stood, and walked the room. "Zack and I are working on a major services contract doing Y2K work for the electric utilities and power transmission companies."

"What? You're kidding."

"And, we have a ton to do and almost no time to do it," Marly said.

"Hello? Do you guys know it's 1998 already?"

"Yeah, of course, we know."

"And, the clock is ticking," Lynne added.

Zack interrupted, "But that's just the reason it's an opportunity. Because the utilities are short on both time and talent."

"Exactly," Marly said. "Those guys are between a rock and a hard place. We may be their only hope."

"But, those losers are lucky if they can find the power switch on their computers."

"That's why we have to get our shit together quickly. Lynne, you and I have to be utility experts in just a few weeks."

Lynne's eyes widened. "Marly, come on. What are you guys smoking? Do you know how much work you're talking about?"

"Sure, damn it, but I also know you and I can do it."

Zack said, "Let's hear Marly's plans."

Marly drew two large circles on a flip chart and began explaining her ideas. "I've been thinking about how we should start. I say we divide and conquer. Lynne, your team has already been doing work for the utilities on their mainframe side, right?"

"Some, yeah."

"OK, you and your team will take the data centers including mainframes and minis. Before I came here, I worked a lot with programmable controls, so I'll take this half, the distributed switches and controls," she said as she labeled the two circles.

"What exactly are we doing?" Lynne asked.

"Well, first we have to get our arms around this beast. We need to have a complete topology, you know a schematic, of the North American power grid. There are four major interconnections, Eastern, Western, Texas, and Quebec. Your team will start by locating all the generator sites and transmission substations, and then trace the high-voltage lines all the way to the power substations. I think we can stop there, though, and not worry about the local transformers and lines."

Zack watched Marly demonstrating why she got her job, combining project level perspective with line item details. But, he also noticed the tension between the two, and wondered if Lynne really was on-board.

"Once we have all that, we can superimpose all the computer systems, control centers, programmable switches and so on. I know it's a ton of frickin' work, but as far as I have been able to learn, that top-level view doesn't exist anywhere. Without that schematic and a detailed plan, there's no frickin' way the utilities can ever be ready in time."

"Marly, you're talking about solving world hunger in three or four weeks."

Zack heard the irritation in Lynne's voice.

Marly said, "I know, but we can do it. We'll use the 'Hermes' conference room by my office as our project center, and keep an updated status on the white board."

Taking a slow deep breath, Lynne looked expectantly at Zack who said nothing. "OK, OK, I'll have my guys start pulling everything we've got on all the generation stations and computer sites we can find. After that, we'll call our contacts to flesh out our grid diagram. How will we ever get all the way down to the local substations, and worse yet, identify all those computerized controls and switches?"

"Do we have to worry about that now?" Zack asked.

"Yeah, she's right," Marly said as she sat down. "I wish I had an easy answer for that. That's the one area I'm worried about. But, I think we can put a team of people on it and just have them systematically follow each high-voltage line to every substation and then go on to the next line. It'll be brutally tedious, but that's the only way I know to get after this. It will take a zillion damn phone calls and lots of leg work, but it can be done."

"Let's say we get this schematic created, then what?" Lynne asked.

"That's when the real fun begins. If we have the overall picture right, then we put a process in place to methodically check each computer, control, switch or whatever to ensure it is Y2K compliant."

"A process is fine, but I think all the computers and even some embedded systems are password protected," Lynne said.

"How big a problem is that?" Zack asked.

"It's something we've got to handle. That's why our teams have to do a couple more things. One, they have to find the software rev levels which should be relatively easy. We're cool there. But then, they have to get the passwords and access rights to the systems or chips. Worse, some of the Supervisory Control and Data Acquisition Systems or SCADAs, as they call them, control multiple Remote Terminal Units or RTUs that are themselves separately password protected."

"Layers of passwords. Just what we need," Lynne said.

"There's more. Many of the systems use automatic algorithms or formulas to regularly change passwords. That way they don't use the same password for long periods because with enough time any second rate hacker can use a PC to "learn" the password. The administrators use the automatic algorithms because no human wants to sit down every thirty days and dream up a couple hundred new passwords. This way it's all automatic. So we need to know which systems have automatic passwords and what algorithms they use."

"Is that all?" Lynne asked. "Excuse me if I seem a little overwhelmed."

"Nope. Some of the SCADAs and RTUs are accessed by direct dial modems. That means we need the telephone numbers for those units. Some of the newer ones are accessed through the Internet, so we need to find those web sites and how to access them."

Zack tried to rationalize all these details and worried, "Is this project even doable?"

"Theoretically yes."

"Theoretically?"

"Yeah. I mean I think we're cool, but truthfully on this, everyone is clueless," Marly answered. "But there is still more. Some of the embedded systems and chips that control the switches and transformers are so old, they can't be fixed with new software. In those cases, we'll need to replace both the hardware and software and then do a full system test."

Lynne rolled her eyes to the ceiling. "My God. We don't have enough time."

"And, we don't have a choice," Marly said.

Zack caught the firmness in her voice and read the body language. Marly's straight spine and fixed jaw made clear she was in charge; Lynne's eye-rolling theatrics, on the other hand, expressed her frustration with this assignment.

Lynne stood and walked to the door. "Well, I obviously have a lot to do and I'd better get started. Just one more thing occurs to me though?"

"What's that?"

"You've described this power grid as kind of a computer seafood chowder with a little of this and a little of that all mixed together. Sounds pretty vulnerable to cyber terrorists, or am I missing something?"

Zack turned, "Is that right?"

"It's dead on. Three years ago the Director of the National Security Agency warned President Clinton about the vulnerability of the power grid. Until now, most of the focus has been on physical security, you know locks and fences. But with all the computerization, there is a real cyber threat. So lately, there's a lot of inspection to ensure passwords are used and regularly changed to protect against hackers and terrorists."

Zack relaxed with the threat seemingly under control.

Lynne said, "So the security issues are being worked."

"Only halfway. There's still a huge threat. Anyway..." Marly waved her arm and cut off further discussion.

"OK," Lynne answered

Zack heard her grumble something to herself as she left the room. He turned to Marly, "Are you sure about her?"

Marly waited, then walked over and closed the door to the conference room. She returned to her chair and directly faced Zack. "Before we get too far into this, you need to understand all the risks."

"What risks?" Zack asked, wondering why all the drama.

"This is really important, Zack. If we take on the Y2K work on the power grid, we're responsible. We're going to wear it."

"Can you cut to the chase?"

"The components on the grid are critically dependent upon each other. I call it the 'cascade factor.' I'll give you an example. Assume an incorrectly set switch causes a high-voltage surge—say in the neighborhood of 250,000 volts—and that surge causes a transformer to overheat and maybe even catch fire. That, in turn, can cause another surge to another transformer somewhere along the grid and then it fails, and so on. The only way anyone can have confidence in the system is if every single component of the grid is guaranteed Y2K compliant, and there are zero mistakes."

"Shit, Marly, are you saying there's a potential for the whole goddamn grid to get wiped out?"

"I'm saying it's possible. If we take on the responsibility for getting the grid Y2K compliant, it's going to be on our heads. You need to understand that."

"Are you suggesting we back off?"

"Zack, that's your decision."

"Is there a way we can make sure we've done things correctly?"

"There are no guarantees, but the key to this is that schematic diagram I was talking about earlier. If, and when, that's done, it will show all the generation units, all the transmission components, the power substations and even some of the distribution substations. That documentation doesn't exist anywhere. If we do that part right, then we should be able to validate each of the components we've identified."

"It sounds like you think we can swing it?"

"I think so, yes. But, I'm so frickin' worried about what happens if I'm wrong."

Zack heard the shakiness in her voice. "What do you mean?"

"Think about what happens if there's a long-term nationwide power outage. It would be catastrophic. Factories would close. Without elevators, high-rises would be useless. Hospitals would switch to emergency generators, but only until their fuel supply is exhausted. Electric pumps would stop pumping. Water would stop flowing. Without fuel pumps, all transportation including cars, trucks and planes would stop moving. Food and other deliveries would halt. There would be no refrigeration. Almost all heating and cooling systems would fail. TV and radio stations would go off the air."

Zack felt his heart pounding. "What happens if we don't work on this? How's it going to get done? The problem isn't going to go away. It might be scary taking it on, but it's better than if we do nothing. At least we understand the danger. I trust you and your people more than someone else, especially the utilities themselves. I don't think we have a choice."

Marly quietly stared at the table. "When you put it that way, I guess you're right. I just hope your trust is well founded."

Zack reached over and put his hand on hers. "I don't believe there is anyone more dedicated to doing a job than you are. Just do what you do. It will be right."

"Thank you," she said, her hands at her eyes. "I pray you're right."

CHAPTER 8

──────────── ▼ ────────────

CHICAGO, OCTOBER 18, 2001: 2:00 P.M.

Annoyed and shaken after being questioned at the police District, Zack went directly home rather than returning to the office. He'd made a wise decision, his blue dress shirt now dark with sweat. It might be early afternoon, but he wanted a drink just the same, and poured himself a sizeable shot of Johnny Walker black label, one ice cube. He paced about his home office. He'd never handled frustration well. "Murder one!" Zack repeated the allegation. It was just too preposterous. He'd been tagged the prime suspect.

The stress exacted its toll; at any other time, his crushing chest pain would be labeled a cardiac event. Zack recognized he had to get beyond this frustration and deal with the situation logically. Worse, he couldn't shake the fear that murder-one was a capital offense. If the case ever went to trial, the sizzling nature of Marly's murder combined with the sensationalistic media would force the District Attorney to push for the death penalty. Fuck, he'd better find a good lawyer. He abhorred the thought, but knew he would need one soon.

There had to be more he could do, and he couldn't wait for the inept Chicago cops to come up with something. Hell, he knew Marly better than anyone; if anybody could find something, damn it, he could. There had to be a clue.

He took a sheet of paper from his desk drawer and began writing everything he knew about the circumstances. He thought better when he wrote himself notes. The dramatic style of her death made it an unlikely random crime. People were murdered every day in the City, but they were shot or stabbed, not tied up naked and thrown off a balcony. No, her assailant must have known her and had some reason for her murder. Zack wrote the names of everyone she had ever mentioned. The list was not long. She had lived her life centered on work and had no family beyond a rarely mentioned uncle. Nearly all the names on Zack's list were co-workers. He personally knew most of them and although at this stage, he couldn't rule anyone out, it seemed unfathomable one of them could be a murderer. More perplexing though, was the lack of a motive, because everyone seemed to like Marly—well apparently not everyone.

As Zack thought about their relationship, he became troubled. The more he thought, the more troubled he became—how little he really knew about Marly. He saw now, the two of them were dedicated work-mates investing endless hours when necessary to meet project deadlines. Beyond that, they shared an incredible physical relationship and little more. He paused, and sadly exhaled. He felt uneasy, something stirring inside himself. Was there something lacking in his makeup? Maybe *he was* incapable of real involvement.

Zack's personal reflections, however, contributed nothing to help him identify her murderer. Distraught and staring wide-eyed at the empty wall across the room, he realized that right on the desk in front of him sat Marly's laptop computer. The police likely found and examined the bigger desktop system in her apartment, but never considered she would have a second computer. Marly often left the machine at Zack's. It was simply more convenient than to take it with her. She used the machine mostly for personal email, but occasionally she would make travel arrangements, or buy books and other things on-line.

Hesitantly, Zack sipped the scotch, opened the case, and violated the privacy of a dead lover. He pressed the power button, the screen brightened, and the Windows software took over with its familiar "ta-da" announcement. Although not in Marly's league technically, he could reasonably navigate through a PC.

Glancing at the screen, Zack realized he had no idea what he was looking for, or expecting to find. He recognized the word processor icon and opened it. The drop down menu listed the last four files that had been opened. He made a note to check each of them, and then closed the program.

He then found the email icon and double-clicked the mouse. There were about seventy-five messages in the mailbox, none of them unread. He checked the sender's names and compared it to the list he'd compiled earlier. Almost all of the names were familiar and the topics appeared sufficiently innocent. Oddly enough, there was one letter from a strange-looking name with a subject line that appeared like a mix of random characters. He chalked that one up as junk email that Marly had neglected to delete. He double-clicked on it and sure enough the body of the letter seemed all garbage. He closed the note and returned to the in-box.

He then decided to check the sent-mail folder. He recognized some of the same names. The last entry, mailed to Lynne Rydahl, contained "Doesn't Fucking Get It" for the subject line, and was sent late at night just a few days before Marly's fall. Intrigued, he clicked on the entry and scanned the note. Painstakingly, he read and reread the letter, dumbfounded by its contents. He discovered himself labeled as "Doesn't Fucking Get It." Marly's note to her friend consisted of a heartbreaking recital of Zack's missed opportunities to demonstrate his love for Marly. This wasn't the first time Zack found himself stunned by the depth of a woman's affection for him. However, what upset him more was his own realization just moments earlier that he knew so little about her beyond the bedroom.

Although Zack knew he had to talk with Lynne and learn more about Marly's affection for him, he saw no link there to her murder. He forced himself to concentrate on his self-imposed task to find some clue to her death. He opened the file manager and quickly scanned Marly's file names looking for anything that might be suspicious or out of place.

He was surprised to find a folder named "grid" and thinking that quite odd, double-clicked to open it. Inside the folder were a series of file names from their Y2K work a couple of years previous. His curiosity piqued, he attempted to open the one named "eastern-interconnection," but instead of the file opening, a dialogue box requesting a password appeared. Zack had no idea of what the password might be. But more importantly, why would Marly have such a file on her home computer almost two years after the project and why she would have it password protected? Marly wrote the rulebook. After project completion the project manager signed-off that all relevant files were either returned to the client or carefully destroyed.

Zack continued looking for other familiar names and sure enough he found folders for "western-interconnection," "Texas-interconnection" and "Quebec-interconnection." He knew these labels represented the four major subsections of the North American electricity power grid. The passwords prevented him from opening the files, but the system let him view the attributes. Incredibly, each of the files had been accessed within just the past two weeks. Why would she still be accessing these files when the project was completed so long ago? He tried to summarize his questions. One, why would Marly have these files on her personal computer? Two, why would she use passwords to protect them and against whom? Three, what reason could she have to be using those files within the past few weeks? None of this made sense to him. There were too many questions and no answers. But more importantly, could any of this be related to her murder? Sweat streamed from Zack's forehead. More than ever, he understood how little he really knew about Marly McCalley and it frightened him.

CHAPTER 9

---------------- ▼ ----------------

CHICAGO, OCTOBER 18, 2001: 3:30 P.M.

Lynne Rydahl answered her phone, taken aback when she heard Zack Dreyben's voice. She wasn't eager to talk to him, considering the horrible situation with Marly's death. Marly had been a friend, and she knew Marly cared for Zack and that he never reciprocated that love. Besides, she was still spooked by the police' questions from yesterday.

"Yes, Zack."

"Lynne, I have to talk to you and the sooner the better."

"Why?"

"It's kind of hard to describe on the phone, you know, but I think it might be important."

"What are you talking about?"

"OK, there are two things I think we should talk about." The words came rapidly. "The first one is that I found Marly's laptop in my condo. I thought there might be some clue there. I found her last email to you about me. I had no idea she was so involved, and…"

Lynne interrupted, "You what? You were reading her mail?"

"Yeah, but like I said, I thought it might help. I know it seems sleazy, but I really do need to talk to you. Can we meet around five o'clock for a drink, please? I promise to make it short and sweet. Besides, there's other stuff on that laptop that could be a lot more serious, and I need your help."

"OK, I'll meet with you, but only because I loved Marly. Whatever you want to talk about will not change that. Meet me around five-thirty in the bar at Barney's. I have some stuff I have to do before then."

"Great, five-thirty at Barney's, and thanks."

Lynne arrived late and expected to find Zack waiting in the bar. Instead, she found him in a booth in the back of the restaurant. He stood to greet her. He looked tired but alert, his dark complexion hiding a day's growth. His breath smelled of alcohol. Her doubts about Zack resurfaced. "OK, Zack, what's so damn important?"

"It's nice to see you, too," Zack replied. "Please sit down. Look Lynne, I can tell you don't like me, and given Marly's note, I guess I understand that. But, what's more important right now is that we find some clue to Marly's killer."

She slid into the opposite side of the booth, thankful for the table that separated them. "Yeah, but what do you want from me?" She remained cautious, not sure where this was going.

"I need your help, because Marly's laptop has some stuff that worries me."

"What does that mean?" Lynne asked, still wary.

"There are some files. I can't open them because they all have passwords."

"So?"

"I think they're the grid files from the Y2K work we did with the utilities in '98."

"OK, two questions," she started. "One, so what? And two, what does that have to do with her murder?"

"Well, to answer your first question, you and I both know how meticulously Marly followed procedures. It's extremely unlike her to retain files that belong to the client."

"I'll give you that, but maybe she just overlooked them."

"I thought that, too, but there are a couple of problems with that. Why would she ever have those files on her personal PC in the first place, when she had a company-supplied laptop? There would be no reason for her to have them on her own machine. But, more importantly, get this. Although the passwords wouldn't let me look at the files, I could check the file attributes, and those files had all been accessed within the last two weeks."

"Maybe they're personal files that just look like the client's stuff," Lynne answered.

"Could be, and I can't say. But the folder names are 'eastern-interconnection,' 'western-interconnection,' 'Texas-interconnection,' and 'Quebec-interconnection.'"

Lynne mulled that over. "Wow, that is weird, but I still don't see what all this has to do with her murder."

"Right now, I don't know, maybe nothing," he said, then leaned forward. "I'm trying to find something, anything that looks suspicious, anything that could be a lead."

"So then, what do you want from me?"

"I need your help to see what's in those files."

"Why don't you just take the PC to the police and let them work it?"

He leaned back in the seat, "Because I don't trust them. They already think I'm their man and besides, I don't believe they'd have a clue what to do."

Lynne agreed with Zack about the police' competence, but she still did not trust him. She decided on a daringly bold move. Her arms were crossed on the table and she stared straight into Zack's eyes. "I want to know, flat out, what happened between you and Marly?"

"What do you mean?" Zack asked.

"Did you have anything, and I mean anything, to do with her death, either directly or indirectly?"

"Hell no! For Christ's sake Lynne, I loved Marly." His eyes flared. "Maybe not the way she loved me, but I'd never do anything to hurt her!"

He could be lying, of course. Knowing Zack's reputation, he probably didn't even know what love meant, but something about his response gave her comfort—maybe it was the eyes. Call it women's intuition, but she believed him.

She sighed and whispered, "OK. I'll try to help."

"Great, thank you," he said. His voice wavered, and she knew he was struggling with his emotions.

"Something else, Zack," she continued. "What about that email?"

"What about it?"

"You really didn't know she was in love with you?"

"Yeah, but..." he stuttered.

"But, what?"

"I guess she was right. Sometimes, I just don't get it," he said.

"How could you not see how much she loved you? And how could you hurt her that way?"

"I never intended to hurt her, and I didn't even know that I had, until I read that letter. The truth is that we never really talked much about 'us.' Most of the time we discussed work stuff. In fact, just before I found her computer, I was thinking about our relationship and I realized then how little I actually knew about her.

"You guys were together for over two years and you didn't know how hung up she was?"

"Yeah, I know. I'm not proud of it, but it's the truth."

"Friggin' men!" Lynne muttered.

"What do we do now?"

She could tell he wanted to get back to the laptop questions. "When can I see her computer?"

"Whenever you want. I have it at my place. You and I can go there now, or I can bring it to you tomorrow morning."

"Tomorrow's fine. By the way, did you find anything else besides the computer? Any manuals or maybe some web site URLs?"

"Not that I remember, but I will look tonight and let you know tomorrow when I bring the PC."

"OK, fine," she said. "I've got to run."

"But I owe you a drink," he said. The two of them had been so intent they'd never ordered.

She slid out of the booth. "Yeah, well, I think I'll pass," she said. She wanted to think. She wished she could be certain his story wasn't just a ruse. Could his involvement with Marly have really been that shallow? Still, his emotions seemed genuine. But then, he was a marketing guy. He made his living persuading people. Down deep, the doubts remained.

CHAPTER 10

▼

SEATTLE, NOVEMBER 30, 1999

November 30 was the official opening day of the World Trade Organization meeting in Seattle. The tension was thick and palpable. There had been minor skirmishes for weeks as idealistic environmentalists joined International Labor unions, farmers, and a hardcore group of anarchists to form an unusual alliance numbering in the tens of thousands. The police and National Guard countered, assembling an overwhelming force of their own, equipped with riot gear, tear gas and rubber bullets.

In many ways this felt like the '68 Chicago Convention to K.P. Forsythe, now the old man in the crowd. But, that event happened a long time ago, and he was different now. This might be his last protest. In 1968, a passionate young activist, he felt the "zing" as he dedicated himself to stopping the war in Vietnam—now, thirty-plus years later, the passion lay stifled, the "zing" quieted. He reflected on all those years and all those protests and what had been achieved. He believed that public pressure and demonstrations had hastened the U.S. exit from Vietnam, but since then, little of note had been accomplished. He had come to Seattle to prevent capitalistic greed from spreading human suffering in the name of Free Trade. In his heart, however, he knew that while this confrontation might generate a little light and a little heat, within days the media's attention would fade and nothing would be different.

His biggest disappointment in life? He had not made a difference—all those years and all those protests, for what?

Those years had taken their toll. He had gained thirty pounds, thanks to the convenience of a fast-food diet. His hair, still long, grew thinner on the crown giving him a monk-like visage. The "Clark Kent" glasses remained, though he squinted now, the old prescription too weak.

Nevertheless, K.P. saw himself as one of the movement's elders and freely offered advice and tales of past protests. K.P. engaged one of the younger activists in conversation. "We ready for tonight?"

"We're cool," his youthful associate replied. "Cops have set up barriers trying to keep us from the delegates, but those barriers won't be a problem."

"Good, but be careful. I know first-hand how bad this can get. I saw my best friend go down from one of those goons." His mind flashed back to that awful night in Chicago. He'd ducked the blow that killed his friend Matthew McCalley. Whether through benevolence or guilt, he had "adopted" his friend's daughter Marly and raised her as his own. He knew deep down he had never been much of a father figure. He'd no desire for a real job, preferring instead to work as needed to cover expenses. Many of the things young girls crave, Marly never had—no Barbie or Ken, no car, no prom gowns. Worse than the material things, he was never able to "be something" for her. Her other friends had fathers they looked up to. K.P. had focused his life on righting the world's wrongs, but in the process lost the opportunity to be there for Marly.

"Hey Man, enough of the fucking, old war stories," the young man shouted. "Dude, we're here, now! It's not like we don't have our own shit. We've got picks and hammers, and we're going to rip up those fuckin' barriers and maybe pop a few of them windows as we go. Man we're stoked."

K.P. continued his warnings, "Watch out for the tear gas and the pepper spray. Be sure you have the lemon juice handy for your eyes."

"Yeah, yeah, Dude, I know," the youngster answered. "Hey, you know what would be way cool?"

K.P. sighed, and rolled his eyes upward behind the thick frames. "What's that?

"I was on the 'net last week. I saw that way back in Desert Storm the army used a special bomb to wipe out Iraq's whole electrical system. These bombs released a real fine cloud of graphite and it shorted out the transformers—burned 'em up. Wouldn't it be way cool to take out all the lights in Seattle?"

K.P. turned to the kid. "Tell me again where you saw this?"

"Shit, I don't know, man. Somewhere on the 'net's all I remember. But, I know it said that when the transformers burned out, that caused other transformers to overload and short out too. Man, they shut down the power across the whole fuckin' country."

"Yeah, well we don't have any special bombs," K.P. replied. Right now, he needed to focus on promoting "the cause." "The cause" meant advancing the philosophy of anarchism. To K.P. any control of the people by the state was unacceptable. Unfortunately, the media had perverted the anarchists' goal to mean chaos, when in fact, the true goal was the liberation of the masses. That goal, of course, meant dismantling governments that by design were intended to limit the rights of people. It also meant the destruction of the capitalistic system, since capitalism exploits the poor and boils down to domination of the masses for the benefit of the few. No thoughtful person could abide one-fifth of the world's population controlling four-fifths of the wealth. K.P. no longer thought about it; he knew in his gut that "the cause" was more important than anyone. He had dedicated his life to it.

"The cause" had to be achieved. If the world freed itself of the horrors of capitalism, workers would share equally in the bounty from their labors. Only then would individuals across the planet enjoy true freedom.

He particularly wanted a better world for his "niece" Marly. Though not truly his niece, she was the only one allowed to call him by his given name. She always called him "Uncle Kevin."

CHAPTER 11

▼

CHICAGO, OCTOBER 19, 2001: 8:00 A.M.

He checked his watch. Zack waited, drumming his fingers on the cluttered desk in Lynne's office. He decided the fewer people that knew about Marly's PC, the better, so he'd buried it deep inside his black Tumi bag to avoid any questions. He wished Lynne would hurry. He had to find what those grid files contained and why Marly still had them. He stole another look at his watch. A single minute had passed, but it seemed longer. He saw Lynne getting off the elevator, walking toward him. He stood to meet her at the door.

"Good morning, Zack," Lynne said, edging past him and hanging her coat behind the door, and closing it. "OK, let's see what you've got."

"Good morning," Zack said, while digging inside the leather case to produce the PC. He slid a stack of papers aside clearing a space and placed the laptop directly in front of her.

Lynne straightened herself in the chair and then turned to Zack. "All right, we need to start at the beginning. What exactly are we trying to do?"

"Find out whatever we can and maybe discover something related to her murder," He replied. It irritated Zack how methodical technical folks could be. Why couldn't they just cut to the chase?

She exhaled a deep breath. "I know that, but what is it that we're looking for exactly?"

"Hell, Lynne, I don't know. Something, anything that looks suspicious or out of the ordinary that might hold some clue."

Lynne opened the PC and waited for the system to boot. "Hmm," she mumbled.

He pulled up a chair opposite her. He found a clear corner of the desk to lean on. "What is it?"

"Well, maybe nothing," Lynne answered. "She didn't set a login password. That's a little strange, but then again, she never expected anyone to be using this machine except her."

Zack studied her as she adeptly tapped the keyboard. He felt lucky to have her help.

"What about the grid files?" Zack wanted to know. "Isn't that where we should start?"

"That's what I'm doing," she answered. "There 's a folder named 'grid' and it has a number of files in it. That includes the four you mentioned, one for each of the major geographies. I can tell from the file attributes that each of them had been accessed within the last couple of weeks, but the passwords won't let me open the files themselves."

"Lynne, damn it, I knew all that. What can we do?" Zack's patience was shot, and time dangerously short. At any time he could find himself in jail, charged with murder, unable to find Marly's killer.

"The passwords are stored with the file. We can try to guess the password and let the operating system check our guess, but there's zero chance we'd be correct. Hell, we don't even know how long they are. You were going to check around and see if there was any other stuff like notes, manuals or something. Did you find anything?"

"Not a thing," Zack answered.

"OK, that means we just have to work it. Let me think. We know Marly worked with computers for a long time, so I am going to guess that she stuck to eight character names. I say eight characters because that used to be the max, and some folks got into the habit of using exactly eight characters."

"Now, Zack," she continued. "Think. Do you have any idea if Marly had either a favorite number or letter?"

"What?"

"I have some software that will automatically generate combinations of letters and numbers and keep trying them in order to guess a password. Some guy wrote it to help people who forgot their own passwords. But, we need to supply the initial character and the number of total bytes in the password so that it has some place to start. Without that starting point, the program would run forever trying every possible combination of letters and numbers until hell freezes over. I'm counting on Marly using eight character names. I'm asking you what you think the first character would most likely be. Hell Zack, you spent the last three years with her. Your guess is better than mine."

"Lynne, no idea. I mean we never talked about our favorite letter of the alphabet, you know."

"Zack, try. Your guess is better than mine."

"Well, we know her first and last names started with 'M'. Let's try that."

"OK, 'M' it is, and eight characters. Keep your fingers crossed."

"How long does the program take?"

"Hard to tell. It tries one combination after another. If we've guessed correctly, then it might find it quickly, maybe in half an hour or less. I'll go find the disk with the software, and get it started."

Minutes later, Lynne returned carrying a floppy disk with a red label. She placed it in the "A" drive and copied the program to the desktop. Double clicking on the program brought up a dialog box asking for three items, "FILENAME," which Lynne typed in, and then "PARAMETERS." Lynne answered "M" to the first and "8" to the second.

"Now what do we do?" Zack asked.

"Hope."

"Lynne, while we're waiting. How the hell did she put passwords on those files to begin with? I didn't know you could do that."

"Don't feel badly. A lot of people, who have Windows 2000, or even NT, are just like you. Actually, it's easy. When you select 'save as' for a file, you get a dialog box. One of the choices on that box is 'tools.' If you select tools, then click on 'options' you can set passwords or access rights so you can let people read the file, but not modify it for example."

Zack listened, impressed.

"I have some other work to do, so I'll check back with you in about an hour or so, OK?" Lynne asked.

"Sure. You'll call me?"

"Yeah, of course."

Zack walked back to his office realizing without exaggeration his future might depend on what Lynne is able to decode from that computer. The strain and fatigue were starting to affect him. He wondered what more could possibly happen?

Lynne poked her head into Zack's office around ten o'clock. She carried Marly's laptop, and she wasn't smiling. "Well, Zack, we struck out."

"What happened?" he asked.

"No luck. Either the password was not eight characters long or it didn't start with an 'M.'"

"What do we do now?"

"All we can do is try something else. Hey, I just got an idea. Let me try this. It's just a hunch, but if it works, I'll buy *you* a drink this time!" She said, a trace of sparkle in her voice.

"What is it?" Zack wanted to know.

"First, let's see if this works," she said as she typed in some new parameters. "I don't want to jinx it."

Zack considered asking her about a techie using the word jinx, but before he got the chance, the program abruptly terminated, and the file opened.

"I knew it." Lynne yelped. "I just knew it."

"What?"

"Well we guessed right with eight characters, but we missed on the first letter. So I had a hunch and it worked."

"What worked?"

"Z, like in Zack!" Lynne explained. "Marly was so hung up on you that she used the word 'Zack' as the first part of the password."

"Holy shit," he breathed. He thought again about Marly, and their relationship, and it hurt.

But then he realized he'd just uncovered a darker side of Marly. She'd been keeping secrets from him, keeping her distance. She'd never shared the depth of her love, for example, and now these suspicious files with his name as a password. Why? What was she up to?

"All right let's see what's in this file," Lynne said, without commenting on Zack's pained expression. "Well, it's the grid files, all right. This one is the eastern interconnection like we thought. Wow, you know what's strange here is that this information has been updated. When we saw that she had recently accessed the files, I kind of assumed that she'd only looked at them. Now, I'm spooked. Why would she keep these files updated? What use could she possibly have for the equipment list and passwords for all the computerized controls in the power grid?"

"What do you think it means?" Zack asked.

"I hoped you'd tell me. We know she passworded the files, so she wanted them to be kept secret. That in itself is spooky enough, but keeping them updated, is really weird. What good would these files be to anyone other than the utility companies, or someone doing work for them?" Lynne asked.

"Maybe that's it. Maybe she thought we would win another contract for some more work for the utilities and she could use the files for that," Zack said.

"Maybe, but I don't think so. Besides, Marly always followed procedures, and all the files were either delivered to the client or deleted. Not only did she not return them, she kept updating them. Let's go back. Who would have any use for this information?"

"Well, someone doing maintenance on the grid, you know, maybe changing some transformers or something, they could use it," he said.

"True, but we have to assume that the utilities themselves already have this information. Why would Marly need to have it?"

"OK, if it's not to do repair on the power grid, what about expanding it?"

"Nope, it still doesn't make sense."

"Oh my god!" Zack's face went pale. "If it's not to improve the grid, what about the opposite?"

"You mean somehow screw it up?" Lynne asked.

"To be honest, I don't know what I mean," he said. "Let me ask you this, what damage could be done to the grid if this info got into the wrong hands?"

"It depends on how much they know. If you remember, we had a hell of a learning curve to go through before we were up to speed. If someone already had a good knowledge of the power grid, it could be ugly."

"What's ugly?"

"How about disastrous then?"

"Isn't that a little melodramatic?" Zack asked.

"No. It could be a lot worse than that. But, I can't believe that Marly would be involved with anything like that. Hell, I knew her; we were friends."

"Lynne, she was my closest companion for over two years, and she kept at least one huge secret from me. Maybe she kept an even bigger secret from both of us."

"Zack, do you know how much damage could result if this data got into the wrong hands?"

"Not really."

"OK here goes. A power blackout across the entire North American continent, how's that for melodramatic?"

"Holy shit!"

"Anyone who has this data, and knows what to do with it, could control the electric power grid for the whole United States and part of Canada."

"But Marly wouldn't be involved in anything crazy like that."

"I don't think so, either, but right now, we don't know."

Zack took a deep breath. "All right, let's step back for a second. Before we do anything, we need to know more. That means we'll have to look at the other files and everything else we can find. That will take some time. What are you doing tonight? Besides, I think you owe me a drink."

"Yeah, OK," Lynne answered.

"Before we get together tonight, can you look through her desk one more time for anything that we or the police might have missed? I'll recheck my place, too. Come to think of it, we should probably work there. I would hate to have this get out before we've figured out what it's all about."

"Good thinking."

"Tonight it is then. I'll take the PC and see you at my place around six o'clock, OK?"

"Six o'clock. I'll be there."

"Good, see you then," Zack said, shutting down the laptop. He tried his best to maintain a normal tone, but inside he was Jello. Surprised before at how well Marly could keep a secret, he feared what they might learn tonight.

CHAPTER 12

--------------- ▼ ---------------

CHICAGO, OCTOBER 19, 2001: 5:00 P.M.

Zack had just enough time to get home, walk Katie, and still meet Lynne at 6:00. He took a shortcut through the Board of Trade building to the Van Buren 'EL' stop. Most often, Zack would drive to the office, but with downtown traffic getting unbearable, he'd opted for the 'EL' today. He barely noticed the gray-haired woman a few paces back as he exited the CBOT and climbed the metal staircase. He found the tiny platform jammed with rush hour commuters, all waiting for the Purple Line train.

He clutched the leather bag holding Marly's computer, allowing his weary mind to drift. Zack and Lynne had hoped to find a clue to Marly's murder, but found instead a bizarre twist. Zack took assurance knowing that the files themselves were not sufficient to initiate a disastrous blackout. It would take someone with an extensive knowledge of the power grid to use the files, and then it would be a challenging and time consuming effort. Even so, the potential was unsettling.

Zack hoped they would find evidence that all this could be easily explained. He wanted his life back. He missed Marly. He missed her teasing and wanted to call her, talk to her. He hadn't slept more than an hour or two in the past three days. He promised himself a strong drink and an early bedtime.

The growing rumble and accompanying shudder of the platform announced the approaching train. During rush hour, the CTA used longer eight-car trains that seemed to enter the stops at higher speeds. Zack aimed to get a spot in the last car, thus placing him at the exit stairway when they reached his stop. He stood on the edge of the platform looking down the tracks for the train, checking its arrival, and knowing the first few cars would race by him as it approached.

He didn't see the subtle nod behind him. The scuffle began just off to his right between two young people, one white and one black. There were rough words. The white youngster called the black one a "worthless nigger" and the black youth retaliated with a swinging left hand. The diversion worked; everyone's attention turned to the pair. Zack also turned, taking little notice of the stout, gray-haired woman standing behind him.

The train decelerated as it raced towards the platform. Zack felt a foot slide between his. Someone first touched his back and then shoved him hard. Panic seized him. His feet were tangled and his arms flailed wildly as he helplessly tried to regain his balance. He was falling to his left, staring straight at the train just two feet away. The operator blasted the alarm and yanked the brake. The crowd turned toward the blaring horn and screeching wheels. Horrified screams erupted from the crowd. In a microsecond flash, Zack saw the horror-struck face of the operator, as he felt the solid impact of the initial car plowing into him. Halfway pinned against the flat front of the train, he continued falling toward the tracks and the electrified 'third rail.' Instinct forced him to reach out and grasp anything to abort his fall. For an instant, the forward momentum of the train actually worked to his benefit as his right hand grabbed the security chain dangling in front of the car. As the brakes took effect, he slid his left arm through the chain so that he was hanging horizontally across the front of the car. Endless seconds passed before the operator finally stopped the train. With the help of a beefy bystander, Zack, dazed and nearly paralyzed with fear, slowly untangled himself from the chain, carefully stepped over the rails and stumbled to the platform.

The crowd swarmed to the scene on the tracks. No one noticed the figure headed for the exit stairs dropping a bulky coat and gray wig into the first trash-can. The two younger men, one white and one black, separated and disappeared into the crowd eventually finding their own way to the exit.

CHAPTER 13

▼

CHICAGO, OCTOBER 19, 2001: 4:00 P.M.

The fall WTO meeting originally planned for the mid-east nation of Qatar was relocated to the U.S. The Director-General felt security would be better in the U.S. following the September 11 attacks. With New York out, Atlanta, San Francisco and Dallas were considered as sites in addition to Chicago, but Chicago won based on the immediate availability of an appropriate venue. Surprising many in the community, Mayor Asa Bradigan had lobbied for the conference and even offered up exclusive use of Navy Pier, a main tourist attraction, as the venue. The press found the offer particularly interesting since the Metropolitan Pier and Exhibition Authority is the Pier's governing body, not the Mayor.

Detective Rob Harrison waited in the hotel ballroom, hot and overcrowded by half. Unexpectedly warm October weather had arrived from the southwest, with the hotel's air conditioning already shut down for the winter. No one told Rob officially why he drew this assignment, but he knew the reason. He'd been sent here to show the FBI that the City and the Police Department were cooperating. Ever since 9/11, the Administration paid more attention to everyone playing nice, but goddamn it, he was a homicide detective, not a fucking traffic cop. He certainly didn't expect to be baby-sitting a bunch of foreign delegates, let alone a shit-load of spoiled-brat, protesting punks. His Dad played that game thirty years ago, and lost.

The FBI and Secret Service called the meeting to review security measures for the upcoming conference, and every city and state agency lined up to make sure their noses were officially counted. Rob attended as the Senior Detective out of the Eighteenth Police District where the WTO conference would be held. He would rather have been chasing down leads and interviewing murder suspects. Hell, couldn't they find some prim and proper new recruit to sit here and look interested? Anyway, knowing the Feds, they were planning on talking, not listening.

A man wearing an ordinary, gray suit, white shirt and blue tie stepped to the podium—his short hair and chiseled face a Xerox copy of the other men sharing the tiny platform. He tapped the microphone twice. Two amplified thumps, signaled he was about to speak.

"Good afternoon," he began. "My name is Gregory K. Johnson. I am the SAC." Blank faces swept the room. "That's Special Agent in Charge. I'm an eleven-year veteran of the FBI and served five years before that in the Uniformed Executive Protection Service."

Rob, thankful he'd claimed a chair in the last row, tilted back against the wall and relaxed. So typical, he thought to himself. Only an arrogant FBI prick would go by "Gregory K." rather than "Greg." Other than two close friends who were agents, Rob didn't have high regard for the "bureau."

Johnson continued, "Today's session is to brief you on our security plans for the upcoming World Trade Organization meeting. As you already know, the session's venue is Navy Pier right here in Chicago. Before I get into the details, I want to welcome the invited security representatives from our guest countries."

Rob scanned the room. Four or five hundred security people from all 142-member countries had packed into the ballroom. What the hell kind of security briefing has hundreds of people attend? How did they think they could keep anything secure? Happily, Rob remembered, he was only there to "show the flag."

"Our primary concern is always The President of the United States, but just as importantly, we have delegates from 141 other countries and their staffs to consider." One of the other men dimmed the lights as Johnson switched on the computer projector on the table in front of him. He held a four-foot wooden pointer. "This morning you will hear detailed reports on the following: surface access control; water-based access control; aerial observation measures; evacuation paths and contingencies; advance sweeps for explosive and bio-terrorism risks; personnel assignments and locations; escort teams; and of course, comprehensive reports on individuals who may pose security risks."

Special Agent Johnson explained that the site selection team had chosen the Navy Pier venue for good reasons. Physically, the Pier is essentially a large peninsula jutting a mile and a half out into Lake Michigan. The Navy used it in World War II as a training facility, thus its name. It had fallen into disrepair until a 1995 renovation transformed it into a Chicago tourist attraction with restaurants, theatres, shops, and dramatic nighttime views of the city skyline.

"OK, let's start on the ground," Johnson said clicking the mouse to the slide titled "Surface Access." The graphic showed a map of all streets and walking paths to the selected site. Johnson continued speaking, but Rob found himself way ahead of the presentation. He mentally reviewed the location's advantages. Being a peninsula meant surface access was limited to one direction. Rob liked that because it meant securing only one highway, but still having close proximity to delegation hotels and an immediate evacuation route to the primary trauma hospital, Northwestern Memorial. Best of all, any demonstrators could be controlled outside the perimeter of the access corridor and away from the delegates. Rob checked the agenda for a break that would let him slip out unnoticed. He had work to get to.

Johnson droned on describing the plans: The Coast Guard would secure a 500 yard clear perimeter on the Lake; the air corridor to O'Hare Airport to and from the east would be closed for the duration of the conference; The Air National Guard would maintain twenty-four hour air reconnaissance; The Presidential Protection Division's Counter Assault Team had set up operations at the nearby executive airport, Meig's Field, and on, and on.

However, even with all the formal trappings, the foreign security staffs would not be informed about *all* the preparations. Long before the venue selection became public, the CIA began planting super-sophisticated electronic eavesdropping equipment, designed especially to listen-in on the most discrete conversations of foreign leaders and their security teams. The National Security Agency and the CIA were hoping to intercept communications between foreign security forces and operatives around the world. The NSA and CIA justified the listening posts claiming that international terrorists would be listening in as well.

Johnson finished his briefing with the plans to control any protests. Lists and pictures of all known security threats were distributed. "Chicago Police are cooperating and will arrest and detain on whatever charges are necessary, the most critical suspects until the conference is over. In addition, riot control teams from the Chicago police and the Illinois National Guard are well equipped and ready. We won't tolerate any problems like they saw in Seattle or Genoa. City officials have promised me that they'll do whatever is necessary to keep a lid on things here in Chicago."

Rob Harrison perked up when he heard the comment and wondered who the hell made that commitment? The answer came immediately.

"We want to thank the Chicago Police Chief and the City administration for their assistance, especially Mayor Bradigan," Special Agent Johnson concluded.

Should have known, Rob thought to himself. This is just like '68 when the honchos downtown screwed Dad. Rob felt uneasy with this riot control shit, but at the same time thankful because there was no way that he would be involved.

CHAPTER 14

▼

CALIFORNIA, OCTOBER 1998

K.P. Forsythe sat on the cushy, old sofa, taking a break. Marly would be arriving soon. He'd been cleaning since morning. The apartment smelled like pine oil, but it was better than the stale smell of the old take-out cartons.

K.P. found it hard to believe he'd lived in this modest two-bedroom since 1968, the year Marly came to live with him. K.P. and the landlord had developed a kind of an understanding. The rent increases would be minimal, but so would the improvements, as evidenced by the gold shag carpeting and harvest gold appliances. The arrangement worked well for K.P. allowing him to work short-term jobs as he liked and continue attending his various protests and demonstrations.

He'd been looking forward to Marly's visit for days. He'd stocked up on her favorites including her weakness, Belgian dark chocolate. An earlier newsstand trip provided the latest computer magazines that were spread across the old coffee table. He wished she'd get here. She'd moved to Chicago just months ago, but he missed her.

*   *   *   *

Stationed at the window, K.P. watched Marly park the rental car and walk toward the front door. Before she even reached the first step, he swung the door open and greeted her, "Hi."

He gave her a nice hug. Their embrace did not last long; they never did. He and Marly never developed much of a touchy-feely relationship.

"I know. I'm late. I'm sorry, Uncle Kevin. We were late getting out of O'Hare."

"No problem. Come on in." As usual she was dressed smartly, this time all in black. "Here, let me take that," K.P. said, reaching for her rolling suitcase.

"Thanks. Oh, it's great to be back. I miss California," she said comfortably sinking into one of the overstuffed, corduroy chairs.

K.P. noticed the dark shadows under her eyes. "You look a little tired. You doing OK?"

"Yeah, fine, just tired. I've been working my ass off. That's why I scheduled this long weekend. I needed a little R & R."

"Well, fill me in on everything. Why are you working so much?"

"We're all going nuts working on this Y2K shit for the electric industry. Zack won this huge contract, but now we're running out of time."

K.P. knew that Zack was Marly's boyfriend. "Tell me about Zack."

"He's great," she answered, her eyes bright.

"OK. I want to hear everything. But first, how about a glass of wine to unwind?"

"Yeah, cool. That sounds great."

He poured two glasses of a Napa' Merlot and handed her one, "Here you go." He sat on the old sofa across from her. "OK. Now about Zack."

She leaned forward. "He's very hip, Uncle Kevin. He's six feet tall and very handsome. He has just a touch of gray hair and the most incredible deep blue eyes."

"You two work together, right?" K.P. asked.

"Yeah, he's the V.P. of Marketing. He joined the Company just a month or so after I did. But, we're keeping it quiet."

"Why's that?"

"You know, the whole thing about dating someone you work with and all."

K.P. nodded that he understood, but he wasn't sure he did. He had never worked for a big company and he definitely didn't understand the corporate world. "OK, so how serious is this thing with Zack?"

"Pretty serious, at least for me."

K.P. frowned. "And Zack?"

"Well, I know he likes me, but we haven't talked much about the two of us. It's kind of hard for Zack to open up. I think a lot of guys are like that."

K.P. wondered about Marly's answer. He knew she hadn't dated "a lot of guys" and he hoped she was right about Zack. She deserved to have a guy that really cared about her. "Is this part of that 'male sensitivity' thing I hear about?"

"I guess. You know, I don't think I'll ever understand how guys think. Why doesn't he just see that we're supposed to be together?" she asked.

"Are you?"

"Ah, yeeahh!"

"How do you know?"

"You just do," she said. "Geez, is 'not getting it' genetically male, like baldness?"

"Well, I don't know, maybe. But as long as you're happy, I'm happy. Other than that, how does he treat you?"

"Great. He's thoughtful; buys me flowers; says the right things—most of the time; and remembers special days like my birthday; that kind of thing."

"Sounds to me like you're hooked."

Marly smiled the smile of a woman in love. "Yeah, I am."

"And the future?" K.P. asked.

The smile left her face as swiftly as it had arrived. "Oh, hell, I don't know. It's way too early."

K.P. thought it wise to change the subject. "OK, so much for Zack. Tell me about work."

"Work's crazy. This huge new Y2K contract with the electric utilities is wearing my ass out."

"Explain to me what Y2K is again?" He'd heard the news reports on TV about the problem. He'd used a computer for years, but pretended ignorance.

As he expected, Marly perked up at the chance to show her expertise. "It's making sure all the computers correctly handle the date changes from 1999 to 2000."

"What will happen if they don't?"

"No one knows for sure. Some people think airplanes won't be able to navigate, or there'll be blackouts because the electric grid will shut down. Others think the banks and ATMs will screw up everybody's records, all kinds of stuff. But, nobody really knows. That's why people are worried."

"So, what exactly are you doing?" he asked.

"I'm leading the project team with the electric utilities and transmission companies. They have a big problem because the power grid has tons of computerized switches that all have to be checked, and they can't do it themselves."

"Why?"

"They don't have the time or the people. So, that's where we come in. We've got a lot of people and they know what they're doing. In this case, we've actually taken over the whole effort, because the time is short and we need to keep moving. Usually, the client monitors the project, but there is too much going on and they can't be everywhere. That's why I've just taken control, to ensure we make it in time."

"Sounds like an awful lot of responsibility."

"Yeah, it is. In a way, I'm not too crazy about it," she added.

"Why? What do you mean?"

"Well, there are a lot of bureaucrats involved because we had to get the North American Electric Reliability Council in the loop. And, it's getting worse. Now, every government agency including Congress wants to stick their fingers into things because everyone's scared about not being ready."

That explanation hit a powerful note with K.P. He detested everything about government and governmental control. "Those bastards," he said under his breath.

"What's that?" Marly asked.

"The government. They keep trying to control people. Can't they see they should help people, not control them? That's the same government that took Matthew, your father. I can never forget that," he said sourly. He'd never been able to distinguish one arm of government from another. Chicago Police, The National Guard, Congress, they were all the same. Thirty years after Grant Park, he still felt the pain, or guilt, maybe both.

"Neither can I," she said with tears forming in her eyes.

"I would love to find a way to show those bastards up," K.P. muttered.

"What do you mean, show them up?" Marly asked.

K.P. waved his arms in frustration. "Hell, I don't know, but I'd love to have the whole goddamn world see how government screws everything up."

"What good would that do?"

"Only demonstrate to the entire world that governments and bureaucrats are not the answer, and maybe we could get even with those bastards for what they did to Matthew." His face was hot. He got angry whenever he remembered.

Marly's expression changed. Her eyes narrowed; she wore a strange wry smile. "What if there was a way to really embarrass the shit out of them?"

"How?"

"Well, I just got an idea. It might be crazy, but if we're careful we might just make the government and some of the bureaucrats look like total losers. Best of all, no one would be the wiser."

"I don't know what you are talking about, but I like it."

"A long time ago when I was just six or seven, I made a promise to get even. Now, I think I might have a way."

Eager to know what Marly was thinking, K.P. asked, "OK, so what is it?"

She scratched her head above her right ear and smiled. "Uncle Kevin, I know how the whole damn power grid works. What if I could come up with a way to black out places for a few minutes? Maybe start on one side of the country and go across to the other. The blackout would last only a minute or so, but long enough to have the government look confused and embarrassed. No one would get hurt. It would just make those responsible look like total asses."

"Can you really do that? Wouldn't you get in a lot of trouble?

"First of all, yes, I think I can do it. And, no, I don't think I'd get into trouble. By the time those losers realized the power was off, it would be back on. I'm only talking about a minute or so. They would never be able to tell exactly what happened. The more I think about it, the more I like it. The blackout would roll across the continent like a shadow passing over the country. Everyone would know that it was intentional, but the bureaucrats wouldn't have a clue of what happened or how."

K.P. got caught up in Marly's enthusiasm. "Wow."

"Can you imagine the headlines? The rolling blackout would be the number one news story for weeks. Politicians from the President on down would be trying to explain it away until the next election."

"When?" K.P. asked.

"That's the important thing. We'd have to be careful. It'd have to be a long time from now. We'd have to get through the Y2K stuff first. Then we'd need enough time to go by that everyone would've forgotten that Magnicin even worked with the grid computers. That may take a couple years or more. We have to be patient."

"Are you sure you can really do it?" K.P. asked.

"I'm pretty sure, but I'd have to do some work before I'm certain. But, I think by controlling the programmable switches, I can quickly turn the power off and back on under program control."

"What does that mean?"

"It means I have to create a computer program that properly sets the grid switches in exactly the right sequence at exactly the right time. Having a program do it ensures it's done correctly and nothing goes wrong."

"And, *you* could do that?"

Marly straightened with pride. "Oh yeah, it would take some careful planning, but I could do it."

"Then what?"

"We'd select a time when we think we'd have the greatest impact, and start the program. From then on, it's automatic."

K.P. knew if Marly set her mind, she'd do it. He remembered when she was eleven; they made a deal. She would make good grades if he would promise not to go to a protest for a whole year. She earned nothing but straight A's from then on. K.P. felt proud, and wanted to tell her, but saying the words was too difficult. Still, he assumed she knew. Anyway, as it turned out, he didn't keep his side of the bargain.

K.P. asked, "How can you be sure this is going to work?"

"That's a good question. I think I should set up a simulation program that would let me play 'what if' games."

"What's that?"

"The program will simulate exactly what would happen based on different parameters like timing, switch settings, power loads, time of day, and so on. It would be complicated, but if the simulation is done well, we'd be able to tell exactly what would happen ahead of time, like going to a movie preview."

"That's amazing," he said. He loved the idea of embarrassing the government. "Could you make it do even more?"

"Like what?" Mary asked.

"I don't know. Maybe shut down the whole grid?"

"It's possible, but I sure don't want to go there. This is just to make those losers squirm a little."

"Oh, I know. I know. Just curious," he said. "I think your Dad would be proud of you. After all, he lost his life fighting the system."

"Yeah. Paybacks can be hell," she said, her mind seemingly elsewhere.

CHAPTER 15

————————— ▼ —————————

CHICAGO, OCTOBER 19, 2001: 6:00 P.M.

With considerable help, Zack managed to sit on the side of the platform, his vision blurred, his head pounding. He was trembling, bruised and thankful to be alive. Zack wasn't religious; but, this near-death experience left him wondering about how he'd survived and even why. His clothes were torn and covered with a grimy sludge from the track base. Inexplicably, his shoes were gone. The flesh on his left arm was ripped open and bleeding badly.

Someone had called 911 and the paramedics were attending to his injured arm and completing their checks of his vital signs.

"What's your name?" the first paramedic asked.

"What?"

"What is your name?" the paramedic repeated more slowly.

"Dreyben. Zack Dreyben."

"You're going to be fine, but we're taking you to the hospital. Can you walk?"

"I don't know. I'm shaking like hell."

"Take it easy. Easy. We've got the gurney right here. Just sit here and swing your legs over."

Trembling, Zack seated himself, and with lots of help laid down.

He had the classic signs of trauma-induced shock: clammy skin, disturbingly low blood pressure, eyes caught in a kind of twilight stare. IV fluids were immediately started and an oxygen mask placed over his nose and mouth. They covered him with an EMS blanket and pulled the security straps taut across him.

"Just take it easy. We'll have you at the hospital in just a couple of minutes," the paramedic assured him. "Do you have all your stuff?"

It wasn't until then that he realized he did not have his bag with Marly's computer. "Wait," he shouted through the mask. "My bag?"

"What bag?"

"My computer bag. I've got to have my computer bag. We can't go yet," he pleaded.

"OK, just one fast look. We need to get rolling," the attendant said.

A few of the onlookers began a quick search. It only took a moment for one of them to point to the flattened Tumi bag lodged beneath the front panel of the train, the contents mangled and useless.

"Forget it. Looks like it got smashed under the train," the paramedic said as he nodded to his partner. "Let's go." Zack felt the paramedics lifting, and then carrying him to the stairs and the waiting ambulance.

His first ambulance ride proved unpleasant. The wailing siren aggravated his pounding headache, and worse yet, laying flat prevented him from anticipating the starts, stops and bumps of city streets. Fortunately, the trip to the hospital took just fifteen minutes.

The paramedic team radioed ahead; the ER stood ready. A second bumpy ride on the gurney, and he was transferred to a bed, surrounded by hospital curtains and sophisticated medical equipment. The trauma team, protected by plastic face shields and latex gloves, immediately went to work. The remains of his clothing were cut away; an automatic blood pressure cuff placed on his arm; a pulse monitor slipped on his finger; his wounds thoroughly cleaned; and injections of antibiotics and tetanus administered.

Soon a staff doctor began examining him and completing a series of questions, looking to uncover any additional injuries, her bedside manner surprisingly polished for a young resident. She engaged Zack in a continuing conversation, listening intently, and judging his clarity and understanding.

"Hi, I'm Doctor Jennings. I'd like to ask you a few questions. First of all, how do you feel? Are you weak or lightheaded?"

"No, just sore, and shaky."

"Where is the pain and how bad?" She asked, apparently concerned about internal injuries.

"Not real bad, and kind of just all over. It's not like in one place."

"Does this hurt?" She questioned while probing his abdomen.

"Not really."

"What about this?" she asked, continuing her check of internal organs, all of which appeared normal.

"Nope."

"How did you fall?" She asked. "Have you had balance problems before?"

"I don't have balance problems. I didn't fall. I was pushed."

"Really?" was her only reaction, but she noted his reply. "Do you know how you cut your arm?"

"I think it was when I reached to grab the chain, you know the one that hangs in front of the train? But, I'm not sure how I cut it."

She continued to examine him. Beaming a mini-flashlight into his eyes, she checked his pupils for dilation. His eyes responded normally. His pulse and blood pressure had returned to normal range.

"Considering the close call you've had, you're in pretty decent shape. Your vital signs are all within normal; you're obviously not confused or disoriented. Regardless, we'd like you to spend the night here for observation."

Zack wasn't eager to spend the night in the hospital and besides he still had to contact Lynne who by now would be wondering what happened to him. "I think I'd rather go home, if that's OK?"

"Well, we can't make you stay, but take it easy for a few days. You've been through a lot. Listen to your body and your brain. If you start to feel unusual—lightheaded, dizzy, disoriented, etc.—get to a hospital. Shock is nothing to take lightly. You can take aspirin or Tylenol for the aches and pains, but nothing else, OK?"

"Sure, and thanks."

"No problem. Remember, anything unusual, get to a doctor immediately." She smiled over her shoulder as she walked away leaving Zack alone for the first time since the incident.

Slowly, as the terror of the event subsided, he regained his composure. He knew for certain he hadn't slipped off the platform in front of that train; someone pushed him. Somebody had murdered Marly and now someone tried to do the same to him. Why? The two situations had to be linked. He'd be nuts to think he and Marly were random victims just three days apart. What could the connection be? An icy shiver shot up his spine. Who would want him dead, and why? And if they tried once, they would try again. He felt himself sweating. He was frightened by what he knew, but more so by what he didn't know.

As if that weren't enough, the train crushed his spirit when it crushed Marly's PC. That computer held his only prospect of clearing himself of suspicion in her murder. His head buzzed like a chainsaw, but he had to think.

Zack realized he had a few issues to deal with before he could leave the hospital. One, he had no clothes. The shreds that remained had been cut away and pitched. The less-than-modest hospital gown concealed nothing. The assistant nurse brought him a telephone and plugged it into the panel behind his head. He called his neighbor Terry asking him to do two things: take care of Katie until he could get home; and use his key to get him a clean set of clothes. He then called Lynne's cell phone hoping to catch her.

"Hello," she answered.

"Lynne, boy am I glad I got you."

"Where the hell are you?" she demanded.

"I'm at Northwestern Hospital. I almost got killed, but I'm OK. Lynne, I need a favor. My neighbor Terry is getting some clothes from my place, could you please pick them up and bring them here?"

"Hold on! You almost got killed?"

Zack didn't feel like going through the whole story just yet. "Yeah, it's a long story. I'll tell you the whole thing later. But right now, I want to get out of here, and I need some clothes. Mine were ruined by the train."

"Train? What train?"

"The one that almost fucking killed me!" Zack sputtered. "Please. Can you just pick up the clothes at my place and bring them here? It won't take you long."

"OK, OK. Calm down. I'm not too far from your place now. I should be there in a few minutes."

"Good, just bring them to the emergency room."

"All right. Then you're going to tell me what this is all about, right?"

"Sure, what I can," he said, knowing there were questions that he couldn't answer.

While he waited for Lynne, he tried to think through how he would explain what happened. His brain just wasn't connecting. He couldn't concentrate. He chalked that up to exhaustion, frustration, and perhaps even shock. Maybe that's what the Doctor was talking about.

His spirit plunged. The last two people in the world he wanted to see, Detectives Harrison and Stockano, were walking across the ER. Dead tired, hurting and bruised all over, he thought what an awful, fucking day this had been. What more could go wrong? He worried he would soon find out.

Rob Harrison greeted him with a slight nod, "Mr. Dreyben."

"Hi," Zack said with a half-wave and no warmth. Why the heck were they here?

"We understand you had a run-in with an 'EL' train."

"Yeah. How did you know?" Zack asked.

"Can you tell us what happened?"

"OK, but how did you guys find out?"

"Standard procedure," Stockano answered.

"What Jimmy means," Harrison said, "is that whenever there is any life-threatening incident—that may not be accidental—the ER automatically contacts the police. You told the Doctor that you were pushed in front of that train?"

"That's right, I did."

"Well, the Doctor took a note of that and contacted the department. We have a computer system with the names of everyone involved in open investigations. If a call comes in regarding any of those people, it's routed to the detectives handling the investigation."

"Oh, OK. So what do you want to know?"

Before the detective could answer, Lynne bolted into the ER, spotted Zack and beelined over. She pushed past the cops and handed Zack his fresh clothes.

"So what's this all about?" she demanded.

"Well, I was just going to tell these guys the story. They are the Detectives investigating Marly's murder." He turned to Harrison, "This is Lynne Rydahl," he said.

"Yes, we know. We've talked before," Harrison answered.

"You have?" Zack asked.

Lynne gaped at him. "Of course, the day after she was murdered. They talked to everyone."

"Oh, OK, sure," Zack said. He felt sheepish. He should have realized.

"Well, go on. Let's hear what happened," Lynne said.

"Is it OK?" Zack asked the detectives.

"Yeah, why not. Go ahead, tell us what happened," Harrison said.

"There's not a hell of a lot to tell. I was standing on the platform waiting for the train home. It was crowded. Just as the train was coming, I felt someone's feet kind of stepping around mine. I looked down and then I felt a push in the middle of my back. I lost my balance and tried to grab anything I could, but there was nothing to grab and I fell towards the train."

"Did you see who pushed you?"

"Not really." Zack tried hard to concentrate. "I mean, there were a bunch of people, and I didn't particularly notice anybody."

"Try to remember. Did you notice anyone or anything?"

"Well, it was an after work crowd. I think there were a couple of traders beside me, you know, wearing those wild colored jackets, and maybe an older lady behind me, but I'm not sure."

"Tell me what you remember about the old lady," Harrison asked.

"Hell, just a fat, old lady for Christ' sake."

"How tall?"

"About his height, I'd guess," Zack said pointing to Stockano.

"So, about five-eight. Anything else? What color hair did she have?"

"Gray, I think. She was old, you know."

"Did anyone else see you get pushed?"

"I don't know, maybe. But, everyone was watching the fight."

"Fight? What fight?"

"Well, just before all this happened, there were a couple of guys pushing and shoving and calling each other names and stuff like that. So, everybody was watching them."

"Where were these two guys?"

"Oh, maybe twenty or thirty feet behind me and off to the right."

"And then, you felt the shove?"

"Yeah, right when the train was coming."

"Can you describe them? Do you think you would recognize them?"

"Hell, I don't know, maybe. They were just a couple of young guys maybe eighteen, twenty years old, kind of wild looking. One of them had spiked blond hair, you know the kind that sticks out about three inches in all directions. The other kid was black, short hair, but he had his back to me, so I didn't see his face. What? Do you think they were involved?"

"I don't know, but it wouldn't be the first time someone set up a diversion," Harrison answered.

"Holy shit," Zack said. The picture appeared clearer and more frightening. No chance now that the accident was a case of being at the wrong place at the wrong time. It had been staged, with Zack the pigeon. But why? Who would want him dead?

Lynne interrupted, "Do you still have the computer?"

"No, damn it. The train smashed it."

"What computer?" Detective Harrison asked staring over his glasses.

"One of the laptops from work," Zack quickly lied. He wasn't ready to share his discoveries about Marly's files with the police. He prayed Lynne would catch on.

Lynne immediately picked up. "Oh, well, that's one way to get a new one," she said.

Harrison hesitated a moment. He removed his glasses and scratched the hump on his nose. He turned to look at Lynne, then directly at Zack. "Anything else you want to tell us?"

"Not really," Zack answered.

"OK, I think we've got what we need for now," Harrison concluded as he and his partner turned to walk away.

Lynne waited until the cops were out the door. "Smashed?"

"Yeah. Hell, I was trying to save my damn life."

"Now what?" Lynne asked.

"I hoped you could tell me."

"I don't know. Marly was always a nut for backing everything up. Maybe she had a backup copy somewhere. We can check. How are you feeling anyway?"

"I'm dead tired. I hurt all over. I'm worried that someone is trying to kill me. I'm worried that the cops think I killed Marly, and I'm worried about the computer. I guess that's all."

"Hey, don't get sarcastic with me. Hell, I've been waiting and waiting, and then all I get is a phone call to go fetch some clothes."

"Sorry. I shouldn't be taking this out on you. By the way, thanks for the quick pick-up on the computer story. I just didn't want those guys knowing about it just yet."

"OK, no harm. Can we get out of here now?"

"Yeah. Just let me put my pants on, OK?"

"That's a first, a guy wanting to put his pants *on*," she said, and she chuckled at her joke.

It was a good line and Zack couldn't help but laugh with her.

"Zack, I'm sorry I was bitchy. I'll turn around and let you get dressed," she said as she turned away.

"Hey, no problem," Zack said. He slowly slid his feet off the bed to the floor, removed the skimpy hospital gown and reached for his clothes. Although Lynne faced away from Zack, he noticed her watching, trying to catch a quick peek as he dressed.

"I've got my car," she said. "I'll give you a lift home."

"That's great, thanks."

Zack finished dressing and they walked the short distance to her car. She watched as he painfully folded himself into the passenger's seat and buckled up.

He leaned back against the seat, closed his eyes and sighed. "I just want to go home, take a hot shower, and relax," Zack said, mostly to himself. He thought about Lynne's favor of getting his clothes for him. He owed her one. "I haven't eaten all day. If you want, we could order something for delivery at my place."

"Works for me," she said as she started the car. "Are you sure you're up to eating?"

"To be honest, I'm not sure. I still feel shaky, but I think something in my stomach might help."

It was a short drive from Northwestern hospital to his place and they made the trip almost without speaking, each caught in their own thoughts.

When they arrived, Zack unlocked the door and let Lynne inside while he went next door to get Katie. He assured his neighbor Terry he was OK, just a little sore, and thanked him for taking care of Katie. They returned to his place, and Lynne watched as Katie wiggled and squirmed and licked Zack's face in her traditional welcome home.

"That's quite a welcome. She must really love you."

"I know. You just can't beat it. Dogs ask so little—a little food, some water—and they give you so much unconditional love. That's my girl," he said patting Katie's head.

"I didn't know you were such a big softy."

"Yeah, that's me. Ol' Mr. Softy."

"Me, too."

Zack's eyebrows lifted, "Really?"

"Oh yeah. When I'm in the office, I am totally "at work," but get me out of there and I'm a different person."

"How so?" he asked.

"Well, you may not believe this, but women still have a higher hill to climb professionally then men do. So at work, I stay focused. Away from the office, I loosen up a lot."

It was true. At the office, Lynne was the consummate pro, in fact, sometimes too sharp and businesslike. When she wasn't around, the guys called her "The Lieutenant" or at times "Lieutenant Lynne," because of her abrupt style. But now, away from the office, he saw little of that edginess. Surprisingly, he'd never really noticed her. Probably, because she did remain so professional and remote, and of course, he was involved with Marly. Marly…the pictures flooded back and took over his brain. Marly…

He forced his mind back to Lynne, "Would you like a drink? Glass of wine?"

"Any Chardonnay?"

"Sure, I'll get it," he said as he went to the kitchen.

He returned with a chilled bottle, and a corkscrew. He popped the cork, poured two glasses and offered her one. He wondered if he should be drinking alcohol, but the Doctor didn't say anything about it. He decided to go easy.

"To better times," he toasted, his voice twinged with sadness.

They made eye contact as they touched glasses.

"Umm," she said, sipping the wine. "How are you feeling? Coming down a little? I know when something throws me out of whack, it takes a while before I feel normal again. God knows, you've been through a lot."

"I think being home helps. You know, familiar surroundings and all? I'm pretty sore, though. I think I'm going to take that hot shower. There are a bunch of delivery food menus in the top drawer of the end table. Pick whatever looks good to you. I'll just be a few minutes. OK?"

"Sure. Do you like Chinese?" she asked.

For the first time, Zack noticed her eyes, more blue than gray—like polished slate. "Yeah, my favorite. Just order whatever looks good and we'll share it."

The hot shower felt wonderful and refreshing. As the warm water beat down, it relieved some of the aches and pains, and he granted himself a few extra minutes of warmth and luxury. He turned off the water and grabbed a towel. He loved thick, oversized towels and after drying, slipped on a blue terry robe. He hand combed his hair, and walked back to see how Lynne was doing.

She had found placemats and dishes, and even had a couple candles burning.

"The food should be here in a few minutes," she said. "And, by the way, you look much better. Feel better?"

"Yeah, lots. The hot water helped."

They both reached for their wine glasses, and there was a quiet, awkward pause. Lynne broke the silence with a question.

"So what do you think is going on? I mean Marly's killed and then someone tries to push you in front of a train?"

"Lynne, I wish I knew. You do believe me? I mean about both Marly and the train?"

"Yeah, of course. Hey, I admit at one point I wondered a little, but I don't think anyone jumps in front of a train to prove a point."

"Lynne, I'm scared shitless," he admitted. "I have no idea what's happening or why. I'm even wondering if I was the real target the night Marly was killed. Hell, I was only gone a few minutes when it happened. And now, there's this train thing. Maybe I was the target all along and Marly just happened to be at the wrong place at the wrong time. But, then again, she was found naked, so that doesn't make sense."

"Why would anyone want to kill you? There must be some reason."

"I have asked myself that a thousand times, but I just don't have an answer."

"Isn't there some way to find out?"

"Well, I was hoping that computer might give us a clue, but now that's over."

"Maybe not," she replied.

"What do you mean?"

"I've been thinking about this. I just know that Marly was too much of a pro to have all that stuff on a computer without some backup, and I think I know where it might be."

"Really?" Hope sprang into Zack's mind. Perhaps after all, there was a chance.

"Well, I don't know for sure, but she had me reserve space for her on one of the servers at the office. I never knew why. Maybe she used that space to backup her laptop. Think about it. It's a great place because anyone who might find those files would believe they were just part of the Y2K project, and not think anything more about it. I'm betting those files are on that server. Tomorrow's Saturday. I'll go into the office and check it out."

"That's the best news I've had all day."

"That's not saying much, and it's just an idea, right now."

"Lynne, if this works out, I owe you big time."

"Even if we do find the files, there's no guarantee that they will lead us somewhere," she cautioned.

"I know that, but it's something," he said. "Besides, it's better than just sitting here while somebody finds a way to kill me that works."

"At least you still have a sense of humor."

Just then the doorbell rang...

CHAPTER 16

▼

CALIFORNIA FEBRUARY, 2000

It was mid-afternoon. K.P. stopped reading *The New Left Review* and looked around the apartment, thinking he might start picking up the place. Marly'd be here soon. Regular cleaning was not on his priority list. He didn't object to cleaning per se; in fact, he fully expected to spend a day or so scrubbing and polishing before Marly's arrival. But, he hated the routine daily pickup, and living by himself, he often postponed the effort.

Lately, he'd spent more time thinking about Marly, particularly her younger years. She seemed especially sensitive then, maybe because of her father's early death; he'd leave that to the shrinks. He knew he would never be "her Daddy," and at the same time, he felt responsible for Matthew's death. Maybe that blocked their efforts to communicate. Doubtless, he'd missed opportunities to be a better parent; too often focusing on other responsibilities. Certainly, he was no less attentive than a suburban dad who disappears daily before breakfast only to return after bedtime. In fact, when looked at this way, his course seemed more virtuous. Still, though, he could have balanced things better.

He smiled as he remembered one of the better occasions. When Marly turned ten, he held a surprise birthday party for her. He took her and a half dozen of her friends to Happy Hollow Park. They loved the puppet shows and the animals. They screamed and ran in huge circles playing tag games until they were exhausted. Marly thrived on the attention and treasured every moment, running faster and playing harder.

Marly had emailed that she would be arriving, although vague about exactly when. This would be her first trip back to California in over a year. She explained that she and her team worked extremely long hours, seven days a week through the end of the year. Fortunately, the Y2K deadline, midnight on December 31,

1999, had come and gone with no real glitches. Marly said she needed a vacation after the pressure of the final days and hours, and wanted to get back to see how her Uncle Kevin was doing.

There was a soft rap on the door—the bell had long since stopped working. K.P., in jeans and a t-shirt, shuffled to the door. He was startled when he found Marly standing there. He didn't expect her for a few days.

"Hi Uncle Kevin," she said. She had that impish smile that came out when she knew she "had him." "Surprised to see me?" She stepped into the apartment that was cluttered with newspapers and a couple old burger bags.

"What are you doing here already?" he asked.

"Aren't you happy to see me?" She looked classy as ever dressed in sharply creased tan pants and starched white blouse.

"Of course," he said, stretching forward to give her a hug, but keeping his usual "personal space" around him. "But you said you'd be here in a couple of days."

"I know. I wanted to surprise you."

"Well, you did. The place is kind of a mess. I've been keeping pretty busy and haven't done too well in the housekeeping department. Glass of wine?"

"Sure, why not. So, what's been keeping you so busy?" she asked, following him to the kitchen.

He rummaged through his catchall drawer for the corkscrew. "Oh, the usual stuff." In truth, he'd been working to organize an anarchist action group. After Seattle, he thought hard about ending his activist lifestyle. The youngsters in Seattle had little use for him—the "old man." But the need to make a difference had not died. He couldn't talk to Marly about his new group; she was apolitical to the core. He never understood that, in fact he resented it. After all, she was around all those years when he traveled to protest after protest.

"Like what?"

K.P. hesitated. Should he answer her question? Marly wouldn't get it. He decided to sanitize his answer, no use getting her all worked up. "Well, some of us were in Seattle for the World Trade protests a couple of months ago. There were so many demonstrators there, it was a rush. You probably saw the reports on television. I felt especially proud of our group." In fact, most of the protestors only waved signs and marched around. What the hell good did that do? His guys made sure they were noticed.

"Did you say, 'our group'? I'm not sure what you mean," Marly said.

"The Global Liberation Front," he said. "It's a group I've organized, but so far, there are only a handful of us. I patterned it after the Earth Liberation Front or the ELFS as they call themselves. But, they're only into environmental stuff. Our goal is to free the people from the bondage of governments and international corporations."

She heard the cork pop. "The ELFS? I've heard of them. Aren't they pretty violent?"

She surprised him; she knew about the ELFS. Interesting. Maybe there was an opportunity here. He would have to choose his words carefully.

He poured two glasses and handed one to Marly. "They worry about fancy hotels that were built by clearing virgin forests, and university labs that tinker with genetic research and screw up the food chain. The ELFS are right about those things. But under the surface, the real problem is capitalism. Wealthy corporations rape the forests under the guise of 'opening up the wilderness,' when in reality it's only money they seek. In order to line their pockets, they fund immoral research and engineer new genetic mutations without regard to the ecological risk. We need to change the system before capitalism ruins the planet."

As he spoke, his face got redder. "We don't want to hurt any living creature, man nor beast. However, we've got to stop the capitalists. So we'll try to strike where they feel the most pain, their wallets."

She took a half-step backward. "Wow. Isn't there some way to compromise?"

K.P. hated it when Marly bailed out like that, and his ire betrayed him. Before he knew it, he blurted a response. "Compromise? With who, the greedy corporations, or their bureaucratic lackeys? Impossible! My bitch is that the ELFS don't go far enough. I'm proud to say that our group, the GLFS, takes over when the ELFS chicken out."

Marly said nothing, and the silence was heavy. He knew he needed to change the subject. "Anyway, enough about me and Seattle and stuff, what's new with you?"

Marly appeared eager to talk about something else. "Well, on my last visit, I told you I had an idea we could use to embarrass the government bureaucrats and make them look like losers."

"Yeah, I remember. You were going to write some computer program that could cause blackouts. What ever happened to that?"

"Actually, I said that I would work on a *simulation* program that would give us a preview of what we might be able to do."

"OK, so what's up?"

"I think what I've done is even better. I think you'll like it. At least, I really hope you do. Wait 'till you see this."

She retrieved her computer bag from the living room and returned to the kitchen. Brushing aside some clutter on the table, she made a space for her laptop, opened it, and pressed the power button. She waited while the computer sprang to life and then selected an item from the desktop. When she double-clicked the program, a large map of the United States and Canada appeared. Superimposed on the map were yellow icons. She explained that the larger ones represented power-generating stations, while smaller icons were critical distribution points and key substations. She waited until K.P. took it all in.

"It works like this. I have a series of menus that I can select from. The program will show on the map what would happen if that selection were really made."

"I don't know what you mean," K.P. admitted.

"OK, it gets pretty complicated, so I'll give you an example." She slid a chair across the linoleum to the chipped white table, took a seat, and placed her fingers on the keyboard. "First, we'll select the geography; we'll pick the Mid-Atlantic region. Then, we'll pick the date and time. Let's use today at noon. Finally, we choose the desired effect, and for that we'll go for a three-minute power interruption. When I click on this 'go' button, the program will simulate what would actually happen under those conditions I selected."

"Wow, that's really cool," K.P. said as he pulled over a chair for himself.

Marly beamed and squirmed about. She spoke rapidly as she explained how the program would accomplish its task. "The system is pre-set to select the right set of programmable switches in a predefined sequence. After that, it's all automatic. First the substation switches are set, and then the distribution centers. I think you'll see how it works when I click the go button. Ready?"

"Yeah, go. I want to see this." K.P. answered, his mind already well beyond temporary blackouts. He remembered the young demonstrator in Seattle who thought it would be "way cool" to black out the city. Hell, this was much better. It would allow them to cause a blackout at the time and location of their choosing. He decided against sharing those ideas with Marly, at least for now.

"OK, here goes," Marly said as she started the simulation. The tiny icons representing the substations first blinked red, then changed to black. Shortly after that, the larger icons representing the distribution centers did the same. Simultaneously, a black shadow began growing near the center of the region and eventually engulfed the entire Mid-Atlantic area. Marly pointed at the screen and explained, "If we were doing this for real, this area would now be totally blacked out. Anyone who didn't have an automatic generator setup would be without power. The lights would go out, elevators would stop between floors, traffic lights would stop working, computers would shut down, radio and TV stations would go off the air, subway trains would be stranded in tunnels and so on. In short, total chaos for a full three minutes! Since this area includes Washington, D.C., can you imagine the so-called experts on the Sunday morning news shows trying to explain the blackout? Everyone from Senators to Cabinet members would be calling for heads to roll. Best of all, there's no way they could find out what happened because the switches are automatically reset to normal within seconds."

"Incredible, just incredible," K.P. said. Of course, he knew it was only a simulation, but if Marly could create the simulation, she might be able to create the real thing. He leaned back in his chair, removed his glasses to clean them, and began thinking how to approach the subject.

Knowing her motivation was to get revenge for her father's death, he said, "That's a remarkable program. You know, you're right. That blackout would make them look like clowns and probably cost them an election. That's one way to get even with them."

"Yeah, I know. Isn't it great?"

"But, how do you go from a computer simulation to being able to do the real thing?" He asked.

A smile popped to her face. "I thought you might ask that. Writing the simulator, I realized that creating the simulator was exactly the same work as doing it 'live.' So, rather than doing double work, I just added a menu selection for making it really happen. Of course, the computer would have to be connected to the Internet so that the program could communicate with all the switches, and naturally, I had to put a password on that selection to protect it."

K.P. had goose bumps. He couldn't believe his ears. This tool could bring "the system" to its knees. His entire life he had been frustrated by the government and the capitalistic system. Now, he had a chance. Things could be different. He wanted so much to share his enthusiasm with Marly. If he could only convince her of the value of "the cause," perhaps she'd join the movement. After all, like the other members of the group she was young, intelligent, educated, and best of all, she had personal reasons to hate the system. K.P. decided on a bold approach. He had to persuade Marly to join the GLFS.

"Marly," he began, "I want to talk to you about something important." How should he say it? It had to sound just right.

"Sure, what?" A puzzled look replaced her smile.

"I think you know that I have been against government and bureaucracy for a long time, but in the past few months, I've realized how important it is to start making a difference, *now*."

"What do you mean?"

He turned and scooted his chair closer to hers. "I know this sounds drastic, but I think the world is literally in trouble. Capitalism has resulted in a tiny wealthy minority dominating the masses, who are just trying to survive."

Her right hand scratched above her ear. "Isn't that a little too simplistic?"

"Only a little. Actually, just a few million people control the entire population of the planet. It's all based on money. Think about it. The wealthy control the international corporations, which in turn 'own' the politicians and the political infrastructure. They have the financial ability to force decisions and policies that increase their wealth at the expense of the people."

"But the people of the United States and other democracies can vote for whatever policies they want," she argued.

He started to get up, to walk. No, stop…less drama. He leveled his voice. "Not really, because corporations control the media, and therefore manage public opinion. After all, international companies own the newspapers and broadcast companies. For example, General Electric owns NBC, MSNBC, and CNBC; Disney owns ABC; AOL owns CNN, *Time Magazine,* and so on. They determine everything you see and hear, both news and entertainment. The stories they promote either increase their domination or limit dissent."

She reached for her wine. "You think they're brainwashing us?"

"It's not brainwashing, exactly. It's just that everyone's mindset is a product of what they hear and see. These companies manipulate all that. They use their power to establish a system that cements their wealth and power. For example, the World Trade Organization that we were protesting in Seattle exists purposely to maintain low wages in the third world. Who benefits from that? The multinational corporations."

"So the corporations are the bad guys?"

"Capitalism, yes. It's human nature. Everyone looks out for himself. The wealthy see their role as controlling everyone else. If they lose control, they lose money. If they lose money, they lose power and influence. Therefore, they have to perpetuate a system that dominates the world's masses. Anything less, they see as a precursor for disaster."

"I thought capitalism was supposed to be the system that works best?" She asked.

He forced his face blank, controlling his passion. "Of course, that's what the media have taught you and everyone else to believe. The U.S. touts the system because the capitalists control both the message and the messengers. How does anyone justify the poverty-ridden third world? If capitalism is so great, why do so many people in the world live in unbearable squalor, while the wealthy few have so much? It just doesn't make sense. Besides, it's easy to be in favor of a system that benefits you. Ask anyone who struggles for the basics of food, water and shelter what they think of capitalism."

"Hey, you're really into this, aren't you?"

"We *all* should be, and we have to act now to save the earth before the greedy corporations destroy it."

"Destroy the earth? Really?"

"Absolutely." He moved his chair even closer, almost touching hers. He reached for her hand, but stopped short. "This is where the ELFS have it right. Our environment is in critical condition. Forests are being leveled; oceans are over fished. Our waters and air are polluted. But the worst and most immediate problem is global warming from burning all those fossil fuels. We're destroying the planet's ecosystem while the government wants more studies. That's because the capitalists control the government. If we don't start protecting the environment immediately, we're risking a total ecological disaster."

She held her glass in front of her with both hands. "So what is it you're doing?"

"We're taking action."

"What does that mean?"

"It means that we're trying to do three things." He counted them with raised fingers. "One, we'll educate the intelligent people of the world and get them to look beyond the messages of the capitalistic media. Two, we'll take whatever actions necessary to stop the capitalists from causing more damage to the planet. Three, we're building our forces by getting smart people like yourself to join us in this struggle against capitalism."

"The GLFS as you call them."

"Yeah, the Global Liberation Front. We want to protect people and planet from the greedy capitalists that control the world's infrastructure for their own benefit."

"That sounds like you're anarchists."

"Yes, and damned proud of it." Well, now he'd said it. Now, it was out there. "But let me explain. Anarchists have been given a bad rap by the media. We've already talked about why the media is against us. The anarchists are the only ones speaking up for the oppressed peoples and distressed environment."

Marly stared into her wine glass.

"I know I've thrown at lot at you," he conceded. "But, I want you to think about it. You're smart. Once you get by all the propaganda and preconceived ideas about anarchists, I think you'll see we're right. Put it this way, if we don't stand up for the environment and the people, who will? Or, should we just abandon the planet earth and its inhabitants so that the rich will get richer? I want you to join me; I mean join the GLFS. We need you. The world needs you."

He thought he saw a glimmer of light in her eyes. Maybe his little speech had gotten through. He had been careful not to talk about exactly *how* the GLFS intended to take action. Although the media proclaimed non-violence as the way to social change, he knew that true non-violence never accomplished anything. When one looked behind the media's oft-touted stories of Gandhi, for example, they would find the issues more complex and riddled with violence in various forms.

He had established the GLFS to take whatever actions were needed to force the necessary changes. He hoped that Marly would join them, but regardless he needed that power-blackout program to advance "the cause." Nothing, and no one would be more important than "the cause." Nothing less than the future of the world depended on it.

*   *   *   *

K.P. watched Marly move around the apartment straightening magazines, dusting, tidying up. He knew the signs. Most of the week had passed and Marly's visit to the west coast neared its end. She made it her habit to clean the place before heading out; a classic "everything in its place" kind of person, she always made sure everything was organized and put away before she left.

She headed to the kitchen with a stack of newspapers destined for the recycling basket. Since their earlier conversation, neither she nor K.P. mentioned her joining the GLFS. The time had come and he brought the subject up. "Have you thought more about what we talked about?" he asked.

Her eyes avoided his. "Uncle Kevin," she said, dropping the papers into the basket, "you know how special you are to me. I'd do anything for you but..."

"But, you don't want to join us," he said, sitting down at the kitchen table and finishing her sentence.

Tiny tears appeared in her eyes.

"Why not?" He wanted to understand, but he couldn't—the picture so clear, the world teetering on the brink of disaster.

"I'm sorry. I really am. I just don't see things as you do. Please don't try to persuade me. I know you're really into this, and that's OK. It's just not for me."

"Damn it Marly, damn it," he said, the anger visible in his clenched jaw. "You didn't talk with anyone else about this did you?"

"Not really." She turned away from him, and began filling the sink with hot water.

"What do you mean, 'not really?'" he asked. Importantly, the GLFS needed to remain unknown until the right time—a time with the greatest impact.

"Well, I talked to Zack on the phone. I asked him what he thought of groups like the ELFS. He said right off that people who commit criminal acts are criminals."

That fucking Zack. "You didn't mention me or the GLFS did you?"

"No, no. I wouldn't do that," she said, squirting piney liquid into the sink.

"Good. He doesn't need to know any of this. What about your friend Lynne? Did you tell her anything?"

"Of course not. If I didn't tell Zack, I sure as hell wouldn't tell Lynne." Marly faced K.P. and stiffened. "Uncle Kevin, I just can't get involved with this stuff. You've been chasing this shit all your life and look where you are. You still have the same dumpy little apartment you had thirty years ago."

Marly stunned him with her frankness; the truth hurt. "What stuff?"

"Demonstrations, boycotts…"

"OK, OK. We'll just have to agree to disagree. But what about the program you showed me?"

"You still want it?" she asked, a wariness in her tone.

He had to have that program, but if Marly suspected his real intentions, she'd never agree to give it to him. "Sure, like you said, it's a great way to embarrass those government losers."

"I guess it's OK. I'll make you a copy of the program and the files I have now. I'll email you the updated files when I get home."

"Updated files? What do you mean?"

"Those grid files are constantly being updated because equipment and switches are always being changed. I still have access to the live files, but to keep current, I need to keep updating my copies. I'll send them to you encrypted, just in case anyone's looking at your email. That way, if someone does see them, they won't be able to tell what they are. I'll give you the encryption software and key before I leave."

"OK, good."

She grabbed a towel, dried her hands and looked directly at him. "Uncle Kevin, you've got to promise me something. I'm serious. This is really important." He knew she was studying him, looking for any revealing expression.

"You'll only use this program like we've talked about. You know, short blackouts just to embarrass the government. *Nothing else.*"

His face remained blank, and he assured her, "Of course." He would agree to any conditions. This program could send a wakeup call to the world. He'd found the Achilles heel of capitalism.

"You promise?" she asked, again.

He held up his right hand. "Yes, I promise." He hated lying to Marly, but "the cause" had to come first. This was his one real chance to make a difference—to be someone. He still had a problem, however. He needed her expertise. A small blackout would be fine if he only wanted to embarrass someone. But in the end, he didn't want to stick his thumb in the capitalists' eyes; he wanted to blind them. He had to be able to leverage the potential of that program. Only if he knew the program inside and out could he be certain that he had the tool that he wanted and needed. He had to persuade Marly to share her expertise, to make him an expert on the program, but how? He knew a philosophical political discussion would be futile. She was not a "believer" and he knew he could not convince her with logic. He decided to play on her emotions, leveraging her father's graphic death and her personal devotion to him.

"Marly, there is something special I want to do. I want to use your program as a tribute to your father. He gave his life trying to make this world better. Ever since that night, I've worked to achieve that goal. I promised your father that I would take care of you. I think you know how much I love you. Right now, I need your help."

"Uncle Kevin, you know I love you. But, what is it you want?"

"I want you to show me how the program works."

"What do you mean?"

"There is a big World Trade meeting coming up. We're already planning the protests. Think of it this way. When the American colonists confronted the British at Lexington Green, everyone called it 'the shot heard round the world.' It was only a skirmish, but the colonists were inspired by it and they began a process that changed the world. We are going to do the same thing. You once said that you'd waited thirty years to avenge your father's death. Well, the time is now. This movement—in your father's honor—will be the new Lexington Green."

"What exactly do you want?" she asked, joining him at the table.

He could tell the appeal moved her. "I want you to teach me everything about the program, how it works, how you set it up, how the various controls work, everything. Just think about it. Government goons caused your father's death. This protest helps make that right."

"I don't know," she replied, her eyes shut tight.

"Marly, you don't have to do anything. I just want you to show me how it works. That's all."

"Promise me no one will get hurt."

"We won't hurt anyone, just some harmless blackouts to embarrass the bureaucrats."

"OK," she whispered.

"Great. When can we start?"

"It won't be easy. There's an awful lot to know," she warned.

"That's all right. How long will it take?"

"What exactly do you want to know?"

"Everything. The places on the grid with the greatest impact."

"OK, but you have to be really careful because of the 'cascade factor.'"

"What's the 'cascade factor?"

"That's a name I made up to describe what could happen where one thing causes more things to happen. It's like dominoes falling where one knocks over the next, except it's a one-to-many scenario instead of one-to-one. For example, if you set the switches wrong, you could burn out a set of key transformers and create a power surge. That surge in turn would burn out more transformers, and so on. From that point on, the failure would cascade throughout the entire grid."

"You mean, literally blackout the whole country?" he asked.

"Worse. It's actually more complicated than that because there are four grids. But, the real problem is that the outage wouldn't be temporary. You'd permanently destroy hundreds or thousands of transformers and transmission controls, and totally shut down the entire power grid."

"Everything could be replaced though, right?" he asked.

"Only theoretically. No one has that much equipment in inventory so a lot of equipment would have to be manufactured. But since the plants all run on electricity, they couldn't build the necessary components. It's a huge chicken-and-egg problem. Essentially, the entire continent would come to a screeching halt for a long, long time. Now you know why I'm making you promise to only use the program as it was setup, for short-term blackouts."

"Yeah, now I see." Incredibly, this program could do more than he'd hoped. He couldn't let Marly know how he felt for fear she might have second thoughts. No, he had to play this straight, at least for now.

Strictly for her benefit, he said, "I guess I have a lot to learn. Just to be safe."

"Now remember, you promised."

"I know. I promised," he said. "It looks like I have a lot of work to do. Can we get started today?"

"Why not? I only have one more day here. That won't be long enough, but it should give us a start. From there, we'll have to trade emails. It's a good thing we'll be using encryption."

"OK, let's get going," KP said. He couldn't believe it, his lifetime dream within reach. If he controlled the power grid, he could force the end of globalization.

Chills ran through him. He intended to do just that.

CHAPTER 17

▼

CHICAGO, OCTOBER 19, 2001: 8:30 P.M.

The Detectives walked two blocks to their car, and then drove up Larrabee to the Eighteenth District. After exchanging greetings with the Friday-night-duty cops, and locating a pot of hot coffee, they sat down to compare notes. Their hospital interview with Dreyben had injected a new wrinkle into their investigation.

Rob Harrison's old wooden chair squeaked as he leaned back and propped his feet up on the desk. Stockano sat on the corner of the desk off to Rob's left, a steaming Styrofoam cup in his right hand.

Rob leaned forward for a tissue from a box on the desk and began cleaning his glasses. "You know, Jimmy, the more I think about it, I believe we got two suspects, not one. One is Dreyben and the other is Rydahl. Look at it this way; the forensics suggest Dreyben, but we got no motive. On the other hand, we got no forensics on Rydahl, but we got two possible motives—McCalley getting the job she wanted, or maybe Rydahl having the hots for McCalley's boy. What do you think?"

"Damn it, Rob," Stockano answered. "If you mean, do I still think Dreyben fucking killed her, the answer is yes."

Harrison restored his glasses to their usual perch. "So you think Dreyben staged the 'EL' accident?" Rob asked, staring over the lenses.

"Rob, you got me there."

"See, that's my problem," Harrison said. "He gives us a story about an old, gray-haired lady standing behind him. You got to remember he has no idea that we found that old coat and wig. That's a ton of coincidence."

"I don't know. Maybe he knew we would find it."

"Ah, come on, Jimmy," Rob answered. "You suggesting that he planted the coat and wig so that we'd discover them? If he went to all that trouble to set up a scam, he'd make goddamn sure he didn't actually die. But, he damn near did die when that train hit him. I don't believe it was a setup."

"Yeah, OK. You're probably right," Stockano said.

This case was complicated enough. Rob wanted to make sure he and Stockano were on the same page. "So we agree that someone tried to take him out?"

Stockano nodded, "Yeah." Then, he paused for a moment and with a puzzled look added, "What if he was involved in McCalley's murder with someone else and that person tried to take him out."

Rob mulled that over and said, "Hell, anything's possible, but that kills your theory about him being some sexual sicko that got carried away."

Stockano shifted his weight on the desk and turned towards Rob. "Maybe not. Maybe they had a threesome that night."

"Jimmy, slow down. Think a minute. The only DNA evidence we found was Dreyben's. That shoots down the Ménage a trois theory."

"Unless..."

"Unless, what?" Rob asked.

"Unless the third party happened to be another female," Stockano said.

"What are you saying?"

"Just listen to me for a second, Rob. What if there were three of them that night, McCalley, Dreyben and another woman? Dreyben's servicing both of them. They play around and tie McCalley up with the scarves; he screws her brains out. When the fun and games are over, the two of them toss her over the railing. Hell, she's already tied up with the scarves, it's nice and easy."

"Holy shit," Harrison said. "But then, who tried to take Dreyben out tonight?"

"The other broad," Stockano said excitedly, as if surprised by his own revelation. "Maybe she's thinking Dreyben will go belly up and tell the truth."

"And implicate her," Harrison said, "because she's the one with the motive."

"Exactly."

"So, if you're right, we need to be looking for a female friend."

"Guess who?" Stockano asked, eyes wide.

"Rydahl."

Stockano pointed at Rob, "Bingo."

Rob played that over in his mind. It could explain why she was in such a hurry to blast into the ER tonight and be there while we talked to him.

Stockano was still talking. "You know, if you think about it, she knew he was taking the 'EL' home tonight. It could explain why the big coat and gray wig were necessary. She'd have to make sure he didn't recognize her on that platform. By the way, how tall is Rydahl?"

Rob answered, "Hmmm, about your height, five-seven, five-eight, something like that. That fits…OK, but what about the diversion, the two guys arguing?"

"Maybe just two guys arguing and not a diversion after all," Stockano offered.

"Regardless, we need another visit with Dreyben, and we need to question Rydahl again."

"If we're right…" Stockano mused.

"We don't know anything yet. Let's just make sure we're not working on a second homicide. It's still early; let's go see our Mr. Dreyben again."

*   *   *   *

When the doorbell rang, Zack went to the door with thirty dollars in hand expecting the Szechwan Pagoda's food delivery. Unfortunately, instead of the food, he found Detectives Harrison and Stockano looking to ask him a few more questions.

Zack wilted. "Ah, come on guys. Can you give me a fucking break? I already told you everything I know at the hospital. I'm tired and I'm sore and I'm waiting for some dinner. Can you make it quick?"

"Can we come in?" Harrison asked.

"Do I have a choice?" he said, standing aside.

Stockano checked out Zack's robe as they walked through the front hallway, "Nice," he said with a crooked smile.

Zack tugged the terry belt tighter. "I just took a hot shower to try and relax some."

"Sure," the Detective replied.

As they entered the living room, the two cops spotted Lynne. "Miss Rydahl, we didn't expect to see you here," Harrison said.

"I told Zack I'd give him a lift home. We decided we were hungry and ordered some food. We're waiting for it now."

"Actually, it's just as well. We'd like to ask both of you a few questions. I think this will be quicker if I talk with Mr. Dreyben here and maybe Detective Stockano and you, Miss Rydahl, could check out the kitchen?"

"Ah, come on. Is this really necessary? Can't this wait until tomorrow?" Zack asked, unable to hide his irritation.

"Yes sir, it is," Harrison responded.

Stockano motioned toward the kitchen. "Miss Rydahl?"

When Stockano and Lynne were safely in the other room, Harrison began asking Zack about Lynne and Marly. "How would you describe their relationship?"

Zack did not offer the Detective a chair. Maybe he'd get the hint. "They were good friends, maybe best friends."

"Can you tell me a little more? Did they go out together socially, or was it mainly an office friendship?"

"I don't think Marly went out with anyone very much, so I guess it was basically in the office, but you should ask Lynne that question."

"We will. How long have you been friends with Miss Rydahl?" Harrison asked.

"Two or three years. Lynne was at the Company when I joined them in '98. But, we really weren't what you would call friends all that time. I guess you'd say that she and I were more acquaintances than friends."

"But, you would call yourselves 'friends' now?"

"Yeah, I think so. Yeah."

"You're uncertain?"

Harrison was sharp. Zack wasn't sure exactly what the situation was with Lynne. To be truthful, he and Lynne were wary of each other. "Well, Marly's death affected both of us. It's kind of brought us together," Zack answered. His mind raced. He thought about Marly's computer and those yet-to-be-answered questions. He wasn't willing to share all that with the cops, however.

Harrison paused. His index finger scratched his nose. "I see. So you'd say you're 'friends' now, and, this a recent thing?"

"What are you getting at?"

"I'm just asking how long you and Rydahl have been friendly?" Harrison said, glancing at Zack's robe.

Zack realized how it must look. Only days after Marly's death, Lynne's at his house having dinner, and he's wearing only a bathrobe.

"Look, Lynne and I are friends. She was nice enough to give me a ride home from the hospital. We were both hungry so we ordered some food to be delivered. While we were waiting, I decided to clean up and take a hot shower for a little relief. That's all."

"So there is no romantic interest between the two of you?"

Zack thought for a split-moment then responded, "Nope."

"If I asked her the same question, would I get the same answer?"

"Yeah, I think so."

"Just think so?"

"Harrison, I am too fucking tired to play word games. If you want to ask Lynne, go ask her."

"Did you ever sense any jealousy? Better yet, did either of them ever mention any tension or rivalry?"

"You mean, was Lynne jealous of Marly? No. They worked great together. Marly did mention once that Lynne felt she should have gotten Marly's job, but that was a long time ago."

"Anything else?"

"Nothing really. They were both good at their jobs, although they challenged each other."

"Interesting. Can you give me an example?"

"One time, Lynne tried to find an especially difficult program bug. Marly bet her lunch that she could find it first. That kind of thing."

"Did she?"

"Marly did find it first, and Lynne had to spring for lunch at The Everest Room."

"How did Rydahl take that?"

"Fine, but she made sure she won the next time. Lynne is wickedly competitive."

"On the whole, what do you think McCalley thought of Rydahl?"

"Lynne was Marly's best friend. She admired Lynne's technical skill, but even more so, her ability to relate to people. Marly used to say that she wished she was more like Lynne that way."

"What way is that?"

"It wasn't easy for Marly to meet people and strike up a conversation. Lynne, on the other hand, has no problem making friends."

"Did McCalley resent that?"

"I don't think resent is the right word, maybe envy."

"Anything else you can think of?"

"Sometimes I thought she wished she had Lynne's looks."

"In what way?"

"Well, Marly was a very attractive woman, no doubt about it. But..."

"But what?" Harrison scrunched his nose to reposition his glasses, keeping his pencil and pad in separate hands.

"Marly would ask me if I liked blondes better, you know, that kind of thing."

"What did you say?"

"I told her I thought she looked great exactly as she was."

"And, how did she take that?"

"OK, I guess. I answered it as well as I could." Zack shrugged, "Why the hell do women do that anyway?"

"Did she mention Rydahl's looks a lot?"

"A couple of times. I don't think it was any big deal."

"How close do you think they were?"

"Well, Marly said a number of times she loved Lynne. You know, the way women talk." Zack wondered why Harrison wanted to know this stuff.

"Do you think there was any other relationship between them?"

"Like what?"

"Romantically maybe?"

"Between Lynne and Marly? Noooo. No way!"

"How can you be so sure?"

"Marly was no lesbian. She was very much into heterosexual sex; I know."

"What about bi-sexual?"

"Nah, no way. Couldn't be," he answered. Actually, he'd never thought about it, but the idea intrigued him.

"What about the three of you? Any three-way parties?"

That did it. Zack pushed his finger in Harrison's face. "No, none! You guys are a real fucking piece of work, you know? First you tell me that I am a prime murder suspect. Then you come over here and ask if Marly and I were having a threesome with her best friend. You guys are sick!" Zack turned away, and walked across the room.

Harrison followed him, and said stiffly, "Mr. Dreyben, calm down. These are questions I got to ask. Jealousy can be a powerful motivator."

"You think Lynne was jealous of Marly?"

"We don't know. It's possible. We're looking at everything."

Zack's eyes bugged out. "Are you saying you think Lynne was somehow involved in Marly's murder?"

"I'm not going to comment on that. We're just doing our job, looking into every possibility."

"Are you about finished?"

"Not quite. I have a couple of questions about your accident earlier."

"I told you everything I know," Zack said

"Did Rydahl know you were taking the 'EL'?"

"Yeah, I think so. She knew I was going home. We planned to meet later."

"Did she know what time you'd be leaving?"

"Probably had a pretty good idea, why?"

"We're just checking; that's all."

"Are you suggesting she had a part in the accident?" Zack asked in disbelief.

Harrison ignored Zack's question. "You remembered an old gray-haired woman behind you, right?"

"Yeah."

"Mr. Dreyben, have you ever purchased a wig?"

"No, why?"

"We found a gray wig in a trashcan on the Van Buren platform. Do you know anything about it? It had a label from a costume shop on Milwaukee Avenue. We're going to check there tomorrow to see if a clerk might remember selling that wig to someone. If you know anything about it, you should tell me now."

"I don't know what you're talking about." Zack answered, his patience sapped.

"OK, I wanted to make sure we asked."

"What the *hell* are you getting at?"

"Don't know. All I know is that you said you saw a gray-haired lady behind you and we found this wig. We're just checking things out."

"You think it was a disguise?"

"Again, don't know."

Zack's head whirled—a wig, a disguise—and, all those earlier questions. Did the cops think it was Lynne? Could Harrison be trying to tip him off? Zack thought back to the list he made of Marly's acquaintances hoping to find a clue to her murder. He knew everyone on the list, so he likely knew her murderer. He recalled Harrison's statement about jealously being a strong motivator. But, they couldn't suspect Lynne. That didn't seem possible. No, it couldn't be.

"Are you finished?" Zack asked.

"Yeah, I think so," he answered, closing his notepad and folding his glasses. Just then, Stockano and Lynne returned from the kitchen.

Stockano looked at Harrison. "Let's go," he said tersely.

Zack and Lynne followed them to the front door. As they opened it, the Szechwan Pagoda deliveryman arrived with their dinner. The two Detectives exited, heading back to their car. Zack fished around in his robe' pocket to find the money, paid the deliveryman, and tipped him five bucks.

They carried the food to the dining room table. The candles were still burning, the wax falling around the candles' base. Lynne divided portions of sesame chicken as Zack refilled their wine glasses.

They picked up the chopsticks and began slowly picking at the food. After a few long moments, Lynne spoke. "What did he ask you?"

"I was just going to ask you the same thing," he said.

"Well, he wanted to know about me and Marly."

"What did you tell him?"

"I told him we were good friends. What else would I tell him?" She replied, then added, "you know, that Stockano guy is a real loser."

"He's an asshole."

"So, tell me what the other guy asked you."

"About the same."

"Anything else?"

"Not really," Zack answered.

Lynne sensed something wasn't right. "Zack, what's up?"

His pounding headache had returned, and his stomach churned; he felt nervous, on edge. He decided to fake knowing about the wig to see how Lynne would react. "Lynne, tell me about the wig."

"What wig?"

"Harrison told me about the gray wig." Zack purposely said as little as possible hoping she would take the bait and fill in any holes.

"What the hell are you talking about?"

"The wig on the platform. The cops know all about it."

"For the last time, I don't know what you're talking about," she answered louder. "If you think you know something, then spit it out."

"The cops found a gray wig on the train platform."

"So?"

"Remember, I saw a gray-haired lady behind me on the platform before I was pushed?"

"And you think I knew about all this?"

"I'm asking."

"OK, I'm telling you. I don't know anything about that wig or anything else that happened on that platform. Now, I understand why Stockano asked so many questions about how late I worked. I'll tell you the same thing I told him. I finished some work for a client. If you want, I'll show you the damn time sheets. I left about twenty minutes to six, which was ten minutes or more *after* your accident. Remember, we were supposed to meet here at six."

"Yeah, OK. With everything going on, I don't know what the hell to think. My mind is like Jello right now."

"You're a real jerk, aren't you? Do you really think I could have anything to do with either your accident or Marly's murder?"

"No, I guess not," he answered uneasily. But then he thought, he hadn't mentioned anything about Marly's murder. Why did Lynne inject that? Did she make some type of psychological slip? He decided he needed sleep and a clear head. He would think through this tomorrow. Right now, he just wanted to go to bed. He thought about saying something to Lynne when he noticed she was already ready to leave.

"You *guess* not? I'm out of here. I know you've been through a lot today, so I'm going to let this go for now. If you want to talk, call me. I am still going to the office tomorrow to see if I can find Marly's backup files. You're welcome to join me if you want. Remember, it was your idea that those files might be a clue to her murder."

Zack said nothing more as Lynne stomped past him to the door. He double locked the door behind her. Leaving the food uneaten, he headed for the bedroom. He was asleep within seconds.

CHAPTER 18

CHICAGO, OCTOBER 20, 2001 9:30 AM

Lynne, carrying her customary French Roast grandé with an extra shot, showed her badge to the security guard and stepped into the waiting elevator. Inside the car, she sipped the scalding coffee through the plastic lid, and waited edgily for the doors to open. Quiet. The best thing about Saturdays was the quiet. She'd get more done in a few early hours than a full day during the week. She often came in weekends—a curse inherited from overachieving, workaholic parents—but why the hell should she do extra work to help him?

God, he had pissed her off last night with those questions about the wig, and what she knew about it. Zack could be a real asshole. Why the hell *was* she here? She could be working out at the East Bank Club or catching up on that growing stack of *Bon Appetites*. She walked the darkened, deserted hallway to her office, so still, it seemed even the air had the weekend off. She parked herself behind her desk, pushed aside Friday's unfinished tasks, and cleared enough space for a fresh, yellow pad to take notes. She wasn't trying to help Zack. She would just clear up the mystery surrounding those grid files Marly had on her laptop. That's all.

She pulled the plastic lid from the cup, freeing the scent of strong coffee. Half the pleasure of Starbucks was the aroma. Her thoughts returned to last night and the wig. So the cops found a gray wig, big deal. What did that have to do with her? Why would he ask *her* about it? Did he really think she knew something, or was this all part of a convincing cover-up, a distraction to take the focus from himself?

She'd gone both ways on Zack. At first, she suspected him, but he convinced her with words and wrenching emotions that he was innocent, and needed help with Marly's computer. He was so persuasive. And then, the train accident—if it was an accident. What a great way to throw suspicion away from yourself. Concoct a story about a gray-haired woman pushing you in front of a train—if you could pull it off safely. She had no idea how close a call he'd really experienced. Could someone do something like that and survive? How the hell could she know? How could anyone know?

For her own peace of mind, she would find Marly's backup files, then she was done. Zack would be on his own. She recalled Detective Harrison's warning about "no one is above suspicion, and no one is safe." A chill trickled down her spine.

She hit the power switch and waited impatiently for Windows to spring to life. She expected the search for Marly's files to be quick. Allowing all of Magnicin's users as much storage as they desired, would be prohibitively expensive, so backup space was rigidly controlled and recorded. Marly, of course, was the exception.

Thanks to an earlier systems administrator, all the backup server names were fictional characters. Lynne sensed the irony as she searched the "Holmes" directory where Marly's files would be stored, if they were there at all.

She sat staring at the screen, massaging her jaw with her left hand, two middle fingers. She checked off sub-directories and files, until she found something unusual. One of the sub-directories, "MAM," did not follow the Company naming conventions, and stood out like a flag on July fourth—"MAM"—Marilyn Anne McCalley.

Marly's files were there all right. Lynne checked the dates on the files and found they'd been updated recently. Knowing how meticulous Marly was, she probably did weekly backups. Lynne wanted to see if Marly had also backed up her email files, so she looked for a ".pst" file. Sure enough it was there. Good.

Now that she'd located the files, she would let Zack know. Based on his reaction from yesterday, she was sure he'd be thrilled. She decided to spend a few minutes reviewing the files, maybe checking the email—just to see. If she found something interesting, she could tell Zack and save him some time. Yeah, she could do that much for him, anyway.

Most of the filenames were familiar from their earlier Y2K work, but the fact that Marly still had them was beyond bizarre. A new file, named "B-OUT-SIM" caught her eye. Her pulse picked up. B-OUT? Like Blackout? Nah, no way. She opened it and when prompted, entered the password she'd deciphered previously.

Her monitor went black and a full screen map of North America appeared. It had pull down menus for "LOCATION" and "DURATION" and a number of tiny icons which dotted the image. She looked for a help menu, but didn't find one, so she checked the LOCATION menu. Her choices were the seven major sections of the continent: North and Northeast, South and Southeast, Midwest, Northwest and Southwest.

Her blood raced. What the hell was this program doing? She tentatively tried the DURATION selection and found options ranging from 1 to 10 minutes. Holy shit! Her hands shook. She ordered herself to slow down and think. Think like Marly. Think logically, methodically.

Only one way to find out…she selected Midwest and 5 minutes. The icons changed colors and a black shadow began growing throughout the mid United States. Oh God! Her hands surrounded her face and sweat dripped from her forehead. It *was* a blackout program. Just a simulator, she hoped? Yeah, sure, SIM for simulator—maybe. She exhaled, never realizing she had been holding her breath.

Quickly, she closed the file. She searched the list for the program that created the simulator. There had to be one, unless it had been deleted. Please, please, let it still be here, she pleaded silently. "B-SIM" caught her eye and she opened it. YES! It was the program. She had to know if B-OUT-SIM was just a simulator, or God forbid, the real thing. She would have to spend a lot of time examining the coding to find out. The program was there, but it would take hours of tedious work to decode Marly's program. Unfortunately, Marly wrote tight code. This would be no easy task.

Zack. She had to call Zack. He had been right. Marly's computer did have suspicious files. So, he was telling the truth.

Her hands shook as she dialed his number. No answer, damn it, just a machine….

CHAPTER 19

---▼---

CHICAGO, OCTOBER 20, 2001: 11:00 A.M.

The telephone woke him; he didn't know how long it'd been ringing. For the first time in days, he'd slept soundly. Katie jumped on the bed, licking his face, wagging her tail. Zack rolled over to check the clock radio. No wonder Katie wanted him to get up. He reached for the phone, but by then it had stopped ringing. No big deal, he'd check his messages in a minute. Whoever called could wait that long. He shook the cobwebs away, pushed his hair off his face and went to get his dog-walking clothes. Anxiously, Katie danced about while he threw on jeans, a shirt and jacket, then stepped into some old loafers, skipping the socks. He made a quick pit stop, grabbed Katie's leash and his cell phone and headed for the door.

Katie, thankful to be outside, immediately took care of business. Enjoying the cool, clear October day, Zack decided to walk Katie over to Lincoln Park. Yesterday's "accident" remained fresh in his mind, but here, close to home, he felt secure. Even so, he reminded himself to be watchful. While they walked, Zack took a quick account of how he felt. His pounding headache had eased, and most of the aches and pains were gone. He found the fresh air invigorating and his head cleared. But, an undefined, uneasy feeling remained.

He flipped the phone open and dialed his machine, retrieving the call he'd missed earlier. He stopped cold when he heard Lynne's voice. The message was terse, only a dozen words, her voice wavering, full of tension. "Zack, it's Lynne. You need to come to the office right away."

Zack thought of last night, and Harrison's suggestion that Lynne might be involved in both Marly's death and the attempt on his life. He hated to think of it. At the same time, someone tried to kill him and he'd be foolish to ignore anyone and let down his guard.

Saturday morning, and Lynne had gone to the office to find Marly's backup files. Zack worried about meeting her. If Harrison's suspicions were right and Lynne had disguised herself as the old woman on the platform, he certainly didn't want to be alone with her in a deserted downtown office. On the other hand, those computer files offered him the only chance of uncovering Marly's killer. The stakes were high. If Lynne really were involved, he'd be walking straight into the lion's den. If she wasn't, those files just might unlock the mystery behind Marly's death and free him from suspicion.

He knew he had to act, and drew a deep breath of the crisp morning air. Even with Lynne's potential involvement, the enigma of Marly's grid files remained. Until he could untangle that puzzle, he had no chance to find the reason for her murder and clear himself with the police. He realized he had no choice but to take the risk and join Lynne at the office. He was glad he'd finally got a good night's sleep; he knew he would need it.

Zack proceeded cautiously. He left a message on Terry's voice mail telling him the time and whom he was meeting. He searched around in the kitchen junk drawer and found a small penknife and decided to take it along, although he wasn't sure why. He didn't bother taking a shower or changing clothes. The office would be abandoned.

He drove to the office—the weekend traffic light. It took him just ten minutes and he lucked out with a nearby parking spot. He entered the nearly deserted lobby, paused briefly to show his badge to the lone security guard, and walked over to the first bank of elevators. Stepping into the car, he punched "20." Strange…Marly's fall from her twentieth floor apartment started this whole sequence. He barely breathed as he stepped off the elevator and guardedly walked to his office.

He unlocked his office door, switched on the light and nervously looked around the room. Seeing no one, he slid into the leather chair behind his desk and reached across to the telephone, pressing the speaker button. He punched in Lynne's extension and waited only a moment for her to answer.

"Zack, I wondered if you were going to make it," she said. "Wait 'til you see what I've found."

"Why, what's up?"

"Can you come up to my office?"

He hesitated a moment. "Ah, yeah, OK," he said. Perspiration danced down the back of his neck.

"Are you all right?" Lynne asked.

"Yeah, yeah. I'm still a little shaky from yesterday, but I'm OK. What did you find?" He struggled to sound as normal as possible with his heart pounding.

"I have to show you."

"OK. I'll be up in a minute," Zack said, although he would have preferred meeting in his office. He checked his pant's pocket for the small knife, bucked himself up, and headed for Lynne's office.

Zack found the door propped open, and Lynne's face inches from her computer monitor with both hands supporting her head. She looked anxious, on edge. Keeping his right hand locked around the penknife deep in his jean's pocket, he stepped into her office, "Hey."

She turned and saw him in dog clothes and unshaven, "Hey, yourself. You still asleep?"

"Slept like a log. If it hadn't been for Katie, I'd probably still be out," he said.

"Zack, you're not going to believe this." Lynne said, stress straining her voice.

"What?"

"It looks like Marly was into a whole bunch of weird shit. I'm still trying to figure it all out. Maybe you can help put the pieces together."

"What the hell are you talking about?"

"It's easier if I show you. Come over here," she said, her right hand motioning to the chair next to her.

Warily, Zack sat on the front edge of the chair next to Lynne, watching her, not the screen.

"I found Marly's backup files on the server, just as I suspected. The dates are only a week old."

"And?"

"This is a program I found. As you can see, this is a map of the North American continent."

"And you think this is somehow related to her murder?"

"Just wait a second. We started this search looking for anything unusual that might be a clue, right?"

"Yeah."

"And the first things we found were the grid files. But we couldn't figure out why she still had them, right?"

"Yeah."

"Well, I think I know why she kept the grid files up to date."

"Why?"

Lynne pointed to the map on the screen. "This is a computer simulation of large scale power blackouts," she said, her voice cracking with tension.

"What do you mean?"

"This program shows how whole areas of the country can be selectively blacked-out."

"You mean cause them…the blackouts?"

"Yes. I still have to study the code, but watch how it works. It's scary."

Lynne started the program. Using the mouse as a pointer, she said, "These tiny yellow icons represent power generators and major substations. Up here at the top are pull down menus to select location and duration." Her index finger tapped the mouse. "So, for example, we'll take the Midwest for location and thirty minutes for duration. Here goes."

Zack stared as the icons flashed to red and a dark shadow expanded over the entire Midwest of the United States.

"What do you think it means?" he asked.

"Well, I think this simulation just demonstrated what would happen if key switches controlling the power grid were thrown in a prescribed sequence."

He began to grasp the significance. "Marly was planning to actually *cause* large-scale power outages? Ah, come on. Could she really do that?"

"It's possible. She certainly knew a hell of a lot more about the grid than the rest of us. I remember talking to her about what she called 'the cascade factor,' her name for what would happen if certain switches were thrown incorrectly. She described it saying as one component failed, it would cause multiple components to fail and in turn even more would fail and that it would just keep getting bigger and bigger."

"You know, I remember her telling me the same thing. Why would she want to screw things up like that?" he asked.

Lynne leaned back in her chair, "That's where I thought you could help."

Zack reflected on his time with Marly. Three years, and he never knew her. Did that say something about Marly, or something about him? "Shit, Lynne, I have no idea. She never said anything about blackouts. Why would *anyone* want to get involved in something like that?"

"I don't know. You know you hear about all those crazy groups protesting this and that, but I don't think Marly would have been into anything like that."

"Where do we go from here?" Zack asked. "You said you were going to look at the program code. Will you be able to tell what it's really doing?" he asked.

"I think so. All I know right now is that the program is a simulation. But, wait Zack, there's more."

"More what?"

"I was looking through all the backup files and I checked her email files."

Zack turned to look at Lynne, "Yeah, and…"

She squinted and frowned; her face wrinkled into a troubled look. "Some of the more recent letters look like they were encrypted."

"What do you think that means?"

"There's only one reason people encrypt stuff; so that no one can read it—no matter what. Marly sent and received a lot of encrypted email. Zack, she was hiding something."

"Lynne, remember when I read Marly's original email about me? There were other notes that looked like garbage and I thought were junk mail. Were those encrypted letters?"

"Probably. Anyway, we wanted to find something suspicious that might lead us to her killer. I think we've found it. Somewhere between those encrypted letters and this program, there's a critical piece to this puzzle, and damn it I am going to find it," Lynne said, spitting the words out.

Lynne's passion surprised Zack, her tone so adamant. Did *she* have something to gain? "How are you going to do that?" he asked.

"First, I have to study this program, then we'll know exactly what it can do. At the same time, we need to find the encryption key she's using. Unlike the passwords, there's no way to break the encryption. That's where you come in. You've got to help me."

"What do I do?"

"Encryption software uses a long string of bits as a key, 128 to be exact. No one's going to remember a string like that. That's why people drop the key onto a floppy and hide the disk in some secure place, maybe with a phony label on it. We have to hope that Marly did the same. It's as simple as this, if we hope to figure out what's going on here, we have to find that disk."

"Where do we look?"

Stress lined her brow. "Everywhere Zack, everywhere! I have a key to her office and I'll check there. You go to your place and look everywhere she might have hidden a floppy disk. We have to find that disk."

"Lynne, what if you're right?"

"What do you mean?"

"What if Marly's program could be used to cause blackouts?"

"If this program can do that, then we're in big trouble."

"Who, we?"

"Zack, I'm assuming that Marly didn't do this on her own. Someone put her up to it, and I'm guessing that's what the encrypted emails are about. If there are more copies of this program, the country could be facing total chaos. Someone killed Marly. If they're willing to murder her, what else are they willing to do?"

"Shouldn't we call the police?" he asked.

"I don't think so, not yet. We can't run to the cops until we have something to talk about. Heck, we know they're already suspicious of both of us. First, we need to figure out this program and find that encryption key. That's the only way we'll know what this is all about."

That comment jolted Zack back to the present. He had his opening. The stakes just got higher—no time now for indecision. "Lynne, you once asked me straight out if I had any part in Marly's murder. Now, I have to ask you the same question. Did you have anything to do with her murder or my accident, either one?"

Lynne's eyes popped wide open and she flared, "Fuck you, Dreyben."

"What does that mean?"

"It means I wouldn't be here busting my ass trying to decode something that would prove my own involvement, asshole!"

Zack expected the denial, of course. But the harsh language from Lynne stunned him. Fortunately, years of sales experience had given him considerable practice reading people's expressions and body language. He could tell more from *how* someone spoke than *what* they spoke. Her eyes stayed straight, not shifting or looking up and away. Her voice, though angry, remained clear, not hesitant. Finally, he watched her hands. People who lied often unconsciously put their hands over their mouth. These traits told him more about a person's veracity than words ever would. Lynne was telling him the truth. He'd bet his life on it.

"OK."

"OK? What does that mean?" she demanded.

"I mean OK. I believe you. But, I had to ask you just as you had to ask me," he reminded her.

"Yeah, but that was different," her tone lighter, less confrontational.

It didn't make sense, but it didn't need to. "Oh, OK," he said, letting it go. He felt better thinking he and Lynne *were* on the same side. "Where do we go from here?"

She sighed, "Is that it? You're OK?"

He nodded yes. Zack realized he hadn't eaten since this time yesterday "Can we get some lunch, I'm starved. I'll buy."

"You're damned right you'll buy," she said.

They walked to the elevator and waited. The confrontation had cleared the tension between them. Both of them were more relaxed and conversational as they made their way to the corner coffee shop. On Saturday, the shop was nearly deserted and they selected a booth towards the rear. Back there, no one could hear their conversation.

"What do you make of all this?" Zack finally asked.

"I don't know," she said. "Marly was hiding something. Who would benefit from blackouts?"

"Somebody who hates utility companies?" he started.

"Or, someone who is trying to make money from a utility failure? Like maybe someone who trades options on utility companies?" she asked.

"Good guess, but would Marly be involved in something like that? No, I think it would have to be something that Marly could identify with." Her image flashed into his mind. He knew so little about her. What were her passions? Encrypted emails, blackout programs, what next?

"Like what?" Lynne asked.

"I don't know. We have to find that encryption key and learn whom she was trading email with. That should tell us a lot," he said.

"Damn, why didn't I think of that sooner?" she said. "The emails. The text and the subject lines are encrypted, but the actual email address is intact. That's the only way it can be delivered. Now, the question is, can we trace it to someone that we know?"

Zack paused and caught Lynne's eyes. "There's something we're overlooking here."

"What's that?" she asked.

His voice strained and cracked, "We're dealing with murderers. They killed Marly and they tried to kill me."

"You're frightening me," she confessed. "Why do you think they're after you?"

"I wish I knew. It has to be linked to Marly. First, she's murdered and then there's an attempt on me. It's just too much coincidence to think these were random occurrences. Whoever is doing this had to know about our relationship."

"Do you think they might try to kill me, too?"

"If they think you were close to Marly, yes. The murderers must think that I know something that will get out if they don't get me first. The same thing would apply to you, I'm afraid."

"I think you're right, Zack, but..." she stopped, did not finish her sentence. Her eyes lifted toward the ceiling. "But, what if they didn't know about you before her death?"

"What?"

"Just thinking out loud. What if the murderer only found out about you and Marly *after* her death?"

"With all the press coverage, that means it could be just about anyone."

"Perhaps, but most people reading about you in the papers don't know much about you two. I'm thinking someone closer to the situation."

"Lynne, what are you talking about?"

"Maybe, just maybe, it's someone really close to the case."

The light bulb went on in Zack's head. "Like the police?"

"Could be. Try this…A rogue cop is out watching couples getting together, starts getting a little itchy himself, and sees the two of you walking to her place. He decides to try to get a little action of his own. He waits for you to leave and then pops in on Marly. It's a better scene than he could hope for because she's wearing nothing but silk scarves. He has his little party and then cleans up the evidence by tossing her over the balcony. Best of all, you're a perfect patsy because you were with her only minutes earlier. They indict you for murder and he's off clean, but there's a problem. You're fighting back. If you're somehow able to prove you're innocent, the investigation has to go on, and he runs the risk of being found out. What's the best solution? You have an accident with an 'EL' train. The investigation of Marly's death is quickly and neatly wrapped up, and no one's the wiser."

"But Stockano told me that the only real evidence at Marly's was from me."

"Of course, he's going to say that." I don't trust that SOB for a second. On top of that, when he sees us talking to each other at the hospital, he comes up with a cockamamie story about you and me and Marly in a threesome. Pretty creative don't you think?"

"Wow."

"Zack, I don't know if this is right, but I *am* sure we can't trust the cops. You and I have got to find Marly's murderers. If not…"

Zack finished her thought, "They will find us."

CHAPTER 20

▼

CHICAGO, OCTOBER 20, 2001: 11:30 A.M.

The frustration gnawed at him and sapped his motivation. For Detective Rob Harrison nothing was going right. A slow news week and McCalley's tabloid-style murder combined to attract the 24-hour news hacks, who otherwise wouldn't have cared less about one more urban homicide. It had only been a week since the killing, but the press and Rob's publicity-adverse Captain were pushing for an arrest. Both MSNBC and CNN had scheduled hourly updates from their Chicago correspondents on the progress of the investigation. Rob found himself pursued by gangs of video-touting cameramen whenever he left the District.

Up to now, Rob had been careful to avoid any statements to the press. Dreyben's accounts of bondage games and oral sex would be just the lurid details the reporters would love to blast across the airways. Unfortunately, someone leaked the autopsy report to the press, complete with photographs, descriptions of semen samples, and DNA comparisons. All hell was breaking loose. He had his suspicions about the source of the leak, but he would deal with that issue later. Right now, he had to subdue the media furor and the mounting pressure for an immediate arrest.

The Department's Media Relations team called a press briefing. The "spin" would be that a thorough, competent investigation was in progress led by an experienced Detective. Rob's role would be to confidently answer the questions while providing no new information that might inflame the situation. He braced himself for the ordeal. After all, he was a homicide detective, not a PR man. He despised these briefings for their intentional obscurity and the resultant absurdity.

The briefing began with the expected barrage of questions about details in the leaked autopsy report. For the most part, Rob successfully deflected the questions without compromising critical information. Just when he began to relax, one of the reporters blindsided him. Reporters…scum-buckets, vermin, experts at half-truths and innuendos—pricks just like this guy destroyed his Dad's reputation.

The portly reporter stood, wearing a bulging, dark blue jacket and unmatched, navy blue pants. His stomach sagged over his belt. With a fat hand he waved the leaked autopsy report and challenged Rob in that haughty, public-has-a-right-to-know tone, "Detective, we have it on good authority that you have the victim's boyfriend as the prime suspect and that you refuse to arrest him, even though these autopsy findings directly link him to the victim at the time of death. How do you respond to that?"

A buzz swept through the briefing room. Rob fumed. He knew who linked that report. Stockano had loaded the dice; played the media to increase the pressure for Dreyben's arrest. Both Detectives knew they had only half a case, but by leaking this report, Stockano tried to swing public opinion, force an early arrest, and make any defense doubly difficult for Dreyben.

"No comment," Rob responded. The tension pinched his throat making him short of breath. "I can't make any statements regarding pending arrests."

"So then you are confirming that an arrest is pending?" the reporter asked.

Rob swallowed half a glass of water. "I can only say that the investigation is proceeding well and that we are tracking every lead. Thank you," Rob said, and walked out the door, ending the press conference. He couldn't wait to find Stockano.

Rob charged up the corridor. It didn't take him long to locate Stockano sitting with his feet on the desk and a portable TV still tuned to the news channel that had carried the briefing.

"What the fuck do you think you're doing?" Rob demanded.

"What?"

"Don't give me that shit, Stockano. There're only two people that know the details about this investigation, you and me. You're the only one who could have released that information about Dreyben."

"Maybe it was Rydahl," Stockano replied.

Rob hadn't considered that. She might have clued the press in, hoping to increase the pressure on Dreyben. Then Rob remembered that the reporter claimed that Rob "refused" to arrest Dreyben. No, it had to be Stockano.

"That's bullshit," Rob shouted. "Rydahl doesn't know I'm reluctant to charge Dreyben. You're the only one that knows that. Just what the fuck did you think you were doing, anyway?"

Stockano looked like a guilty kid with chocolate on his face. "Oh, OK, OK. I gave them a little lead. I threw 'em a bone. It's no big deal for Christ's sake."

"Yeah, it is a big deal."

"Rob, the son of a bitch did it. You and I both know it. I say we bring him in and let the prosecutor worry about getting the conviction. At least we'll get the press off our butts."

"Is that what this is about? Listen, I hate those bastards more than you do, but I am not going to half-ass this investigation, and I'll be goddamned if I'll let a dirty cop with an agenda sabotage me. You're off the case as of right now!"

"What?"

"You heard me. I'm having you reassigned. I need a partner I can trust. You just proved that's not you."

It was Stockano's turn to be upset, his face crimson with anger. "Rob, you're fucking crazy. You're going to let that little shit Dreyben get away with this?"

"See, that's just it," Rob sputtered. "I can't prove that Dreyben has done anything. You got him convicted…no evidence…no trial. This Department has done too much of that in the past, and I'll be damned if I'm going to let that happen on this case."

"Fuck you," Stockano grumbled. His short legs churned as he stormed out of the office, slamming the door behind him.

It took a long time for Rob to calm down. He pondered why Stockano seemed so adamant about Dreyben's guilt. He had worked with Stockano for years and never known him to be so focused on a single suspect. Something just didn't fit, and inside, Rob was afraid to find out why.

CHAPTER 21

▼

CHICAGO, OCTOBER 20, 2001: 1:00 P.M.

A sun-faded sign on the glass door claimed the coffee shop had been owned by the same Greek family for thirty years. The food was good and fast, and priced right. Best of all, they believed in generous portions and big baskets of warm Greek bread.

Zack and Lynne sat in a secluded booth in the back with cushions so meager they felt like original equipment. The stress had spiked their appetites, and they pounded through Chicago-sized servings of Caesar salad with grilled chicken.

As they ate, Zack mulled over Lynne's suspicion about Stockano being involved in Marly's murder. The mere idea left Zack feeling exposed and powerless. If the police were perpetrators instead of protectors, no one was safe. Given his own experiences, he had gained a new empathy for those minorities who see the police as their persecutors.

Zack made himself think. He despised Stockano as an overdressed, unyielding, dogmatic dick, and Stockano did seem to have an odd interest in lurid details. But, the rest of Lynne's supposition was just that, supposition.

Zack sucked the last swallow of his Diet Coke through the ice cubes and looked over to Lynne. "You know, about Stockano? I just can't buy it. Not that I think the prick would be above doing something like that, it's just that I can't see how it could be. He was at Marly's place with Harrison when I got back there after she was killed. How could he murder her, and then link up with Harrison in such a short time? We're only talking minutes. Anything's possible, but I don't see how."

Lynne nodded her understanding, her lips strangely pressed together. Then, he watched as she found a mirror in her purse, and plucked a bit of lettuce from her teeth, leaving Zack to wonder if he had a similar problem. He ran his tongue across his upper teeth. She smiled at him and gave him the OK sign.

"I know," she replied. "And, that blackout simulator on her computer doesn't fit."

"What do you mean?"

"Well, look at it this way. If—just if—Marly was involved with something ugly, then it's a ton of coincidence that she gets murdered in a random attack at just that time, don't you think?"

"Yeah, I see what you mean. Possible, but pretty damn unlikely," he agreed.

"Exactly."

"So then, the only way we'll know for sure is to find that encryption disk. We'll worry about Stockano later," he said.

"Sounds right, and based on the fact that someone already took one shot at you, I think we'd better find that disk pretty damn fast."

The comment hit home, and the squeezing pain in Zack's chest reappeared. "Let's go. We have to find that floppy."

"We? Now?"

"Why not? The only clues we have are in those encrypted files, and I'm not crazy about waiting around while someone's trying to kill me. My place is a good point to start, and with the two of us we should find that disk in no time. Besides, I have to confess, I'd feel a lot more comfortable with some company."

"You're assuming the disk is there."

"I don't know. Hell, at least it's a place to look. Come on." Zack paid the tab. They left the coffee shop and walked around the corner to his car. The weather was changing with the wind blowing in off the lake, bringing the first hint of a Chicago winter. Without heavy coats, they walked briskly toward his car, thankful that he'd parked close by. Zack pressed the remote and the 540i dutifully unlocked their doors. They jumped in and paused a second to catch their breath. Zack watched Lynne as she raked both hands through her hair, adjusted herself in the seat, and reached for the shoulder belt.

"Set?" he asked, starting the car.

She nodded, "Let's do it."

Zack loved the light Saturday traffic in the City. He looked around, whipped a U'y and headed north on LaSalle. Luck with the traffic lights and the 540i's quickness put them in Lincoln Park in less than fifteen minutes; he guided the BMW into his assigned space.

A horde of media people charged them on their arrival. The crews had arrived within the hour after the police department's latest press briefing. A tangled scene emerged. News trucks pointed microwave dishes high and south to unseen towers. Burly cameramen were tethered to the rookie reporters, who had drawn the short-straw, weekend assignment.

The swarm descended on Zack and Lynne, pushing and shoving ever closer, each trying to out-shout the others, all eager for an on-camera statement or, better yet, a careless remark. Zack clutched Lynne's arm firmly and escorted her through the crowd of reporters and their out-thrust microphones.

Not surprisingly, with all the commotion, no one noticed two houses down, a pair of young punks and a man in his fifties, dumpy, with thick black-framed glasses. The three were leaning on the bumper of a deteriorating Jeep Cherokee. They had been there for two days.

Once inside, Lynne said, "You could have warned me."

"Hell, I didn't know they were here."

"What a bunch of sharks."

"More like weasels," he said.

Zack checked his message-waiting light and noticed that his neighbor Terry had called. In the voice mail, Terry was irate. He had heard a news report from this morning's police briefing, saying one of the reporters had named Zack in Marly's murder, and asked why the police refused to arrest him. Terry went on to explain that the media circus outside began shortly after that, and that the reporters had even bugged him for comments. He said he'd called the police, but they told him the press had their right to be there. The message ended with a colorful stream of obscenities describing the police and the press. Zack smiled knowing no comment from Terry would ever clear the airwaves. Terry had been more than a good friend through all this and Zack scribbled himself a reminder to somehow make it up to him.

Zack knew that the media attention would only grow worse until someone solved Marly's murder. Zack offered Lynne an opportunity to get out.

She straightened, "No way. I'm not going to let those losers intimidate me."

"Are you sure you're up to the assault?"

"Zack, I know you want to be the big guy in-control, but I can take care of myself. You've got to trust me, OK? I'm here because I want to be. I know what I'm doing. I want to find out who killed Marly. Besides, my butt's on the line here, too."

They were under a lot of pressure, and the stress exposed more of the true, unadulterated Lynne. He admitted he liked the picture, the strength. Self-assured women fascinated him. Through the years, many women were attracted to him and offered themselves easily; and, he hadn't declined. But somewhere deep inside, he respected strength as much as he admired beauty.

"I'm sorry. I underestimated you. It won't happen again. I'm a little uptight, but I am glad you're on my side."

Characteristically, Lynne's left hand went to her face, and the two middle fingers massaged her cheek. "OK, OK. So let's get to work. By the way, you know there's a good chance that disk isn't here, don't you? I mean, why would Marly leave it at your place instead of hers?" she asked

"I don't know. Maybe it's not here, but maybe it is. She left her laptop here, perhaps she hid the floppy here too. Let's start in my home office. That's where all the computer stuff is. Maybe she hid it there."

They walked to the office and began looking. Unfortunately, a single floppy disk could be almost anywhere. They started with the desk and found several floppies, but all of them checked out. The barrister bookcase became the next target; books were removed, inverted and shaken—nothing. The closet contained boxes with software manuals and disks buried in Styrofoam packing. Painstakingly, they checked the disks and repacked the contents. In all they'd spent nearly two hours, but no disk.

Zack, never much for patience, became frustrated. "Where the hell could she have put that goddamn disk?" Clueless where to look next he turned to Lynne. "OK, you're a woman, where would you hide it?"

"I'm glad you noticed…I think I'd put it somewhere that you don't look."

"Somewhere that I don't look?" he asked. "What do you mean?"

"You know, someplace so obvious you wouldn't notice it, sort of hidden in plain sight."

"Like?"

Lynne shrugged as she strained to think of an example, "Maybe under the divider in your silverware drawer or something like that."

He thought her idea sounded pretty lame. "OK, where else?"

"Gees, maybe an old recipe book, or the back of a lingerie drawer, or with the old dishes in the kitchen, or behind the refrigerator or under the TV, or…"

"Hey," Zack interrupted.

"Under the TV?"

"No, no, you mentioned the lingerie drawer. She didn't have a lingerie drawer, but she did have a 'favorite' drawer. This'll only take a second," Zack said as he turned and headed for the bedroom. Lynne surprised him by tagging closely behind.

He walked to the nightstand on the far side of the bed and opened the drawer. Inside was a collection of exotic items including jars of massage lotions, scented candles, and more.

Lynne edged her way around Zack. "Let me look."

Zack turned red and stuttered, "Well, er, we ah, just some stuff, you know."

Lynne spotted his crimson face and smiled. "Yeah, I see."

"The disk, remember?"

"I'm looking," she answered. "Wait a minute, I have something."

"Did you find it?"

"No, but I did find something reeeaally exciting," Lynne teased.

"Lynne, damn it, the disk!"

"OK, OK."

"Well?"

"Got it!" she shouted. "It's unlabeled, but I'll bet this is it. Quick, let's get your computer."

They ran to his office and powered up the laptop, and anxiously waited while it booted. Lynne inserted the disk and opened the files.

"There it is, but let's make sure," she said. Her fingers flew across the keyboard. When the screen displayed a long string of random characters, Lynne pumped her fist, "Yes. Yes! Now for the real test."

"What's that?" he asked.

"I'm going to log-in to the office net and see if this really is the key by opening those encrypted emails." Lynne dialed the server and waited for the link to connect and then entered her password to clear the firewall. Successfully on the LAN, she located the archived email messages and then applied the newfound key.

"That's it!" she screamed and spontaneously jumped up and hugged Zack in celebration.

"Awesome, just awesome," Zack said returning the hug. "Now what?"

"We start by finding out who sent the encrypted mail," she mumbled, already hard at work. "Weird, very weird."

"What?"

"A couple of things. This is going to take a little effort, but I have a feeling something is really crazy here. First of all, the email identity is "Black Beacon" which doesn't tell us too much, but we can work on it. The second thing is some of the mail looks like it's automatically created. I mean it looks like the kind of stuff that viruses or worms would generate."

"What does it mean?"

"I don't know yet, but we've just gone from one puzzle to another. Before we didn't know anything. Now, we can read the mail, but understanding it is another thing. I think we need to back up, and follow the mail threads from the beginning. Are you OK with that?"

Zack trusted Lynne's judgment, "Sure, if that's the best way."

"OK, then. I'll search the server to recover the files as far back as possible. Then we'll just keep following this Black Beacon's mail to Marly until we have a complete picture. This could take all night, you know?"

"Lynne, this is our only shot. I don't care how long it takes. If we don't find someone with a smoking gun, then I'm afraid he or she is going to find us. I don't know about you, but I am scared down to my toes and not ashamed to admit it. I say let's find out who Black Beacon is, and what the hell Marly was involved with before something else happens."

"OK then, let me work on this. There's not much for you to do right now until I get all this email a little more organized."

"All right. Maybe I'll just take Katie for a quick walk in the back courtyard. Hopefully, that press mob won't see us out there. We'll be back in a couple of minutes."

When Zack returned, Lynne had systematically examined the repository, and begun placing the letters in chronological sequence. She eschewed Zack's offer of help to avoid the confusion of a second set of hands and eyes.

*   *   *   *

Lynne stood and stretched, pushing her arms over her head, palms to the ceiling, fingers intertwined. A glance at the desk clock showed six even. Wow, four hours staring at that computer. She visually toured Zack's home office as she tilted her head side to side, ears to shoulders, freeing the tension in her neck.

Her eyes scanned full circle. The room was comfortable, homey and male. A richly detailed rug protected the dark hardwood floor, and the exposed brick gave the office a sturdy, warm feeling. She imagined the photo layout in *Architectural Digest,* "Successful Executive: at Work and Home." For sure, it looked like a professional decorator's work—carefully arranged furnishings, an expensive oriental rug, designer lighting.

Tiny, halogen lamps illuminated one wall with an official looking plaque and a large, framed picture of a younger Zack in a scarlet football uniform. She stepped closer to read the three lines engraved on a small brass plate: "Zack Dreyben, Ohio State Buckeyes, Go Ohio." Scotch taped in the corner of the picture was a snapshot—apparently taken some time ago judging by the clothing—that looked like a proud parent with his arm on the shoulders of a peewee football player. She studied the picture and a sad-clown's smile washed over her face.

Zack called from the other room, "Lynne, you want anything to drink?"

"Yeah, water'd be great," she answered as she scooted back to her chair. She didn't want to be caught snooping.

He walked in and handed her a chilled bottle. "Well?"

She looked straight at him, "Zack, you'd better hold on."

His head twitched slightly, a quizzical look on his face. "That sounds pretty ominous."

"It's worse than that. I'm afraid Marly got messed up in some pretty scary stuff."

"How scary?"

"Do you remember that blackout simulator?" she asked.

"Sure."

"Well, believe it or not, these email letters amount to a tutorial on how to shut down the electrical power grid of the United States."

"What?" Zack asked, his voice elevating in volume and pitch.

"You got it. Marly provided this "Black Beacon" person the ability to black out electrical power to whomever he or she wants. Marly sent him—I'm assuming it's a guy—the blackout program, instructions on how to use it, updated grid files and all the background knowledge he would need."

"Is that as bad as it sounds?"

"Worse," Lynne said. "If it's in the wrong hands, it's a damned terrorist's dream. She told him everything, even warning him about the cascade factor. If Black Beacon is a good learner, he can figure out how to destroy the electrical infrastructure for the entire North American Continent."

Zack leaned forward, both hands on the corner of the desk. "Are you sure?"

"She obviously trusted this Black Beacon. I don't know why. But the evidence is all here. Look for yourself."

"No, no, I believe you. It's just hard to think that Marly helped some terrorist."

"Based on what I can get from the letters, she felt some kind of bond with this Black Beacon guy. She wanted to be helpful to him but at the same time she constantly warned him about the dangers of misusing this capability. Even so, she must have been awfully damn naïve."

Eyes wide, Zack straightened, a fist at his face. "So, bottom line, right now, this Black Beacon guy is running around with Marly's blackout program and the ability to burn up the entire power system in the United States?"

"Yeah, that's right," she said and shivered. She felt shaky. Hell, she had never faced anything like this. Other than the pain of her divorce, the toughest thing she'd ever experienced were final exams.

"Shit...do you think that's why she was killed?" Zack asked.

"I don't know. But, I do think Marly started to get scared."

"Why? What do you mean?"

Lynne took a deep breath and it helped. "Do you remember I said some of the email messages looked like something a computer virus would generate?"

"Yeah..."

"Marly planted a worm in Black Beacon's computer. She outsmarted him. She set it up so that it gave her automatic updates on what he was doing with the grid files and so forth."

Zack furiously paced back and forth, finally asking, "Do you think he found out about it and killed her?"

"Zack, I don't know," she said in frustration. "As far as I can tell from the emails, he never caught on to it."

"What do we do now? Go to the police?"

"Not yet. We can't trust the cops."

"You're right, but we've got to *do something*," Zack said, his voice cracking.

Helplessly, the two looked at each other. Finally, Lynne broke the silence. "You know, when I went through the files, I focused on Marly's mail to Black Beacon. There's a bunch of email from him back to her. I think that somewhere in his letters to Marly may be the smoking gun you've been looking for. If we can find that, then we'll go to the police. Until then, I think we've just got to keep this between us."

Zack looked rattled. He was sweating and pasty. He'd been through a tough time what with Marly's murder, the cops grilling him, the accident, and now this. Amazing, she thought, that he could keep it together. "Zack, one more thing..."

"What?"

"Black Beacon kept referring to '*the event*' like it's the most important thing ever. Do you have any idea what '*the event*' might be?"

Slowly, he shook his head. Lynne saw her own fear reflected in Zack's eyes as she heard him say, "No. Let's just hope it's not soon."

CHAPTER 22

———— ▼ ————

CHICAGO, OCTOBER 20, 2001: 8:00 P.M.

With Lynne buried in Black Beacon's numerous emails to Marly, Zack decided to clean up. He took his time and enjoyed the luxury of a long shower, allowing the hot water to beat on his back, and relieve some of the tightness. He toweled off, brushed his teeth, hastily pushed a comb through his hair, and went to get a fresh change of clothes. He pulled a pair of khakis from their hanger and reached for a blue denim shirt. The shower and clean clothes transformed him; he felt fresh and invigorated.

Zack found Lynne still at it, the pressure of the past few days taking its toll. Her normally faint color now ashen; dark circles hung from each eye, and the natural lift of her eyebrows had disappeared. He thought she could use a hot shower as well, and a good night's rest.

Lynne pushed the leather chair back from the desk. "What are we going to do?" she asked, a tiny quiver in her voice.

He wished he had a comforting suggestion, but didn't. "I don't know, but we can't lose our heads. We've come a long way. We know Marly gave Black Beacon the blackout program with instructions on how to shut down the power grid. We also know that she worried enough about him that she planted that worm in his computer."

"But, we still don't know who murdered her, or why. And, for that matter, why someone tried to kill you."

Zack sat in a matching chair and leaned forward. "You're right, and it scares the hell out of me. We can't link any of this to her murder. Maybe if we knew who Black Beacon is, or what that 'event' is, we could go to the police, but right now they'd laugh me out of the station or worse. They're working a homicide. We're talking about power blackouts by somebody we can't even identify. We have to find the link between Black Beacon and her killer. It's only a gut feeling, but I think they're one and the same. But how can we prove it?"

Lynne's face brightened, "Maybe we let him prove it."

"What do you mean?"

There was a fresh enthusiasm in her voice. "The worm! If Black Beacon hasn't discovered it yet—and I bet he hasn't—then we can look through everything on his computer, just like it was right here. Why didn't I think of this sooner? Zack, that's it. With the worm Marly planted, we can log into his system and do whatever we want."

"Are you sure?"

"Yeah. Marly planted a version of a program called 'Back Orifice' that's floating around the web. She obviously duped him into executing some file that installed the worm on his system. Since he trusted her, he had no reason to suspect the file was really a Trojan horse. All we have to do is hop on the Internet and go fishing."

"You mean we can actually look at everything on his computer?"

"Absolutely. All we need is his IP address and I'll get that. Then, we just connect to his computer."

Zack walked over behind Lynne. "What the hell are we waiting for?"

She pulled the chair back up to the desk and quickly connected to Black Beacon's computer.

"Won't he know we've invaded his machine?" Zack asked.

"Nope. We're just going to watch for a minute. If he is using the computer, we can see exactly what he sees on his monitor. If nothing is going on, then we'll operate his system right from here. OK, here goes...."

"What's he doing?"

"Nothing right now. No programs are running."

"Awesome, awesome. So what now?"

"Well, let's take a look at his file manager and see if we recognize any of the folder or file names."

Zack watched Lynne attack the keyboard. Only a few moments ago, he worried that she'd pushed herself too hard, but now, suddenly she had new vigor. He'd learned something important about Lynne. Like most overachievers, she was goal driven. Given a target, she would break through walls to hit it.

Zack checked his watch and saw that it was after eight. "Hey, how about some dinner? I'll order some food." Zack said.

"Yeah, OK," Lynne answered, engrossed in the scrolling images on the monitor.

"I still have a taste for Chinese." he said, remembering that the last time they ordered Chinese, they argued and neither ate it. "I could go for something with a little spicy kick to it."

"OK. I'll keep working on these Black Beacon's files."

Zack reached for the cordless phone, punched the memory code for his favorite Chinese restaurant, the Szechwan Pagoda, and placed a delivery order for Spicy Szechwan Broccoli with shitake mushrooms and a side of vegetable fried rice.

Lynne was still searching through Black Beacon's computer, "Zack, look at this."

"What?"

"There are some very interesting things here." She pointed to the rapidly changing list of folders and files in front of her.

"What?"

"There's a folder named "GRID" which we probably could have guessed. One named "GLFS" whatever that means. And, get this...there's a folder named 'WTO CONF'. Zack, isn't there some big World Trade meeting here in the next week or so?"

"Maybe, but to tell you the truth, I've been so tied up with all this Marly stuff, I haven't been watching the news much."

Lynne squirmed in her chair. "Zack, don't you get it?" she asked.

"Oh my God. 'The event.'"

"Exactly. Maybe we shouldn't jump to conclusions. Let me look at some of these files to be sure."

"You think Black Beacon is planning to blow up the power grid during that WTO meeting? When is it anyway?"

"The answer to your first question is yes, based on what I see here. However, I don't see a date. We're probably the only people in the city who don't know."

"What do we do?"

"Right now, I'm going to keep checking these files as fast as I can. There's no telling when Mr. Beacon might decide to use his computer and we certainly don't want him to find out about us and that worm-hole."

Zack said, "I have an idea. I'll call the 311 information number. They'll know when the conference is." With that, he again grabbed the phone and tapped 311.

The operator answered on the third ring, "Chicago 311. Can I help you?"

"Yes, can you tell me the dates of the WTO meeting?" Zack asked.

"The meeting starts Tuesday, the twenty-third and ends Wednesday night. Anything else?"

"Can you tell me where it is?"

"Navy Pier. The entire Pier will be closed to the public. Also, there is restricted access from Randolph Street to Chicago Avenue from Monday midnight until Wednesday midnight."

"Thank you," Zack said and hung up.

"It starts Tuesday morning and lasts until Wednesday night. Do you know whether Beacon plans to do it at the beginning or the end or when?"

"Well, I've found a timetable file. According to this, it's the Closing Ceremony. Isn't that when all the leaders stand together and smile for pictures and so on? It looks like he wants the blackout to happen right when everyone is gathered together."

"Do you think this is all for real?" Zack asked. He hoped for the answer that would make him feel better, but knew it wouldn't come.

"Yeah, I think so, but it's not that simple."

"Why?"

"If he wants the actual blackout to happen during the Closing Ceremony, he has to start the 'cascade' earlier. I don't know exactly how long it takes for the whole sequence to execute. It's impossible to predict the amount of time before a transformer overheats, shorts out, and causes the next circuit to overload. So, that means he has to start the process early. Just how early, I don't know, and he doesn't know either."

"What does that mean?"

"It means that the best he can do is make a guess. That's good news to whomever is going to try to stop him. Every minute might be important."

"Do we tell the cops now?" Zack asked.

"What do you think? They're not going to believe you because they think you killed Marly. You said it yourself; they're working the homicide."

"Hell, then, I'll try 911. Somebody has to give a shit," Zack shouted in frustration. Something was clicking in his brain.

"Zack, what exactly are you going to tell them?"

He shook his arm toward the computer and stammered, "That, that, this Black Beacon guy is going to blow up the power grid for Christ's sake."

"And what do you say when they ask who is Black Beacon, and how do you know all this?"

"I'll tell them that we saw it on his computer, just like it happened."

"And, then they'll ask how you broke into his computer, and what computer, and where is he, etc. etc. What do you say then? You know, you'll look like a complete idiot?"

"We can't just let it go, damn it," Zack shot back.

"I know that. I need more time."

"Time for what?"

"Time to get enough real information about who Black Beacon is and so on. We know he's not planning to do anything until the conference. That's on Tuesday."

"Yeah, you're right. But hell…"

She interrupted him. "Tell me about it. My hands are so sweaty I can hardly type, and I can feel the pounding in my temples. But, we don't have any other choice. Like it or not, Zack, this is in our hands. We own it."

Zack heard the words, "we own it," and his brain rocketed back. He remembered, Marly had warned him early on the danger of the cascade factor saying, "If we take on the Y2K work on the power grid, we're responsible. We're going to wear it."

There it was again, that same clicking in his brain. The awareness-switch had been thrown and he knew now a purpose, a real purpose—not some transient sales target or marketing pitch, but something real, something vital, something necessary.

Lynne was still talking. "I need to go through all these files. With any luck, I will find something to identify him and maybe even uncover that smoking gun you've been talking about."

"God, I hope you're right. If my hunch is correct and Black Beacon murdered Marly, then he won't hesitate a second to kill both of us, especially if he finds out we've been reading these files."

"Yeah, I know," she said. A vein popped on the side of her head. "That thought already occurred to me, as if I wasn't frightened enough. One thing still bothers me, though. Why do you think Black Beacon killed Marly? She obviously gave him all the information he wanted. Why would he have to take her out? Maybe he discovered how much she knew about his plans—even if he didn't know how she knew?"

"Could be. Maybe he feared she would tell the cops before the conference and spoil his big show. I wonder why he is waiting for the conference. Shutting down the grid would be a big deal no matter what. What does the WTO meeting have to do with it?"

"I think you just hit it."

"Hit what?" Zack asked.

"The WTO conference, his big show! He's put this entire thing together to make some kind of statement. Remember he referred to this as 'the event?' Black

Beacon is a political terrorist and he's using the World Trade meeting to dramatize some political message. If I keep looking, I'll bet that message is in these files. When we find it, we'll have an answer as to who he is and probably that smoking gun."

With a protective look, Zack said, "Lynne, please be careful. Make sure there is no way he can know you're doing this. He's already killed once, and he's tried to kill me. I don't want to give him another shot at either of us."

Beacon had to be stopped. Zack knew *he* had to stop him and prevent the unthinkable. He knew *he* owned it.

*   *   *   *

Outside Zack's unit, a Chinese man pulled up in a small car with a Szechwan Pagoda banner. The news teams were focused on the house and each other and not particularly paying attention. The dumpy man with the thick black glasses had been waiting patiently down the street. He was nothing if not a planner. He had assembled a selection of lethal tools waiting until an opportunity presented itself. Included in his death kit were the makings for Molotov cocktails, toxic gas canisters, various poisons including some particularly potent mushrooms and more.

He'd previously observed the same guy deliver food to that unit. He knew if he waited his opportunity would come, and he was thankful for this one—simpler and cleaner than a fire, he thought. Quickly, he walked to greet the Chinese driver, paid him, thanked him for the fast service and then graciously took the food, saying he would take it in. Grateful for the large tip and happy to avoid the news crowd, the man drove off to make his next delivery. Then the man with the glasses and his two young lackeys added the mushrooms to the food. Given the potency of the "destroying angel," both Dreyben and his female friend would soon be out of the picture. After carefully repacking the delivery, the man, unruffled, calmly walked past the reporters to Zack's door, pressed the bell and responded "Szechwan Pagoda" loudly into the intercom. Zack answered the door and traded cash for the poison-laced fare.

As the man turned and walked away, Zack had an ominous feeling he had seen him before.

Zack chalked up the feeling to paranoia and announced to Lynne, "The Chinese chow is here. I'll get some plates and some beers. Come join me. You can finish those files later."

"Oh good. I'm starved," Lynne said.

Zack carried the food to the kitchen table. He divided the Szechwan Broccoli onto two plates and opened the beers. "You know. There was something about that delivery guy. I can't put my finger on it, but I just don't like it. I know I have seen him somewhere before, but where?"

CHAPTER 23

▼

CHICAGO, OCTOBER 20, 2001: 9:00 P.M.

Zack divided the Spicy Szechwan Broccoli with mushrooms and Vegetable Fried Rice onto their plates. Burgundy placemats, paper napkins, chopsticks, and a couple fresh beers completed the table. Lynne joined him in the kitchen, sporting a set of red, puffy eyes. After staring at the laptop for hours, the fatigue showed. She used both hands to pull one of the hefty chairs away from the worn oak table. The chair squealed as it raked across the terra cotta tile floor. She brought it around so that she was sitting across the corner from Zack instead of opposite him at the table.

He squeezed the chopsticks, snagged a floret of broccoli, and lifted it to his mouth. Instantly, his eyes popped wide and he grabbed his beer, yelling, "Wow, that's hot!" His eyes watered and tiny beads of sweat appeared on his forehead. "That stuff's spicy, even for me."

"If it's too hot for you, I know it is for me," Lynne said.

The fieriness notwithstanding, they were hungry, and managed to still finish about a third of the vegetable dish while devouring the full order of fried rice.

Zack washed down his last bite with the beer, "You know, that delivery guy still bugs me. I know him, but damn it, I can't remember why."

"Maybe he reminded you of somebody you knew before you moved to Chicago," Lynne suggested.

"Could be, but I don't think so. It's kind of strange. It's like when you want to remember someone, you might recall how he walks or what his voice sounds like. I can't place anything about him. This is going to drive me crazy until I can remember."

"Well, while you're walking down memory lane, I have to get back to Mr. Beacon's files. I hope we can find everything we need before the night's over. After that, we'll just monitor whatever he does."

Zack worried that Lynne was pushing herself too hard. "You're beat. You've been at it for almost eight hours, and just look at your eyes. Hell, it's after nine o'clock, and Beacon hasn't been on the computer all day. Chances are he's not going to be working on it anymore tonight. What don't you take a long break and a shower? You could use it."

Lynne turned toward him smiling, "You saying I look like hell?"

His honesty yielded to diplomacy. "No, no, you look great."

"Yeah, yeah. Like I believe that," she said. "Actually, I could use a shower. Do you mind?"

"No, not at all. I'll get you some fresh clothes. They won't fit too well, but they'll feel a lot better. Follow me." With that he headed to the bedroom with a quick stop at the linen closet to fetch a fresh towel. From the dresser, he retrieved a pair of jeans and a scarlet and gray Ohio State Buckeye sweatshirt. He handed the towel and clothes to Lynne.

"You'll feel a lot better after a good, hot shower. I'll go clean up the kitchen. Enjoy!"

Lynne closed the bathroom door, and Zack heard the shower start. He was glad she took a break; she'd certainly earned it. Hell, they were both pushing themselves. He wondered how they would get beyond this nightmare and what their relationship would be like without the stress. Could they ever just sit and talk like normal people, or have a quiet dinner together? He caught himself. Wait a minute. What the hell was he thinking? This wasn't right. They were here to uncover Marly's—his lover's—murderer. Feeling like someone from *The Jerry Springer Show*, he scoured the images from his mind, and started for the kitchen and some dirty dishes.

Zack was just finishing up when Lynne emerged with a fresh, crisp look. She was dressed in the jeans and sweatshirt Zack had given her, with the towel wrapped around her head turban-style. The bulky jeans didn't flatter her, but at the same time, she looked sexy in the oversized sweatshirt.

"Feel better?" Zack asked. He took a second look. In the big sweatshirt he couldn't be certain, but it looked like she was braless.

"Yeah, lots. But they're not quite my size," she said. With a big grin she tightly held the waist of the jeans for security. "Can you at least loan me a belt?"

Zack went to the closet and found her a military-style belt that could be pulled tight to any size. That solved the problem.

"I think I should get back to Black Beacon's files," Lynne said.

"OK, but be careful."

"Oh, I will. The more I read, the more I see how strange this deal is. You know, Zack, I am really scared that this guy would actually try to destroy the whole electrical grid. What kind of off-balance wacko would do that?"

"Beats me. I don't get it. It's like those bastards that flew the planes into the World Trade Center."

"Anyway, back to work. I think we need to finish this tonight. Who knows when we'll get another chance." With that, Lynne headed back to Zack's home office.

She cautiously connected to Black Beacon's computer and found his system idle. "Thank God," she mumbled quietly. She continued her search through the file system for details regarding his plans for starting the "cascade."

Midnight just passed, when Lynne made the discovery. "Zack, come see this, hurry," she screamed.

Zack had been dozing on the couch. "What is it?" he asked.

"There's a file named 'COMMUN.' It turns out that it is a Communiqué that he apparently intends to send to the media when he shuts down the grid."

"What?"

"Just look," Lynne leaned aside as Zack peered over her shoulder to see the laptop screen.

> The Communiqué
> The Black Beacon is sending this communiqué to the major news networks and press syndicates. There will be only one notice—this one.
>
> Who is Black Beacon?
> The Black Beacon is a network of World Citizens, representing all the people of this planet, irrespective of traditional, but illegitimate national borders. We are dedicated to ending the oppression and exploitation of the world's people in the name of Globalization, Capitalism and World Trade.
>
> What is the reason for this communiqué?
> This is the end of oppressive World Capitalism. Today, Black Beacon will shine darkness across this continent. The Black Beacon will cause the entire North American Electrical Power Grid to self-destruct. This is not a prank or a hoax. Be assured, we have the means to accomplish this goal.
>
> Why this notice?
> This is a warning, your only warning! We are allowing you time to save your citizens. We are neither terrorists nor religious zealots. We are anarchists.

Our goal is the elimination of the structures and rules that limit personal freedom. Unfortunately, some lives may be lost in this struggle as in any great socio-economic metamorphosis. We regret any loss of life, but the greed and oppression of World Capitalism is responsible—we are not. We have already lost some closest to us in this great effort. We will not let their sacrifice be in vain. The elimination of Capitalism is our Cause, and the Cause is more important than any individual.

What will happen?
Today, Black Beacon will free the world's people. When the flow of electricity stops, oppressive governments and capitalistic greed will disappear. The exploitative infrastructure of North America will be permanently destroyed, and the economic and social effects will "cascade" throughout the world.

- Governmental control will cease. Power will return to the people. Stoplights will go black. Courts will be dark. Police and armed forces will be unable to transmit or receive orders. There will be no effectual means to enforce laws or wage war.

- Social infrastructures will change. Lights will go out. Subways, elevators, and more will stop. Hospitals, high-rises, and convention centers will be emptied. Radios will be quiet. TVs will be dark. Networks and broadcasters will be irrelevant.

- Economic controls will end. Computers will no longer run our lives. Privacy will be returned to the people as databases become useless. Shopping centers will close. Stock exchanges will be silent. Banks and ATMs will be impotent.

- Lives will be more important than machines. Factories will close. The people will become powerful as assembly lines become powerless. Refineries will no longer distill oil raped from an oppressed third world. Cars, trucks, trains and planes will grind to a halt without fuel. The pollution and destruction of our planet will end.

- People will return to the land. Water will be pumped by hand. Personal tools will replace power tools. Sunlight will replace incandescents. Gardens will replace groceries.

Zack turned to Lynne. "Can you believe that? He says they aren't terrorists. What an asshole! Do you think he's referring to Marly when he says they have already lost lives close to them?"

Zack spotted the wide-eyed trepidation in Lynne's face. Unconsciously, two middle fingers on her left hand rubbed her cheek. "I don't know, but we're playing with dynamite. It's pretty clear that his damn 'cause' ranks higher than anyone's life. Zack, I'm more frightened than ever. Before, this all seemed kind of remote—a cyber game of sorts. Now, we know it's for real. We know what he's planning. What we need is some evidence of what he has already done."

"Is there anything else in those files?"

"I'm looking now. There are so many of them that it takes a long time to check each one. Here's an interesting file named 'LEADER.'"

"Anything in particular?" Zack asked.

"Yeah," she said. "This guy is a fucking nut!"

"What do you mean?"

"This is what he gets from shutting down the grid. Listen to this:"

> Black Beacon will be *the* number one political action group in the world. We will be more important than the religious terrorists who attacked the World Trade Center. Their efforts disrupted air travel; interrupted the financial exchanges; and terrified a nation, but the world went on. When Black Beacon shines darkness, the effect will be both worldwide and permanent. But, destruction of the grid will be accomplished without terror. Ever since the World Trade Center attack, physical security has increased everywhere. We will take down capitalism without a confrontation. Black Beacon will destroy all vestiges of capitalism and end exploitation of the downtrodden. When the world panics, Black Beacon will rise and shine.

"We've got to go to the police, even if we can't prove he murdered Marly or tried to get me. This is way too scary," Zack said.

"Maybe we should call the FBI. They're the ones who are in charge of security for that conference."

Zack looked at the clock on the desk. "You're right, but it's after midnight. I'll call first thing. But, we still don't know Black Beacon's name. I just hope they'll listen."

"Me too," Lynne added. "Hey, I'm beat. Do you mind if I crash on your couch tonight?"

"Of course not. I'll get some blankets and a pillow. I hope you sleep well. I have a feeling tomorrow will be a long day." Zack tried hard to sound normal as he went to the closet for the bedding. His heart was beating way too fast. This lunatic Beacon had to be stopped, and tomorrow they would tell the FBI, the police, anyone they could get to listen. And then, his future would be in their hands. His murder charge was still pending. Anxiety burned in his chest.

He handed the unfolded blankets and pillow to Lynne and watched her quickly wrap herself in the blanket and cozy into the sofa. He smiled at her before he switched off the lights and headed for the bedroom. Tomorrow would come early.

CHAPTER 24

▼

CHICAGO, OCTOBER 21, 2001: 4:00 A.M.

Zack awoke feeling gassy and crampy. He shifted to his side and shook away enough cobwebs to check the clock. It was 4:00 A.M. He'd slept only a few hours.

He rolled out of bed and trudged the few steps to the master bath. He'd walked only a couple of paces, but that was far enough. He didn't feel good. In fact, he felt lousy.

He reviewed what he'd had to eat and drink: fried rice, some Chinese vegetables, and a couple beers. All that seemed innocent enough. Nonetheless, the rumblings in his belly were getting worse, much worse. He sat on the john, hoping to pass enough gas to get relief. However, within seconds, he experienced explosive diarrhea, and instead of relief, only more diarrhea.

Worse yet, waves of nausea overwhelmed him and an awful sour taste announced his illness. He clutched the wastebasket. He had never experienced projectile vomiting, and the force surprised him. For the next twenty-five minutes his system worked to cleanse itself. His abdominal muscles clenched in repeated spasms to purge the toxins, even after there was nothing to expel. The results were painful "dry heaves" that would leave reminders for days. Zack felt weak and exhausted. His mouth had the rancid taste of vomit. He rinsed his mouth with a fistful of water.

He grabbed his robe and stumbled to the kitchen looking for a glass for a drink; that's when he heard her.

He could hear Lynne retching behind the partially closed door.

"Are you OK?" he called to her.

"No. I feel like shit," she answered. "You got it too?"

"Yeah. I've been sitting on the can and holding the wastebasket in front of me."

"Are you OK, now?"

"Maybe, I don't know." His response was premature as another wave of diarrhea and vomiting swept over him and he rushed back to the bathroom.

Another fifteen minutes passed before the two of them could speak again. "Zack, we must have food poisoning. We need to get help," Lynne said.

"From what? All we had was vegetables and rice."

"I don't know, and I don't give a shit. We should call 911."

"For food poisoning?" he asked. "Isn't that a little overkill?"

"Forget it." Not waiting for Zack, she picked up the phone and punched 911.

The emergency operator picked up on the second ring. "Chicago 911. Officer Symanski. What is your emergency?"

"My friend and I are both very sick. We're vomiting violently and have terrible diarrhea. I think we may have food poisoning."

The operator asked the pertinent questions of name and address and dispatched help. Fortunately, the ambulance arrived quickly; the firehouse was just blocks away at Armitage and Larrabee.

The paramedics walked directly to Zack's door, announcing themselves over the security intercom. Lynne, still wearing Zack's oversized clothes, opened the door.

"You called 911?"

Lynne's voice was quivering. "Yes, we're both violently ill," she said, as Zack joined her and showed them in.

"OK. Let's see," the paramedic said. "Let me check your vitals, then we'll run you over to Northwestern."

The paramedics went to work on Zack and Lynne as they laid on separate gurneys. The two were experienced EMTs, and immediately determined the illness was serious. The lead medic squawked into his radio that they had two people with severe GI problems, possible food poisoning, and they were heading to Northwestern Hospital. His partner alertly ventured into the kitchen where he found the remains of last night's dinner in the trash. He placed the aluminum pan with the vegetables and the rice' cardboard carton in separate plastic bags on the chance the origin of the poisoning could be established.

The EMTs rolled Zack and Lynne out the front door to the waiting ambulance and headed to the hospital.

A couple of houses down, a short, overweight man watched approvingly through thick framed glasses.

*   *   *   *

At the hospital, the ER staff physicians examined both Zack and Lynne. The staff physician introduced herself. "Mr. Dreyben, I'm Doctor Jennings. You might remember me. I treated you the afternoon you had your accident with the 'EL' train. We weren't expecting you back so quickly."

"Sure, I remember." Zack couldn't believe how long ago that seemed, yet he knew that only a few days had passed. So much had happened.

"I see you're having some real GI problems. We're trying to determine the cause. We don't want to move too hastily and make a wrong judgment. Given the severity of your symptoms and Ms. Rydahl's, we're going to admit you for at least twenty-four hours. That way, we'll have time to monitor you and complete some further tests. Actually, having both of you with identical symptoms might help us diagnose this. Do you mind if I ask you a few questions?"

"No, not at all."

"Did either you or Ms. Rydahl prepare any of the food you ate last night, say anytime after six or seven o'clock?"

"Nope. We ordered delivery from my favorite Chinese place, the Szechwan Pagoda."

"Can you remember exactly what you ate?"

"Yeah, we ordered the Szechwan Broccoli with mushrooms and Vegetable Fried Rice."

The Doctor made some notes on her pad. "Did you have anything else?"

"We each had a couple of beers."

Dr. Jennings scratched a final note and closed the cover. "OK, I think that about covers it for now, Mr. Dreyben. Until we know what caused this, we're going to continue monitoring your vital signs and give you some more IV fluids to prevent dehydration and replace the electrolytes. Also, we're going to do some toxicology tests. We're not ruling anything out, but I don't believe that it's e-coli because of the absence of meat products in the food samples. When we have a better handle on this, we'll be more specific in our treatment. Try to rest comfortably."

"Pretty hard to do," Zack said with a weak smile.

Shortly after that, an orderly appeared and moved Zack to a semi-private room upstairs. Normally, Zack would have protested even a short stay in the hospital, but the ordeal had taken its toll and he felt weak and shaky. Besides, he took comfort in knowing that help was nearby, should he need it. Better yet, the patient in the adjoining bed was being released, so Zack would have the room to himself. Also, the IVs were on a rolling stand, which would allow him to get up and go to the bathroom as needed. Exhausted, he laid back and soon fell asleep.

He slept a few hours before being awakened by the need to again visit the bathroom. By now, he had a routine of simultaneously sitting on the toilet and throwing up. At least the process provided some temporary relief from the cramping. He wondered how long this would continue.

Dr. Jennings came to visit, and Zack wondered if ER Doctors would typically visit the wards, but she explained she'd finished her shift and was curious to know how Zack and Lynne were doing.

She smiled in her best, bedside manner, "Hi. How are you feeling?"

"About the same. I'm worried about Lynne, though. How is she doing?"

"She's about the same, too. But, I have some interesting news. We think we know what happened. One of the interns happened to look at your food samples. He's an avid hiker and outdoorsman. He noticed some of the mushrooms in your vegetable dish. Let me ask you, did you add any mushrooms of your own to the dish?"

"No, why?"

"He noticed some of the mushrooms looked a little strange to him. You know, he sees a lot of wild mushrooms when he's hiking. Anyway, there's a certain kind of wild mushroom, grows about anywhere, but is very poisonous. The official name is Amanita Virosa, but it's commonly called "the destroying angel" because it is so dangerous. He thought the mushrooms in your food looked a little unusual. Fortunately, there's a simple test to determine if a mushroom is an Amanita. Guess what? Your vegetable dish had enough "destroying angels" to kill both you and Ms. Rydahl. Our formal toxicology tests would have given us the same information, but this saved us a lot of time. You two were very lucky that you didn't eat it all."

"Are you saying that the restaurant screwed up and used the wrong kind of mushrooms?"

"Not likely. Everything they use would be commercially processed. Considering this and your previous encounter with the 'EL' train, I have alerted the police. Mr. Dreyben, I don't know who or why, but someone deliberately tried to poison you and Ms. Rydahl."

Poison! Fear stabbed his chest. He said it aloud, "Poison?" He wondered, who? Someone at the restaurant? The deliveryman? Then he remembered, the deliveryman! He knew he'd seen him before, but where? Who was he, but more importantly, why did he want me dead?

CHAPTER 25

━━━━━━━━━━ ▼ ━━━━━━━━━━

CHICAGO, OCTOBER 21, 2001: 3:00 P.M

"That *was* the good news," Dr. Jennings said.

"Good news?" Zack asked, shocked. "You gotta be kidding! You just said someone tried to poison me, and that was the 'good' news?"

"In one sense, yes."

"What do you mean?"

"Well, the treatment…"

Zack interrupted, "What treatment?" His stomach ached from the spasms, and his frustration grew. "But I'm better."

"Yes, I know that, but there's more to it," Dr. Jennings explained.

"Now what?"

"We've consulted the Poison Control Center. The Amanita poison you were given has three stages of activity. The initial stage typically begins about six to ten hours after ingestion, and lasts up to a day. Stage one symptoms are the violent cramping, diarrhea and vomiting you've already experienced. The second phase is more insidious because the symptoms disappear, making the victim believe that he or she is past danger. The third stage sets in about three or four days as damage to the liver and kidneys occurs. Eventually, the injury to those organs is so severe the victim passes into a coma and never awakens. We believe that both you and Ms. Rydahl are in stage two, and should begin immediate treatment."

"What's the treatment?"

"We have to do everything we can to cleanse your body of the remaining toxins. Believe it or not, that means diuretics and laxatives, plus activated charcoal to absorb the poison and IV antibiotics to counter the effects. I won't kid you. It's an aggressive regimen."

"Laxatives? That's incredible. I'm so clean now, I whistle from air rushing through me!"

Dr. Jennings smiled. "I'm afraid so. Even then, we need to keep monitoring your vital signs, and we'll be taking regular blood samples to check for diminished liver function, just to be sure. I don't want to scare you, but we're dealing with a deadly poison. Whoever gave you the poison, knew what he or she was doing. I don't think it's likely, but you could be facing a potential liver transplant."

"You can't be serious," Zack replied. "I don't feel that bad."

"I know. Stage two."

Zack resigned himself to more abuse of his GI tract, and the sooner he got it over with, the better. "When do we start?"

"Right away. The doctors here in the ward will schedule the tests and procedures. I just wanted to be the one who delivered the news," she said with a smile. "I'll be checking up on you. I'm sure we'll have you out of here within a week."

"A week? I don't have a week."

"I'm sorry, Mr. Dreyben. It's just too risky."

"You don't understand. I can't stay here that long. It is vitally important..."

Black Beacon's plan was already in progress. He and Lynne would have to convince the authorities of the danger to the power grid, and he knew that words alone wouldn't hack it. He would need Lynne to show the FBI or whomever, how the two of them broke into Beacon's computer. Even then, someone would have to find a way to stop Beacon before the WTO closing ceremonies in three days. Worst of all, they still didn't know Black Beacon's real identity.

"Sorry," she said shaking her head. "But until we know your liver and kidneys are OK, we can't take a chance."

"Then, I have to talk to the police or the FBI. It's urgent."

"Actually, you can do that right away. Detective Harrison is on his way here. I called him when you were admitted. I think you know the police give us a list with names from active cases. If any of those people comes to the ER, they want to be notified. I have to go now. I'll check back later to see how you're doing."

Zack tried to lie back and relax. He still felt weak and shaky. The ordeal had left him dehydrated, his throat dry, and his eyes burning. His abdominal muscles ached from the vicious tugging and pulling, and the prospect of more "purging" wasn't something he looked forward to. Still, he closed his eyes and tried to organize his thoughts. Lynne and he were virtually caged here in the hospital. Meanwhile Beacon prepared to launch his lunatic plan to end capitalism by destroying the U.S. electrical power grid. The authorities would never believe his off-the-wall story without proof. The frustration tore at his gut. Somehow, he and Lynne would have to show them, and that meant they had to leave the hospital. Like it or not, the economy and culture of the modern world depended on convincing the authorities of the threat of Black Beacon. But, he also well understood the Doctor's warning about the short window of stage two and the lethal risks that came with stage three. He hadn't asked for this bizarre role; it had been handed to him. He didn't consider himself the hero type, but the time had come to step up. There was no one else. He had to get to Lynne. They had work to do. Maybe they could worry about themselves later—maybe.

He called the hospital switchboard and rang Lynne's room.

"Hi, it's me. How are you doing?" he asked.

"Other than dying from the inside out, I'm probably OK," she answered. "How about you?"

"About the same, I guess. I just talked with Dr. Jennings and got the scoop on what got us. Have you talked to anyone yet?"

"No. What was it?"

"Turns out to be a poisonous mushroom called "the destroying angel" that someone put it in that vegetable dish we ate."

"What? Who?" Lynne asked, her voice rising two octaves.

"Yep, someone purposely tried to poison us."

"Who?"

"Don't know. Probably the same folks who pushed me in front of the 'EL'. Now they're after you, too. Lynne, I feel awful I got you into all this."

Lynne would have none of it. "Stop right there. I told you before that I was a big girl and that I knew what I was doing. We both got into this mess trying to solve Marly's murder. We knew whoever was behind her death was dangerous. I walked in with my eyes open; so don't start thinking it's your fault. The question is, what happens now?"

"Well, the doctors want to keep us here a week for treatment," Zack answered. "They say we're not out of the woods because that mushroom makes you think you're getting better and then things get really bad and you go into a coma and die."

"We don't have a week. What are we going to do? That Beacon guy is planning to burn up the power grid and we're the only ones that know what he's up to. "How long before we start feeling the effects and risk the coma?" Lynne asked.

"Dr. Jennings said maybe three or four days."

"That's when Beacon plans his big show. If we can convince the cops in time, we should be able to come back here for whatever treatment we need."

Zack admired her courage. "Exactly." He and Lynne thought alike. He also felt something new, a sense of connecting with someone else. Comfortable? Yeah, in a sense, like knowing yourself all the way to your bones.

"By the way," she asked. "What is the treatment?"

"More of what we've already been through, more IVs, laxatives and diuretics plus activated charcoal to absorb the toxins and some antibiotics."

She let out a giggle. "Now, I know I want out of here. I've spent enough time on the john."

"Yeah, me too," he said. "Detective Harrison is supposed to be here soon. I'm not sure what he wants, but we can tell him what we've found out. Do you want to join in?"

"Why not? In the meantime, I'm going to tell the doctors that I'm leaving. I'm sure they'll pitch a fit, but that's too bad. Call me when Harrison gets here?"

"OK," Zack said and hung up. He thought about what he would tell the police when they arrived. He might be able to reason with Harrison, but not Stockano, and he hoped Stockano wouldn't be coming along. Just then he heard a knock and Detective Harrison cracked open the door.

"Mr. Dreyben," Harrison greeted him. "Do you feel up to a few questions?"

Zack waved him in. "Yeah, sure, and I want to talk to you about something, too."

Harrison walked in and pointed to the empty bed across the room. "Private room?"

"For a while, at least. Just you today?" Zack asked.

"Yeah, Stockano's been reassigned, so I'm working your case solo."

Zack's spirits picked up with the news. "What's up?"

"The ER called. Apparently, you had another accident?"

"No. No accident, damn it. Somebody deliberately tried to poison both Lynne and me." His nerves were shot, and his response sharper than he intended.

"Any idea who?"

"We ordered delivery from a Chinese restaurant, so it had to be either someone at the restaurant or the delivery guy. I doubt it's the restaurant—I order from them all the time—but the delivery guy's a different story. Is there any way you can check on him?"

"To tell you the truth, I already have. The folks in the ER gave me your story. I ran a quick check before I came here. Your delivery guy wasn't Chinese was he?"

"No, why?"

"Seems your guy met the real deliveryman and took the food, saying he'd take it in. The Chinese guy didn't think too much about it, and he was happy because he got a big tip."

"Do you know who the fake guy is?"

"No. I hoped you might be able to help."

"I know I have seen him somewhere, but I can't remember where."

"I'm trying to get a description from the reporters who were camped in front of your place, but so far, no luck. We'll come up with something, though. That's all I've got. You said you wanted to talk about something?"

"Yeah, let me call Lynne." He picked up the bedside phone and punched in Lynne's number.

"Hi, it's me. Detective Harrison is here. Guess what? They found out the food delivery guy was a phony. Interesting huh? Anyway, want to join us?"

"I'll be there in two minutes," she answered. "Just let me finish dressing. I just told the docs I was leaving. They're a pretty unhappy crew."

Zack turned to the Detective. "Lynne's going to join us. We have a pretty incredible story to tell you. To tell you the truth, I'm not sure if I'm talking to the right people. Maybe I should be working with the FBI."

"What are you talking about?" Harrison asked. "Tell you what. Fill me in. I've been around long enough to have a couple friends who are Feds. Maybe we can work together here."

The spirit of cooperation dumbfounded Zack. "What?"

"I'll be upfront with you. I was suspicious of you at first. I've heard a thousand tales of innocence that don't hold water, and your story sounded like more of the same. But, I have to admit these attempts on your life change things a bit. Don't get me wrong. I still don't know who killed McCalley, and if I see some indication that you were involved, I'll come down on you with both feet. Right now though, it seems that whoever is trying to smoke you, looks like our best bet. I think we can work together to find him or her and then we'll see where we are."

"What about Stockano? What's his role in this?" Zack asked.

"Stockano's off the case. I canned him."

"Why?" Zack asked, still suspicious.

"He tipped the press about you being the prime suspect. That's why that hoard of reporters camped at your place, looking for a story. I'm sorry about that. Anyway, nobody's going to goad me into taking action until the evidence supports it. I dumped him, plain and simple."

Lynne knocked twice and walked in wearing the oversized clothes Zack loaned her—not a great looking picture. The last twenty-four hours had been tough.

Her uncombed hair half covered the pallid, washed-out face. Vomiting and diarrhea cost her pounds she didn't need to lose. Regardless, she moved with that easy grace and unmistakably feminine swing.

"Hi," she said nodding to both men.

Detective Harrison returned the nod. "Ms. Rydahl." She was wearing an Ohio State sweatshirt, not real common in Illinois. "Hey, did you go to OSU?"

Zack responded before Lynne, "No, I'm the Buckeye."

Harrison examined Zack, head to toe, "You play?"

Zack nodded, knowing he meant football, a guy-thing from big-time football schools. "Walk-on, second, third string safety. You?"

"ND, tight-end." An unconscious smile appeared on Harrison's face. "The wife busts me all the time saying that's how I got the extra lumps in the snoot."

Zack studied Harrison and wondered why he'd never put it together before: tall; broad-shoulders; busted nose; big, beefy hands…

Lynne endured this exchange with a confused look, and cleared her throat.

Zack glanced at Lynne and turned serious. "Detective, Lynne and I have a story to share with you. You'll probably think we're crazy, but I promise you we're deadly serious. We'll give you all the details, but the bottom line is there is a wacko who is planning to destroy the electrical power grid of the U.S. during the WTO closing ceremonies."

"What?"

Zack took a deep breath and spoke with confidence. "I know it sounds crazy, but we have proof."

"Proof? What kind of proof?" Harrison asked.

"His own computer files. It's a long story. When you and Stockano told me I was the prime suspect, I had to do something to clear myself. I found Marly McCalley's laptop computer and started looking for anything suspicious. Well, to make a long story short, we found plenty that was suspicious. Most of it encrypted. Thankfully, Lynne is a computer wiz and figured out how to decipher it. Turns out Marly helped this guy named Black Beacon by setting up a computer program to cause temporary power blackouts. Well, Beacon apparently expanded the idea and is planning to use the program to actually destroy the grid. Marly got suspicious and planted a worm, you know like a virus, in his computer. Lynne has been using that worm to examine his files. We know what he's planning and when. But, we don't know who he is or how he's going to launch the program. His plan is to use the WTO closing ceremonies this week."

Harrison looked around for a chair. "Holy shit. Do you guys know what you're saying?" Harrison asked.

"Yeah, that's why I wanted to talk to you," Zack said. "Should we be talking to the FBI?"

"Probably. But let me go back. You say you have proof? I don't want to run to the Feds with some crazy story only to find that it's some seventeen-year-old's idea of a prank."

"Harrison, damn it. I can't guarantee anything. But Lynne here worked with Marly on the Y2K power project. She's looked at the program and she thinks it's the real thing."

"I *know* it is," Lynne joined. "I just wish I could think of a way to stop somebody using it."

"Looks to me like we will have to get the Feds involved," Harrison said.

Zack willingly responded, "OK, go ahead and alert the FBI; they have to warn the power companies, anyway. You decide if we need to tie in anyone else like the Secret Service. In the meantime, we've got to work together here to figure out who Black Beacon is, and grab him before he can launch that program. But, we only have a couple days before the closing ceremonies on Wednesday, and we've got to have everybody together."

Lynne said, "I'll keep working on Beacon's computer and try to find a way to disable the program. If the FBI has a top computer jock that knows the power grid, I could use some help."

"Is there anybody you know of?" Zack asked her.

"Not really. When Marly and I worked the Y2K project, we knew we were on our own. Nobody ever looked at the grid as one entity. And, I don't think anyone's ever thought of using the web to destroy the grid itself. It's a new twist. It's destruction without force, but it's destruction just the same."

They had thrown a lot at Harrison and Zack could see the uncertainty in his expression. Zack knew Harrison was key to catching Beacon. There was no way either he or Lynne could do that. He turned back and looked Harrison straight in the eyes, "We need your help. Without you, we'll never stop Beacon."

CHAPTER 26

▼

CHICAGO, OCTOBER 21, 2001: 5:00 P.M.

If the Doctor were any more adamant, he'd have been stomping his feet, "I'm afraid not."

"But, it's important," Zack said, in no mood for a debate.

"What is this, a new way to commit suicide? Death by stupidity?"

"Look, I have to check out, *now*."

"Mr. Dreyben, I'm going to try one last time. This is crazy. Whatever you have to do can wait."

"Wrong."

"OK, OK. You know we can't force you to stay. At least listen to me for two minutes so that I can tell you the danger signs. If you notice any of these things, get your butt back here immediately. I can't say it strongly enough. Your life depends on it."

"OK. Two minutes. What do I look for?"

"Any weakness like unsteady legs, trouble maintaining your balance, difficulty standing straight without leaning, these are all serious indicators. Since liver damage is a real risk, look for any hint of jaundice or yellowing of the skin or eyes. Most importantly, any mental disorientation is a major red flag. If you sense yourself becoming confused, return here to the hospital immediately, it may be your last chance to save your life. Do you understand?"

Zack nodded that he understood. He wanted to get going.

"In the meantime, consume lots of water because you are still dehydrated and need to flush your system." He handed Zack a small plastic bottle. "Finally, take these activated charcoal tablets every two hours. They should help absorb the remaining toxins. And, oh yes, good luck. You're going to need it."

"Thanks. I'll be fine," Zack said, praying he was right.

Lynne and Harrison agreed to meet Zack at his place in an hour. They had no time to waste, the WTO closing ceremonies were only three days away. Time was especially critical for Lynne and Zack. The stage three effects of the Amanita poison could begin anytime—initially there would be coma, then death.

But first, Lynne wanted to go home, shower and change, and Harrison intended to call his friends at the FBI.

Lynne arrived before Harrison, and amazingly after only an hour, she looked like a different woman. Her complexion had regained a healthier pinkish cast. The clothes helped a lot. She had changed into a cranberry V-neck and tight charcoal pants. Her eyes again had their familiar glimmer.

She greeted Zack with a tense smile. "Hi, I see you were able to escape."

"Yeah, but the docs weren't happy. In fact, the Resident ran through the symptoms to watch for. I think he tried to scare me. At least now, I know. How about some water? The Doc said we should keep drinking."

"Water sounds good," Lynne answered. "I'll get it." She headed to the kitchen pausing a moment for a few soft pats to Katie's head.

The intercom buzzer rang, and Katie barked, to announce someone at the front door. Harrison stood there holding three huge Starbucks cups.

"Missed lunch," the Detective explained. "Hope you guys like coffee."

Zack checked his watch; six o'clock. The day was shot. "Sure. Come on, we're in the kitchen."

The three took seats at the distressed oak table. Lynne declined Harrison's offer of a muffin. "Sorry, not much appetite for solid food."

Something clicked inside Zack's head, inside his gut. Maybe adrenaline, maybe not, but he knew it was his time. "OK, before we put a plan together to stop Beacon, we need to make sure we're on the same page. Lynne, that means we need to prove to Harrison here that we're not crazy. You'll have to link into Beacon's computer and show the Detective what we know and how we found out."

Lynne nodded. "Got it." She turned to Harrison, "That work for you?"

"Yeah, maybe. You know, I need hard evidence. I called my contact at the FBI and told him the gist of your story, and…"

"What did he say?" Zack interrupted.

"You guys need to understand something. The Feds are so damn busy these days; they don't know which way they're running. The World Trade Center thing has them chasing a couple hundred thousand leads. They ain't got time to shit, let alone take on something new. Don't get me wrong. They're basically good folks, but there are only so many hours in a day. This terrorism crap isn't really my patch, but I told him I'd work with you and that we'd call him when we really needed his help."

"Can you do that? What's your department say?"

"I told them this is part of the McCalley case. Hell, they don't need to know nothing more," he said, a devious sort of smile on his face.

"OK, great," Zack said. "Lynne can show you how she got into Beacon's computer and what she found. The real question is what do we do to stop him?"

Harrison turned to Lynne, "If you can link into his computer, can't you figure out where he is?"

"Unfortunately, no," she answered. "All I have is what is called an Internet Protocol or IP address. Since you're the police, you can take that IP address to a Domain Registry Service and demand they tell you the Internet Service Provider that controls it. The ISP probably has some name associated with that IP address, but there's no guarantee it would be a valid name, and if they even had an address listed, it'd probably be phony. Besides, I think we have a different problem."

"What do you mean?" Zack asked.

"We don't even know who Black Beacon is. Assume we catch him. That doesn't mean that one of his cohorts won't be able to start the 'cascade' from a different computer. No, our problem is that we have to find a way to actually *stop* the 'cascade.'"

Harrison stopped chewing his cranberry muffin long enough to ask, "How the hell do we do that?"

"I'm not sure. If we had more time—maybe a week or so—it'd be easy. We'd work with all the control centers to change the passwords and access rights. But given the thousands of switches involved…We just don't have that much time. We have to find a way to stop the cascade program before it gets started."

"Does anybody know how to do that?" Zack asked.

"Not that I know of. The only person that I knew that could do that was Marly," Lynne said.

"That's probably why she was killed," Zack said.

Harrison squared himself to the table, "Anyway, we have to deal with what we do now."

Zack eyed both of them. "We only have two options. One is to figure out a way to stop the cascade ourselves, or two, find out who Beacon is, arrest him and make him stop the cascade. We can't be positive either approach will work. So, I think we have to work both."

Zack turned to Lynne, "You've got to get inside that program and find a way to stop it, no matter who starts it."

"I don't know…" Harrison began.

Zack interrupted, "We've got to find a way. We have no choice. If Beacon's successful in burning up the grid, we're all lost. It's up to us, guys. There's nobody else."

Lynne stood and motioned to Harrison. "Let's go log on. I have an idea that might give you a way to get started." She led the way to Zack's home office and cranked up the computer. Zack never saw Lynne more spirited.

She explained as she logged on that the office server had backup copies of Marly's computer to show him how she first learned about Black Beacon. Once connected, she spent a few minutes reviewing Marly's email files for Harrison. She explained how Marly gave Beacon a virtual tutorial on the power grid and provided a copy of the cascade program that could be used to cause blackouts by electronically controlling switches on the grid. She also showed the Detective the computer worm that allowed her access to his system without his knowledge.

"Why would she do that, I mean give him that program?" Harrison asked.

"We don't know. Marly must have thought Beacon would use the cascade program as she intended, as a way to embarrass government officials. It's not entirely clear why she wanted to embarrass the government, although we do know that she had a healthy dislike for bureaucrats. As it turned out, Beacon had bigger, uglier plans and wanted to use the program to actually destroy the grid. Marly must have become suspicious, because she secretly planted a worm in his computer that would allow her to monitor everything he did on his system. I'm presuming she intended to disable the cascade program. Anyway, the worm is still functional, and that's how we're able to gain access to Beacon's machine without him knowing it."

Harrison looked at Lynne. "I see. I think. This computer stuff is a little beyond me."

She pointed back to the screen. "I'm now going to switch out of the office server and link into Beacon's system. That's where you'll find your evidence." Zack and Harrison watched as Lynne deftly switched computer connections.

After completing the link to Beacon's machine, she paused.

Harrison looked to Zack, then back to Lynne. "Are we waiting for something?"

"I want to make sure he's not using his computer. Everything I do shows up on his monitor just as if he were hitting the keys himself. I don't want him to know that we have penetrated his system."

After what seemed an eternity to Zack, she began searching Beacon's files and email. She walked Harrison through several encrypted emails between Marly and Beacon that explained the use of the blackout program and Marly's warnings about the cascade factor. Harrison seemed impressed but unconvinced. She retrieved the communiqué file and allowed him time to read it. He insisted on still more hard evidence. Lynne continued checking and deciphering the email messages, even going beyond the ones she had previously read.

"Oh my god," she yelled. "Read this."

Zack leaned next to Lynne to see the monitor. "What is it?"

"Marly's telling Black Beacon she knows what he's planning and that she's going to go to the police."

"We never heard from her," Harrison said defensively.

"She was killed before she could," Lynne answered. "Here's Beacon's encrypted response, 'I can't let you do that. We hold the world's only chance to abolish capitalism. For far too long, too few have exploited too many, only to enrich themselves. You have provided me the opportunity to set the world right. No one has the right to stop us. Love you as I do, I must stop you, and as I am sure you've talked to your boyfriend, I must stop him as well. Progress for the world is more important than any of us.' Look at this, he signed the letter 'love, Kevin.'"

"Uncle Kevin," Zack shouted, as the memory flashed across his brain. He had heard Marly talk of her "Uncle Kevin," but it seemed so long ago. "I have an idea. Lynne, does Marly have any pictures stashed in her files?"

Lynne answered, "Let me see. Give me just a minute." Again, she switched computers to re-establish the link to the office server. "Yeah, here we go." With that Lynne began exploring pictures that Marly had saved. "Here's one labeled UK."

"Quick, open it," Zack said. A picture of an ordinary, middle-aged man with heavy glasses appeared.

Zack jumped. "That's him. Goddamn it, that's him."

"Who?" Harrison asked.

"The food delivery guy. I told you I knew him from somewhere. That delivery guy was Marly's Uncle Kevin. He's the one who tried to poison us."

Harrison put down his coffee, "Are you sure?"

"Hell yes. I've been trying to remember all this time. Do you guys have anything on him? Surely, you contacted him after Marly's death."

"As I recall, we talked to him by telephone. He's not actually her uncle, more like a family friend. He said he hadn't spoken to Marly in years and unless it was absolutely necessary, he didn't plan to come to Chicago. We had no reason to take it any further than that."

"Did you call him in California?" Lynne asked.

"I think we called and left a message. He called back later."

"Which means, he could have picked up that message and returned the call from anywhere, even here in Chicago."

"Could be," Harrison conceded. "Like I said, at the time, we didn't suspect him of anything."

Lynne turned back to the computer. "I think we're done. I'm going to go back to Beacon's machine and close up the files so we don't leave any clues we were there." She switched to Beacon's computer.

"Oh my god," Lynne screamed. "Oh no."

"What?"

"He's on the computer. He's online." Lynne was hysterical. "He must have just stepped away for a while. He knows we've linked into him. Oh my god."

"What's he doing?" Zack asked.

"He's looking at the all the files I've opened. He knows we're here. He can see everything we've learned."

"Oh shit," Zack said. "Does he know who we are?"

"No, he can't tell that, just like we couldn't tell who he was."

"So, all he knows is that someone is in his system?"

"Yeah, that's enough isn't it? I mean this guy's a murderer. I'm scared, Zack." She grabbed his arm instinctually seeking protection. Zack wrapped his arm around her providing what comfort he could.

"Me, too," was all he could add. He remembered that Beacon had tried to kill him not once, but twice. He felt himself sweating.

"That's it," Lynne stated.

"What's it?" Harrison asked.

"He just disconnected. He knew we were watching him through the net so he pulled the plug. He probably won't reconnect until he's ready to launch the cascade."

"Can't we trace him somehow?"

Zack turned to Harrison. "Nothing more than we talked about earlier. I suggest you call in your chits and get some folks in touch with a Registry Service and find the ISP he's using. Maybe we'll get lucky and they'll have a legit address and you can go get him—but I'd bet otherwise. I am going to do what I can to help Lynne figure out a way to stop that cascade program. Lynne, is there any way to know when Beacon reconnects?"

"Not that I know of," she answered. "All we can do is try connecting and see if he's online. Worse, if he's smart, he'll find that worm that we've been using and remove it from his system. If he does that, we're dead in the water."

"So, unless we're really lucky, he'll be able to reconnect and launch the cascade program, and we'll never know," he said.

"Not until the lights go out," she answered.

CHAPTER 27

▼

SUNDAY, OCTOBER 21, 2001: 6:00 PM

Someone, somehow, was operating his computer! Astounded, he kept his patience and watched the monitor as the intruder examined file after file. He realized the files were his "Black Beacon" notes. The hacker apparently knew what he or she wanted. K.P. could not let the surveillance continue, and immediately unplugged the Internet cable. Who could the hackers be? Did they know his plans? Hurriedly, he packed up and abandoned the cheesy apartment.

*　　　*　　　*　　　*

K.P. soon found a cheap motel room. He sat on the lumpy bed numbing his emotions with a tasteless burrito and Coke from a drive-thru window. Sure, he worried about the hacker, but other things had his attention. He wiped his eyes. Excitement and exhilaration didn't mix well with sadness. He'd passed up a lot to get to this point and he wanted that "zing," the satisfaction he expected to feel; had a right to feel. After all, he was about to win the super bowl. This time he would make a difference. This time the world would know. Zing! He would not let the hacker ruin this for him.

Marly had given him the means to change the world. Demonstrations were fine, but in the end, impotent. He'd invested thirty years traipsing from one protest to the next, each time hoping that someone of influence would recognize the righteousness of "the cause" and change the course of events. It never happened, of course.

Now, thanks to Marly's program, the world would take notice. More than that, the world would be changed, and for the better. Sure, there would be chaos at first. Every advance of civilization faced hurdles. The Roman army crushed their enemies before Rome installed a higher order of civilization. The American colonies fought a revolution to establish government by consent of the governed. Those advances were long, hard and bloody, but necessary. Yes, these changes would be chaotic, but no one would die from his hand. He wasn't some religious nut. He would cause no violence.

He had thought through the situation over and over, his logic sound. The rich capitalists have no incentive to correct their own excesses, to make the world better. Only if the foundation of capitalism crumbles, will progress be made. Didn't the very Declaration of Independence itself declare every human is born with unalienable rights, including "Life, Liberty and the pursuit of Happiness," and that "when any form of government becomes destructive of those ends, it is the Right of the People to alter or abolish it?"

He had the right—wrong—he had the *duty* to do exactly that; abolish capitalism. Certainly, no one could dispute that capitalism and government were intimately linked. Nor, could anyone dispute that capitalism had become destructive of the goals of life, liberty and pursuit of happiness. How could poverty-ridden people lay claim to those lofty goals, while from their very lives and labors, the rich get richer? No, he was right; he knew it.

This would be his big show, after thirty years. Hell, he'd do more for people than those weak sister labor unions or the pandering politicians ever did. The world would have to recognize him; credit him for his contribution. Zing!

But, the zing yielded to sadness. Damn it, he loved her; he really did. His eyes welled up and the flood of tears came again. She gave him the gift, then threatened to take it away. Somehow she'd uncovered his plans. It was almost as if she were watching him. He tried to explain, but she refused to understand. Goddamn it, why couldn't she see that the whole world would be better off?

"The cause" *had* to come first. She just didn't get it. The future of civilization depended on it. Just one opportunity, sometimes the world gets just one opportunity to advance.

He wiped his eyes with the soaked handkerchief. He'd had to do it—he knew that. Still, he cried that night. Pain ripped through his chest and tore at his heart. That fucking Zack, it had to be him. If it hadn't been for Zack, everything would have been OK. K.P. knew he could have convinced Marly; Zack deserved the blame, it was all his fault.

Well, K.P. had settled the score with Mr. Zack. After adding his "special" mushrooms to Dreyben's food, he watched and waited, and wasn't disappointed. The ambulance arrived within hours, just as expected. He applauded himself.

Zack had lucked out and survived the train platform, but K.P. knew his chances were nil of beating the stage three effects of the Amanita.

K.P. wondered why the police hadn't arrested Zack; the timing and the scene at Marly's should've led the cops to a quick decision. K.P. knew for certain he'd left no evidence; the latex gloves prevented prints.

In any case, he had made sure that Zack and that other woman would be out of the way long enough for him to launch the cascade. Zing!

CHAPTER 28

▼

CHICAGO, OCTOBER 23, 2001: 5:30 A.M.

Zack forced down the charcoal with a swallow of water, and spent a minute at the mirror checking his eyes and skin for any trace of yellow. A few quick exercises proved his balance and strength were OK. Conducting this mini-inspection convinced him his mental acuity remained intact. All stage three warning signs were negative.

He called Lynne. "Morning, you ready?"

"What time is it?" She asked through a yawn.

"About five-thirty. I'll pick you up in fifteen minutes."

"Give me twenty. I'm still in bed."

"Well, get out of whatever skimpy thing you sleep in, get dressed and meet me outside."

"OK. I'll brush my teeth, and get something to wear. And, why are you thinking about what I sleep in?"

"Oh, just a thought. Anyway, we need to get rolling. I'll get us some coffee. See ya' in twenty minutes."

Time was short. Beacon had to be stopped, and there were only two ways that could happen. Harrison might luck out and find a legitimate street address to match Beacon's IP address and arrest him, or Lynne could find a way to prevent the cascade program from working. Zack knew they were both long shots. Nevertheless, one of them had to succeed. The alternative was unthinkable. The panic caused by people hoarding food and water would result in vicious, citizen-against-citizen riots, and that would be only the beginning. A nationwide power blackout would destroy America's way of life. They had to stop Beacon. There simply was no next-best option.

They decided to work out of Zack's place. Only a few junior reporters were still camped there; the first team reassigned to cover a bigger story, the WTO meeting and the huge number of protestors.

As he drove to pick up Lynne, Zack glanced at the front page of the *Tribune* on the seat beside him. Chicago was thick with tension. The WTO conference had begun badly. The police established their concrete and chain-link barrier defining a no-access Red Zone, and the demonstrators immediately tested it. Governor Evan Devoncourt, expecting trouble, activated the National Guard. Round-the-clock news hawks were everywhere, searching for stories to fill airtime, the more sensational the better. An ominous feeling swept the city. And, for a city experienced in demonstrations and confrontations, the tension was unusual—a pot full of uneasy residents; vocal retailers; foreign security teams; anxious Guardsmen; overworked fire and police forces, and 100,000 potentially violent protestors.

With the area surrounding Navy Pier cordoned off, protest organizers used two city parks as assembly sites, Lincoln Park on the north and Grant Park on the south. Mayor Asa Bradigan ordered police restraint, but orders were easy to issue, results difficult to achieve. Pundits explained these same two sites were Richard J. Daley's undoing in 1968 when demonstrators proclaimed, "The whole world is watching. The whole world is watching."

Outside Lynne's apartment, Zack waited behind the wheel, index fingers tapping in rhythm, sipping his half-decaf. He rechecked his watch. Finally, Lynne appeared wearing jeans, a Cubbies sweatshirt and ball cap. His frustration faded as she jogged to the car.

"You're looking good," he said.

"Don't be sarcastic. I'm barely awake."

"No, I'm serious."

"Yeah, sure. Anyway, thanks." She pointed to the second cup. "This for me?"

"Yep, black with an extra shot of espresso," he answered.

"Hey, you remembered."

He pulled the "bimmer" out and headed to his place. "I bought some bagels, too. Help yourself."

"Thanks, I think I'll wait," she answered. "By the way, what are you going to be doing while I'm working on the cascade program?"

"Well, I'll help if I can; otherwise I provide the 'incentive' program."

She laughed, "What the hell is the 'incentive' program?"

"If you get tired, I get coffee. If you get tensed up, I provide the massage."

"All right."

"Seriously, I hope I can help. But, the first thing I'm going to do is check with Harrison and see how he's doing chasing down Beacon or Kevin, whatever we're calling him now."

"Will Harrison even be up yet?"

"He'd better be. This is no time to be screwing around. Either he grabs Beacon in time, or you find a way to stop the cascade. Regardless, we only have today and tomorrow."

Her face turned grim and her voice cracked, "Zack, what if we don't make it in time?"

"I don't even want to imagine that. In no time, cities will run out of food and water. Cold and hungry people will riot; lots of them could end up dead. Everything will stop working. It'll be the end of the American way of life. That's why right now, we have to think positively. And you have to focus on finding a way to stop that program."

Lynne's voice wavered as she whispered, "I know. I know."

Zack pulled into his space and parked. They walked with purpose past the few remaining reporters still assigned to the old news of Marly's death. Zack thought it ironic, how close they were to their biggest story ever. He hoped, they would never know.

Once inside, Zack told Lynne, "You go get started. I'm going to check with Harrison. If you need anything…"

Lynne stood at attention and saluted. "Aye, Aye, sir."

Zack stopped short. "OK, OK. Sorry about the orders. I'm just scared with all that's happening." Inside, he was more than scared, he was quaking. But, he knew they *had* to stop Beacon. If that meant applying pressure to Lynne and Harrison, then so be it. He would mend fences later.

Lynne put her hand on his arm. "I'm just having fun." A tense smile appeared on her face. "Believe me, I'm as worried as you are, probably more. It's my way of handling the stress. Don't get me wrong. I'm glad you're here with me. I don't know how good I would be if I didn't have you here. I mean that. OK?"

Hearing those words made Zack feel better. He covered her hand with his. "OK. And I promise not to be so uptight."

"Yeah, right. Like I believe that." This time the smile seemed a bit warmer.

Zack's eyes blinked as he turned to go call Harrison.

*   *   *   *

He tried to reach Harrison at the District, but the phone just kept ringing. He decided to try his cell phone.

"Harrison."

"Harrison, this is Zack Dreyben. I'm glad I got you. Lynne's still working on the cascade program. Any news on your end?"

"Some. I've had our computer guys working on that IP address. They had some luck coming up with the ISP that controls that domain. I think they said it's something like 'Personal-Selections-Internet.com.' It's a shoestring outfit out of Palo Alto. We're trying to find a human to talk to, but it's four in the morning out there. We're waking people up as we speak and we're going to stay on it, but don't expect anything for a couple of hours."

"Shit. We need to get to someone. What can we do to shake this faster?"

"Zack, we're running wide open. Oh, by the way, I've also clued in my FBI guy. He's gonna' get us help on the ground in California. I think we'll have a street address by ten our time. Then we'll see. I'll keep you in the loop. For what it's worth, we've got the attention of the FBI. They're on the horn to me as much as you are. They're not saying too much, but I think they're nervous."

"Good. It's about damn time. Call me back in an hour," Zack said as he hung up. He knew that having the FBI in the loop would help keep the pressure on Harrison. That much was good news.

Zack went to the kitchen. Snatching a couple of bottles of spring water, he walked to his home office to check on Lynne.

He found her hunched over printed pages, head down, the baseball cap turned backwards.

"Any luck?" he asked. He could almost see the tension in her.

"Not yet," she answered leaning back and stretching. "Marly certainly wrote tight code. You know it's been a while since I worked on the grid and I'm a little rusty. It's going to take some time."

"I know. I know," he said handing her one of the bottles. "By the way, how are you feeling? You don't have any signs of stage three do you?"

"Not yet. How about you?"

"Nope. Checked my eyes this morning, just their normal blue with a few streaks of red, but no yellow."

"I didn't think of that. Check mine?" she asked, standing up and facing him.

She moved toward him and tilted her head. He cautiously held first one eye open and then the other, checking for any discoloration. He could feel her warmth. The awareness, and bewilderment, returned. Lynne and Marly, one so exacting and buttoned-down, the other so unruffled. Marly's uptight, compartmentalized lifestyle included niches Zack never even knew about, while Lynne was open, relaxed, seemingly comfortable with herself.

Had Marly been compensating for something she'd missed early on? Zack glanced at the football photograph on the wall and wondered if he'd been doing the same. He worried; he'd been so close to Marly for three years and only now, after her death, he was gaining focus. Strange, in becoming closer to Lynne, he was beginning to see Marly—and himself. The guilty feeling washed over him again. Marly'd been murdered only days ago, but how does someone stop his thoughts, his feelings?

He forced himself to the present. "Just your basic red, white, and blue," he said reassuringly. "Are you taking the charcoal?"

"Yes Doctor," she answered.

"Good." He delayed a few extra seconds before stepping back. "What's your best estimate?"

"Zack, I just don't know. I'm working as fast as I can. Just get the hell out of here and let me concentrate. Check with me later, OK? If I come up with something before that, I'll call you. Now get the hell out of here and let me work."

Zack decided to catch the noon TV news. So far, the WTO demonstrations were generally non-violent, but the city remained on edge. The on-air reporters noted the conspicuous absence of the black-shirted radicals who were so prominent in Genoa and speculated on why the black shirts had not appeared. Other comments centered on tonight's scheduled protests. The news anchors predicted a huge demonstration for this evening, with the fear of increased hostility. Authorities warned of zero tolerance for violence. Thankfully, no one mentioned Beacon's Communiqué. There might still be time, Zack told himself.

He hadn't talked to Harrison since early this morning, and decided to call. Just as he reached for the phone, it rang with that wimpy musical ring. He hated that ring.

"Hello."

"Harrison here. It took longer than I thought, but we got an address."

"Great. Where?"

"Not so fast. It's not good news. The address turned out to be legit, that is, I mean, a real address. It's a small, low-rent apartment house on the near west side, the kind of place where tenants don't stay long. The problem is that our buddy Beacon is no longer there. I'm betting that when he found out you were on to him, he bolted."

"Fuck. I was afraid of that," Zack said.

"What do we do now?" Harrison asked.

"Why can't you guys find where he went? Isn't that what police do?"

"Easy Zack. We're trying. You climbing on me don't help none. Landlords in that neighborhood don't ask too many questions. But sometimes you can catch a break when you shake somebody."

"What does that mean?"

"Let's just say we ask in a persuasive way, OK?"

"OK. I got it. So what's the bottom line?" Zack asked.

"It's going to take some time. I know you don't want to hear that, but, damn it, it's the truth. I'm calling in favors all over the department. We'll come up with a lead, but you gotta have patience."

"Patience is not my strong suite. Call me when you have anything at all."

"OK. Will do. Has Lynne come up with anything yet?" Harrison asked.

"Not yet. She says she needs more time, too. I just hope something breaks before Beacon throws the switch. Once it starts, the game's over. Harrison, I'll tell you straight out. I'm scared shitless. If he lights up the grid, this whole country's fucked!"

"Zack, trust me. We'll get him," Harrison said confidently as he hung up. Zack hoped to God he was right.

*   *   *   *

Zack spent the next few hours examining their situation, struggling to come up with a new approach to stop Beacon. Nothing. Zack estimated that they had about twenty hours max, although it was anybody's guess when Beacon might start the program. Zack didn't want to think about the outcome anymore. He'd invested too much time imagining the unspeakable. His headache had returned. He found himself both wide-awake and exhausted, like a caffeine-high after an all-nighter.

Zack went to look in on Lynne. Maybe his imagination was working over-time, but she looked paler. "Thought I'd check with you. Anything new?"

She shook her head "no" without looking up.

"By the way I talked to Harrison. They found the street address, but Beacon's gone. Apparently grabbed his stuff and split."

"What? Oh no. Zack that's awful!" Lynne screamed. She stood up and turned around, fear stretched across her face.

"Why?"

She explained, "I've been working to see how I could modify the cascade program so that it wouldn't work once Beacon launched it, figuring I could find a chance to make the program changes."

"Yeah?" Zack asked, obviously missing the point.

"That means I have to use the worm, and that means he has to be on that same IP address. If he's moved, that IP address is guaranteed to change. Zack we're screwed."

Frustration added to fear and fatigue. She started to cry, first softly, then in torrents. She struggled to regain her composure only to succumb to a new wave of tears. Zack held her as she shook with swell after swell. She buried her head in his shoulder weeping uncontrollably until finally all the suppressed tension was released. She looked up at him, her face soaked with tears. Their eyes locked. A long moment passed. He slowly bent his head to hers and they kissed.

"I didn't want this," she pleaded.

He nodded. No words were needed. They held each other tightly, knowing that something had changed, something very fundamental.

The telephone rang breaking the moment. With his arm still around Lynne, Zack picked up the extension. "Hello."

"Harrison here. I've got good news and bad news. The bad news is that we still don't know where Beacon is hiding—a couple of leads but nothing solid yet. The good news is that we're going to have some more help from the FBI. I guess my old friend started to think about a nationwide blackout, and it scared him to death."

"What kind of help?" Zack asked.

"The FBI is going to issue an alert within the hour to the utilities and power transmission companies, plus all the state and municipal emergency action departments. It's apparently part of the new homeland defense program out of Washington."

"What will that do?"

"Good question. Maybe nothing. Maybe just raise more questions," Harrison said.

"What does the alert say?"

"I don't have the exact wording, but it's something to the effect that there's the possibility of an attack on the national power grid and they should be on alert for anything suspicious. They also talk about measures to protect the grid using the National Guard."

"Great. Ah, that's great. They don't get it, do they? They still think the only way to blow up the grid is to use explosives. Hell, Beacon's not going to try and bomb a transformer. He doesn't need to. The goddamn things are going to burn themselves up. About all that alert will do is cause panic."

"Maybe so."

"Well, one thing we do know."

"What's that?"

"It won't take long to find out."

CHAPTER 29

▼

CHICAGO, OCTOBER 24, 2001: 11:00 A.M.

They were out of time. The Closing Ceremonies, when they expected Beacon to launch the blackout program, were scheduled for just seven hours from now. Once he started the program, key transformers would short out across the country, followed by hundreds more as power surges rippled through the grid.

Zack observed Lynne as she pored over paper and PC, the weight of the moment evident on her hunched shoulders. In twenty-four hours she had taken only one break, ten-minutes—two hours ago. Exhausted, she continued pounding away, seemingly more determined to stop Beacon from executing the cascade.

He interrupted her thoughts. "How about some coffee? I've got some brewing, double strong."

Dazed, she turned, "Huh? Oh, OK. Sure. Thanks."

Zack watched with trepidation. She had passed dead-tired hours ago, but something else bothered him, her computer-fast mind running at three-quarters speed. He blamed fatigue, refusing to accept a more dire rationale. He went to the kitchen, poured a mug of the extra strong coffee, returned to the office and delivered it with a kiss on the cheek. She smiled and placed the cup on the desk securing it with both hands. Her eyes blinked and squinted.

If Lynne was unsuccessful, that left Harrison, the police, and the FBI, to locate and arrest Beacon before he pulled the switch. Zack believed Harrison when he said he'd called in favors all across the department, but that and a buck would get him another cup of coffee.

Surprisingly, Beacon had not yet sent his "Communiqué" to the press. Zack expected Beacon to send his statement to the media early, scoring the morning-news' headline. Zack smiled to himself, happily realizing Beacon didn't understand a damn thing about marketing. Perhaps, Beacon did not grasp that the cascade process would take time. According to Lynne, there was no way to predict exactly how long. Maybe Beacon's lack of knowledge of the grid had given them some time. Maybe they had a few more hours. Maybe.

Zack's head renewed its pounding and he felt more tired than ever. He also felt a little wobbly and chalked it up to weariness. He'd spent the night thinking of a new plan to catch Beacon, and he'd asked Harrison to join Lynne and him at the house. They had one last shot. They took their now familiar places at Zack's rustic kitchen table, Lynne to Zack's left, Harrison on his right. He asked Lynne her progress on the program.

"I do have some good news. I can disable the program if I can link into his computer," she said.

"But, he has to use that same IP address so that you can do that, right?" Zack asked.

"Yeah, and that's not likely." She paused for a moment, as if struggling to catch a thought. "Unless, that's his only access to the Internet. You know, that's not so crazy after all. He may just be waiting until the final minute to connect. If I can catch it just right, I still might be able to stop him."

"How will you know?" Harrison asked.

"That's just it. I won't. I'll just have to keep checking to see if he's logged in."

"OK. Keep at it. Good luck," Zack said. His eyes caught hers briefly, not long enough for Harrison to notice.

"While I'm waiting for him, I have one other brainstorm. It might be crazy, but I'm going to work on it," Lynne added.

"OK, good," Zack said and then turned to the Detective. "What's happening?"

"Nothing solid," Harrison sighed, his forearms resting on the table. "We pushed on our regular sources, but they're all locals and don't know anything about him. The FBI leaned on some of their leftwing wack-jobs, and either they don't know this Beacon guy, or they're not talking. But, they did say that if this guy is planning something big for the closing ceremonies, they thought he would want to be there."

"Exactly," Zack responded. "That's exactly what I was thinking. Lynne, let me ask you a techie question?"

"OK, what?"

"Is there any way that Beacon can launch that blackout program remotely? You know, wireless?"

Her fingers stroked her cheek the way they did when she was thinking. "He could probably use a PDA."

"What's a PDA?" Harrison asked.

"Personal Digital Assistant," Zack quickly replied. "It's a handheld computer people used to use only for their calendar and phone directory, but now they're more sophisticated with wireless connections to the Internet."

"He'd have to set it up, but it could work," Lynne added.

"Harrison, I have a hunch. I think the reason Beacon hasn't issued his 'Communiqué' is because he wants to wait. He wants to be there when the word goes out."

"Be where?" Harrison asked.

"Right in the middle of the biggest, ugliest demonstration. He hates the WTO. The protestors out there are his people. He thinks they'll all love him. He needs to feel that 'high' of acceptance."

Zack's marketing experience had taught him that people are motivated by different drivers. If you knew someone's button, you could motivate them to do anything. The writings had tipped Zack off. Beacon's "button" was acceptance. He had tried so hard to explain himself, to justify himself. Knowing Beacon would seek approval, and the fact that he was in Chicago at this time, meant he wanted to be the center of attention and that meant the WTO demonstration.

Harrison straightened. "If you're right, we might be able to pinch him before he starts the program," he replied, fresh enthusiasm evident in his voice.

"Exactly, but we have to move fast. Lynne, can you get us a copy of that picture of Beacon we saw before?"

"Yeah, no problem. Take me about two minutes," she said.

"Harrison, how long will it take to get that photograph to every cop and Guardsmen at the conference?"

"An hour, max. I'll drive the picture downtown myself."

"I have another idea. You and I are going to the protest site to find Beacon. We'll get the whole team looking for this nut case."

"Then, let's roll," Harrison said.

"Zack," Lynne interrupted. "Be careful. You look a little strange. Are you OK?"

"I'm a little tired," he answered and hugged her, the bony frame frail and unsteady in this arms. His anxiety grew. "More important, are you all right?"

Lynne smiled weakly and nodded yes.

Lynne went back to her computer to work on her brainstorm. Zack and Harrison headed for Navy Pier.

CHAPTER 30

▼

CHICAGO, OCTOBER 24, 2001: 5:00 P.M.

"I'll drive," Harrison said. "That way we can get through the vehicle access to the conference site." They fastened their belts and Harrison placed a flashing blue gumdrop on the Crown Vic's roof and cranked the engine. "Where exactly is this protest?"

Zack answered, "According to the morning news, it's right outside the Pier where lower Lake Shore Drive crosses Illinois Street. The reporters said there might be 100,000 demonstrators. If that number's even close, they'll completely block Lake Shore and fill Illinois for blocks. They plan to meet at Illinois Street and force their way into the Red Zone. Any word from City Hall?"

"From what I heard, they're doing their best to be non-confrontational and letting the demonstrators march, but they're cutting off access to the Pier area. Police and Guardsmen in riot gear are already deployed at the Red Zone. It's been pretty quiet 'til now, but today could get messy." Harrison rolled his eyes. "You know…I *cannot* figure out why the hell we pamper those bastards."

"Do the guys in charge know what we're facing?" Zack asked.

Harrison, steering with his left hand, grabbed his cell phone in his right and thumbed in a number from memory. He nodded to Zack and said, "I'll check with my FBI guy just to make sure."

Zack listened as Harrison talked with his FBI contact. "Felix, Rob Harrison here…OK, and you?…No, nothing yet and we're down to the short strokes. Hey, quick question. I just wanted to make sure you guys passed the word up the ladder about what we're facing here with this blackout thing?….NO? Why the fuck not?…Well, who's goddamn job is it, then?…For Christ's sake, forget the fucking protocol. Never mind. I'll goddamn do it." He slammed the phone down.

He reached for the police radio, and alerted the dispatcher. "10-17 Lake Shore Drive and Illinois. Listen up, short and sweet. Terrorist threat at WTO demonstration. Repeat. terrorist threat. Alert FBI conference security. Do it now!"

Harrison's face and neck blazed red. He turned to Zack. "Can you believe the dumb bastards never alerted the Conference security team? Shit, they issued a warning to the power companies. You'd think they'd have the sense to tell the conference honchos. Hell, the Feds own the security for this goddamn fiasco. Them and their fucking protocols. Not one of 'em has a set of balls."

Harrison pulled up to the access gate and showed his identification. The uniformed officers let him drive forward about fifty yards to a second gate. At this checkpoint, Harrison and Zack had to get out and be frisked. FBI security people in blue jackets approached the car, examined the trunk and using poles with mirrors, checked underneath. Harrison again provided his identification and explained Zack's presence to a young agent who would have none of it. The discussion became heated until a supervisor was called, and they were permitted to pass.

They decided the fastest way to find Beacon was to wade right into the crowd, so they left the car and walked the two blocks to Illinois Street. Hundreds, maybe thousands, of protestors from students to "suits" had already gathered in a colorful mélange of getups, many sporting blue-green dragons, red dripping blood, and other assorted tattoos. The scene looked like a Halloween party gone bad. Some wore masks hiding their faces from the closed circuit TV cameras installed to identify demonstrators for later prosecution. Others, more bold, marched and beat drums painted with vulgar epithets of globalization. They carried hand-painted signs condemning garment makers, oil companies, banks, governments, capitalism and a hundred more offenders. Overhead, police and TV helicopters with their chopping rotors and engine roar forced words to screams. The air cracked with tension.

Wearing street clothes, Zack and Harrison edged their way through the growing crowd, swimming upstream. Bad as that was, the uniformed cops were having a tougher time. The protestors detested the police presence, and although there were no physical confrontations, the pressure rose. Demonstrators called the policemen names, each time using a form of "fuck" as an adjective, flipped them off, and impeded their steps. They weren't about to let them pass easily. Still, pairs of cops knifed their way forward trying to match an older man's photograph with mostly younger faces.

Painstakingly, Zack studied each face. He forced himself to focus. Face after face pushed past him; none of them looked like Beacon. Zack started to feel light-headed and dizzy. They had to find Beacon, and soon.

People were moving everywhere. He turned to ask Harrison how he was doing. He had to shout to be heard, "Any luck?"

"No. We'll never find him this way," Harrison screamed. "I think we should split up. We'll double our chances of seeing him."

A demonstrator shoved past them. Zack lost his balance and fell hard to the pavement. Harrison rushed to him, "You OK?"

Zack ignored Harrison's outstretched hand as he struggled to stand. "Yeah, I'm OK," he said. "I'll start to the left. You go to the right. Remember, we're looking for a short, pudgy guy in his fifties. It should be easy to spot him; he's got to be the oldest guy here."

"Right," Harrison said. "Are you sure you're OK?"

"Yeah. No problem. Let's go. We got to find him," Zack said.

Harrison turned to his right and edged his way into the crowd, his left hand holding Beacon's picture, the other hand the police radio. Zack stumbled off to his left.

Lynne waited until Zack and Harrison left, then trudged to the medicine cabinet, and downed thick gulps of a pink liquid. She turned on the TV in Zack's home office, where folded over and nauseous, she watched the demonstration and worked frantically at the computer. Periodically, she tried to catch Beacon on-line hoping to disable the cascade program before he could launch it. But as often as she tried, she had no luck. Maybe Zack was right; Beacon planned to use a wireless device to launch the program from the demonstration.

She worried about Zack. The poison's stage three symptoms had started, and as brave as Zack tried to be, Lynne saw that he knew it, too. At the same time, she knew the upset stomach and shakiness were warnings of her own stage three problems.

How did she get here? Amazingly, only a few days ago, she'd described him as a lightweight, a 'simple marketing guy.'

She forced herself to work on her new idea, her brainstorm. Step by step, she walked through the logic, ordering her brain to focus, to concentrate. It might work. It'd take guts to try—she'd only get one chance. If she miscalculated, she would start the cascade herself, and destroy the power grid. Not a risk taker, did she dare take the gamble? Her judgment, hers alone. She had to be careful—more careful than anytime in her life. Her fingers flew across the keyboard. Maybe, just maybe.

Fear and anger gripped Zack, his guts squeezed like a python's prey. That bastard murdered Marly, poisoned Lynne and himself, and now was threatening the whole damn country. Face-by-face, Zack pushed through the demonstrators. He knew the Amanita's stage three symptoms had started, but this was no time to quit.

He continued his struggle through the crowd searching for Beacon. He thought about Lynne and how unsteady she felt when he hugged her. He'd tried to convince himself otherwise, but he knew. Using the cell phone's earpiece to hear above the noise, he called her. "How're you doing?"

"Zack, how are *you*?" she responded, her non-answer more telling than words.

"Do me a favor, OK?"

"What?" she answered.

"I should have said something before, but I didn't even want to believe it. You know, you've got stage three symptoms. You *have* to go to the hospital. Please don't wait. It's too risky. Remember what that doctor told me? 'Your life depends on it.'"

"Zack, think about it. Going to the hospital can't help me if Beacon cuts the power. The hospital will shut down as soon as their emergency generator's fuel is gone. The only way we'll get through this is to stop him."

"You're right. I know you're right, but I'm still damned worried." He stopped short of saying it. Not the time. Not the place.

"Zack, please be careful. Promise me you'll let the cops get him? He's tried twice. He'll try again. Promise me?"

"Sure," he promised. He hated himself.

"You're lying. *Please*, let the *cops* get him."

"I'll do what I can," he said, honestly. "I got to go. Bye." He ended the call abruptly. Maybe there'd be time for talk later.

His task grew impossible as thousands more streamed onto Illinois Street. Vitriolic leaders shouted into bullhorns, cranking up the fervor. Rhythmic chants of "No. No. WTO. No. No. WTO," echoed in the concrete canyon.

Sunset came just short of six o'clock. As daylight faded, streetlights and retail signs washed the crowd. High behind the barricades, blinding lights glared down and out toward the demonstrators. The highway repair stanchions, generator motors chugging away, gave police the advantage. The protestors faced the blazing lights while the troops below blended into shadows.

Anxious and disoriented, Zack stared at the amalgamated mass of people crammed into the street. The police barricades stood at his back, the crowd deepening in front of him. His frustration grew; he feared he'd never find the prick, his issues with Beacon now way past personal.

Gregory Johnson, the FBI's Special Agent in Charge, watched the surveillance screens in the Conference Control Center, banged his hand on the table, and screamed at the young agent. "Are you shitting me? Just now? Why wasn't I told before?"

Johnson couldn't believe that a terrorist threat had just come from a Chicago Police Dispatcher. Who? What? How? Where? How could he take action when he had no details? He turned to the young agent and commanded, "Find out where this came from. Make sure it's credible and get me some fucking details, goddamn it. Move!" Since 9/11 every terrorist threat was taken seriously, but the communications between agencies still sucked.

Johnson turned to the "playbook" containing the plans for every anticipated contingency. The correct response depended on the particular threat and that's the one thing he didn't know. All he knew was a Chicago police dispatcher received a radio call that a terrorist threat existed at the WTO demonstration.

He had to act now. The playbook was useless without a specific danger. He had no way to know how long it would take to verify the threat. Better to act, do something, than sit on his hands while some unknown disaster occurred. Quickly, he reviewed. From the limited information he'd received, the risk existed at the demonstration, not the conference venue. He put a preliminary plan in place. Until he had more information, he would follow this strategy. First, the delegates would be escorted from the venue using the most secure of the three exit options. Secondly, the protest site would be cleared; the demonstrators dispersed, using force if necessary. After one warning, the police and National Guard would move them out. Third, bomb squads and environmental specialists would move to the demonstration site and sweep the area.

He ordered an immediate announcement to the protestors to disperse immediately. No specifics to be provided. Perhaps, they could dupe the potential terrorists into believing their plans had been discovered and influence them to abort the threat.

He knew this wasn't the best plan, but right now, it was his only plan.

Harrison worried about Zack. He didn't look good, kind of sickly, and he fell hard when that demonstrator shoved past him. Harrison decided to check with him by phone. "Zack, you still there?"

"Yeah, I'm here, but this isn't working. I don't think I can spot him like this."

"Same thing," Harrison answered. "I need to get up higher to look over the crowd instead of being buried down here. I have an idea. Do you see the cherry picker with the TV camera in the corner by the barricade?"

"You mean the white truck?" Zack answered.

"Yeah. I'm going up in that thing," he barked.

Harrison "persuaded" the cameraman to lower the basket and took over the truck. He climbed into the bucket and was soon twenty feet up. He surveyed the crowd and found Zack struggling through the masses and waved to make contact.

From his perch he spotted a group of about 200, black-shirted, helmeted radicals carrying gas masks. He yelled into the phone, "Hey, off to your right, in front of the lights, are the guys that caused all hell to break loose in Genoa. They'll learn Chicago ain't no Genoa."

"A demonstrator got killed in Genoa," Zack screamed into the microphone hanging on the cord from his earpiece.

"His own goddamn fault. If he wasn't there, he wouldn't have gotten hurt."

With binoculars borrowed from the truck driver, Harrison searched the sea of faces. The crowd moved about making it difficult to know who had been checked. Some protestors wore bandanas; others carried signs hiding their faces behind them.

His radio screeched with activity as riot clad police and Guardsmen took their positions defending the chain link barricade. The crowd, urged on by bullhorn touting leaders, abandoned their rhythmic chant and began shouting anti-American and anti-globalization slogans.

The radical black-shirts charged the barricade, and the melee began. The police fired teargas into the crowd, scattering the demonstrators. One of the black-shirts wearing a gas mask picked up a canister and lobbed it back over to the police side. Some of the choking fumes reached "the basket." Harrison began coughing and his eyes watered.

His time had come! K.P. stumbled through the crowd, bumping into one protestor after another, a human pinball. His spirits soared. He wanted desperately to engage in conversation, and gloat and brag about his coming triumph, although he remained wary. Someone had hacked into his computer. But, he took comfort, assured that he was the only one who knew his plans.

Just in case, though, he had scouted out the area and devised an escape path. He planned to use the Chicago Pedway, an interconnected series of lower level walkways between Loop buildings. Populated with novelty shops and coffee stops, residents used the Pedway to avoid harsh weather and surface traffic. Although the twists and turns of the Pedway could be confusing, K.P. knew this underground walkway was the perfect emergency exit. The surface streets would be crammed with protestors thus making a quick getaway a problem. If anyone were after him, he'd abandon the demonstration and scramble the few blocks to the lower level of Columbus drive, where for protection, he would meet his two associates. Together they would disappear into the Pedway while searchers waded through the masses on the street level.

Again, he tested his handheld computer, and again, it responded perfectly. He congratulated himself on his genius—destroying capitalism from a protest against capitalism. The irony pleased him. There would be time for accolades later, when others recognized his achievement.

He noticed police pairing off, moving through the crowd. He'd been to countless demonstrations and never knew cops to directly flout the protestors that way. What were they up to? Uneasily, he watched one team of patrolmen knife through the mob. No way, it couldn't be. They couldn't know; he'd told no one. The pungent smell of marijuana floated from the twenty-somethings behind him. He relaxed. Of course, how typical, Chicago cops worried about weed. He remembered 1968.

Zack heard Harrison on the phone choking on the tear gas even before he smelled it himself. People in front of him began coughing and wheezing as the fumes floated their way. With his symptoms growing worse, he knew he had to stay away from the gas.

He screamed into the phone's microphone, "I can't take the gas. I'm going to move. I'll keep searching this side of the crowd."

Zack had never seen such a mass of bodies. The hunt for Beacon proved exhausting and he needed to conserve energy. He pressed to his left toward Lake Shore Drive putting him near the south edge of the crowd. Although farther away from the Pier, he could still see Harrison in the cherry picker. The bright stanchion lights previously behind him were now to his right.

Harrison began screaming. The vibrating earpiece nearly jumped out of Zack's ear. "I think I see him. Yeah, yeah, over there."

Zack strained to see Harrison frantically pointing in his direction. Zack scoured the faces around him but couldn't see Beacon. "Where? Where?"

"More to your left, away from me. He's wearing a plain brown jacket." Harrison's frustrated voice blared in his ear. Zack could hear him directing the other cops on his radio. "Get that bastard. He's over there. Get him."

From his perch, Harrison watched as the black-shirts charged the barricade a second time, this attack more violent, more organized. Gas-masked protestors led the group, prepared for more canisters. One black-shirt held a glass jar of amber liquid and a rag. He pulled a lighter from his pocket, ignited the rag and heaved the "cocktail" without looking. It sailed in Zack's direction.

Harrison screamed into his phone, "Zack watch out!"

A huge, orange fireball erupted on impact. One of the policemen near the flames began rolling on the pavement. Another cop fired a rubber bullet at the offender who fell back. Mob mentality took over.

Harrison watched for a moment, worried about Zack buried in that crowd. He turned back to lock in on Beacon, but couldn't find him. "Fuck, I've lost him. I lost him. All this crap…I fucking lost him. Damn it," he yelled.

The police teams chasing Beacon were also distracted. Worse, a riot had started. Unrulies smashed windows of expensive shops. Opportunists found looting more profitable than demonstrating. Cars on the street were torched. The scream of fire sirens added to the echoing din of megaphones, helicopters and howling demonstrators. Riot-clad police methodically advanced, loudly banging their batons on Plexiglas shields.

An announcement blared over the makeshift public address system. "This is an order from the FBI. Repeat, this is an order from the FBI. This demonstration has been declared illegal. Immediately disperse and leave the area. Repeat, you must immediately disperse and leave the area. This area will be cleared. This is your only warning. You must disperse and leave the area."

Many in the crowd never heard the announcement and those who did, weren't about to be dissuaded so easily. Harrison yelled into the phone for Zack, "I can't believe the dumb bastards are trying this. This crowd ain't going away just because the FBI says so. This'll just cause *more* trouble."

K.P. heard the glass breaking a few yards in front of him and turned to see the fireball erupt. Dumb-ass black-shirts! He faded back quickly knowing it would attract the attention of the police and National Guard. He felt safe as long as he remained anonymous, buried in the pack.

The cops swarmed the black-shirt who threw the Molotov cocktail, and K.P. watched as uncertainty swept the crowd. He knew through experience the sirens meant the fire department and probably more cops were on the way.

But then, he heard the announcement. The FBI was ordering everyone to disperse. No! No! Not now. Not yet! He was so close. Bastards were ruining everything. Shit!

What the hell happened? Did the FBI hack into his computer? How could they declare the protest illegal? Damn them and their orders, the fucking pigs. His mind flashed back to 1968.

Well, this time *he* had the answer. He pulled his PDA from the pocket of the plain brown jacket. He lingered, inspecting the situation. Cops and Guardsmen were everywhere. Soon *they* would be helpless.

He moved deliberately, savoring the experience. Proudly erect, he touched the stylus to the screen. It beeped its response. Done. But, instead of elation, he felt cheated. He deserved the credit, and he looked over the crowd. They didn't even know what he'd done for them.

Then, he saw him. The man in the cherry picker wildly waving his arms and pointing in his direction. A cop! Up in that basket, he had to be a cop.

Quickly, K.P. waved to his young associates knowing they knew what to do. He turned toward Columbus Drive, executing his emergency exit plan, confident he'd be long gone by the time anyone could push through the crowd to get him.

Finally, he spotted him again, the short, dumpy guy with thinning hair in a worn brown jacket. Losing track of Beacon had ripped at the Detective's heart. When the Molotov cocktail ignited, he'd looked away long enough to warn Zack—only a second, but long enough. Harrison pressed the talk button on his police radio. "Got him! I got him. He's by himself, same area, about ten yards farther away from the barricade."

Harrison yelled again over the phone to Zack as he waved and pointed. "He's still there, almost the same spot, just a few yards farther away. I knew we'd get him."

Harrison's elation proved short-lived. He watched Beacon retrieve something from his jacket pocket. Too soon, he realized it was a handheld computer. He saw Beacon look over the demonstration and then touch the screen with the stylus. Harrison knew he would never forget that smile, that bastard's arrogant smile.

He was still yelling and waving to Zack when he noticed Beacon staring back at him. Suddenly, Beacon put the little computer into his pocket, waved to somebody and ran into the crowd. Harrison tried to visually follow but Beacon managed to disappear into the mass of people amid all the confusion from the fireball and the police response. Gone.

Harrison felt helpless. He was sure Beacon had started the cascade. Harrison howled in Zack's ear what happened and heard Zack's terse response, "Oh fuck."

Harrison answered, "Zack, that's it. We'll get him, but *you've* got to go to the hospital. I'll call for help for you."

"Not yet. Not yet," was the answer. "I'm going to get him."

"I'll call you back in a minute." Harrison hung up the phone and began lowering the basket.

Before long, the streetlights flickered and dimmed. Flashy, neon signs faded to a dull glow. Protestors and police paused. A sinister air settled over the crowd. Only the generator powered lights on the stanchions remained bright, their broad beams shining over dark seas. Harrison wondered how it could happen so soon. Lynne said it would take time.

He'd seen almost everything, but he was never more scared. All hell would break loose, beyond anything he could imagine. Harrison's stomach churned, the acid raw in his throat. He called his wife to tell her he loved her. Then, he tried to call Zack.

No answer.

The black shirts' success in launching a riot made it doubly difficult for K.P. to make his emergency exit to Columbus Drive. He'd rehearsed his getaway days ago, but there were no crowds then. These multi-level streets were a maze at any time, but with 100,000 people, everything looked different.

The cops must have been looking for him. That pig in the cherry picker obviously recognized him, knew who he was. In a way, that felt good. Whoever hacked into his computer must be very smart. He'd been extra careful never to mention the WTO demonstration, but they were here just the same.

His escape plan called for him to meet his two associates and slip into the Pedway together. He felt safer that way. If anything happened, he'd let the youngsters deal with it. He'd be long gone.

They should have been here by now. Maybe they were lost—worse, maybe he was. Thankfully, he spotted them—one, white with spiked blonde hair, the other, black with a tight Afro. He jumped and yelled. Being short helped him hide in the crowd from the cops, but made it difficult to attract his friends' attention. Finally, they heard him and headed over.

"Hey dude, we got lost. It, like, looks all different," the spiked-blonde said. "We in the right place?"

"It doesn't matter," K.P. said, "let's get going. There's a Pedway sign right over there." K.P. was confident he could navigate the Pedway's twists and turns once he was in the corridor, but he wished he'd brought the map in any case.

They entered the building, part of the Illinois Center Complex, and followed the signs to the Pedway. K.P. began to relax; the plan was working.

The lights in the walkway flickered and dimmed. K.P. smiled. His two companions looked confused and uneasy.

He had never explained the whole plan to them. No need.

Zack remembered that spiked blonde hair from the "EL" platform, and his black friend as well. He decided to follow them. Nothing to lose. Harrison lost track of Beacon after he'd started the cascade, so this was the next best, and only, option. Maybe the punks would lead him to Beacon

He tagged behind them as they pushed through the protestors then headed away from the demonstration towards Columbus Drive. Strange? What would they be doing here in an area of high-rise offices, hotels, and condos? They looked confused and lost, stopping to check their bearings, pointing to different buildings.

Then, in an instant, he saw *him*, short, fat, thinning hair and wearing a plain brown jacket. The man faced away, and looked to be searching for someone. Zack quickly slipped behind one of the columns that supported the upper roadway and waited. He heard some yelling and saw the two lackeys waving to the older man and walking over to him. The man turned in Zack's direction. It *was* him, Black Beacon!

Adrenalin flooded Zack's system. His heart rate red-lined, fight winning over flight. Primal instincts demanded he charge over to him, pin him down and pummel him. He formed both hands into fists so tight the nails dug deep into the palms. He hated Beacon for the pain Marly must have felt, his own close call, and the deadly poison now threatening Lynne and himself. But, Zack could not let anger defeat him. Sanity challenged him to think. His goal had to be Beacon's capture.

Where were they headed? He had no choice but to pursue the trio as they led him into Illinois Center. So that's it, the Pedway. Smart. What better way to drop out of sight?

Down the stairs into the corridor, he remained twenty yards or so behind, the Pedway sufficiently busy that he was not obvious. But then, the lights began to dim and the corridor darkened. He had one last glance at Beacon, time enough to see that smug smile, that cocky smirk.

Emergency beacons popped on in the walkway like train lights in tunnels. Those unfamiliar with the walkway panicked and quickly found exits. Since he worked in the Loop, Zack often used the Pedway and felt comfortable finding his way. This section, he knew, was never connected to the main walkway on the other side of Michigan Avenue, resulting in unexpected dead ends in some corridors.

Zack stalked the trio as they made their way further into the maze; the corridor silent save the squeaky sneakers of the two lackeys. Beacon had a small flashlight he used to help navigate; seemingly he had thought of everything. Suddenly, Zack realized they had made an incredible mistake. Instead of heading in a direction that would let them safely exit at Randolph Street, they'd turned into a dead end hallway. They'd walked themselves into a trap!

Now what? He couldn't just let them turn around and walk past him and get away. No…he had to stop them, but how? Adrenalin had temporarily blunted his stage three symptoms, but he knew he lacked strength and endurance. No way he could physically stop three of them.

He had about *one* minute. Then, they would turn to face him.

He had them cornered. Without fresh air or ventilation fans, the deserted underground passage reminded Zack of an Egyptian tomb. His brain raced, a side benefit of the adrenaline. He approached behind them, close enough to hear.

"Shit," Beacon muttered. "This is a goddamn dead end. We got to turn around."

It took only seconds. Zack watched first confusion, then recognition, fire across his eyes. He glared at Zack. "You? What are *you* doing here?" Beacon challenged.

"You're here. Why else? Do you realize what you've done?" Zack had a plan. He had to keep Beacon talking.

"Yes," K.P. answered defiantly. "I've set the world on a course for freedom."

Zack's right hand crept into his pocket and palmed the cell phone. He hoped K.P. hadn't noticed the earpiece.

K.P. glanced at his two lackeys and proclaimed, "Based on the numbers, I don't see that *you're* going to do anything. Besides," he said, shining the flashlight in Zack's face, "with those yellow eyes, I'd say the Amanita has worked. Your liver's shot. You're down to your last couple hours."

Zack needed him to keep talking. His mind pictured the keypad as his thumb traced the buttons. This wouldn't be easy. If he could dial Harrison, and the connection held, he could keep talking, and clue Harrison in on their location. Long shot, but a shot.

Zack's brain pumped into overdrive. Recognition—Beacon's button was recognition. "You might get me, but nobody knows who the brains are behind this blackout. Someone else is going to take the credit. You've blown your chance."

Dial tone…beeps…ringing…"Harrison," the voice in the earpiece answered.

"By the way, why did you use the name Black Beacon? You ashamed of your real name? I remember Marly talking about you. You know she loved you?"

"Zack, is that you? Where are you? What's going on?" Harrison asked.

"Shut up," K.P. screamed. "If it hadn't been for you, I wouldn't have had to kill her. She'd be here helping us."

Zack could hear the urgency in Harrison's voice in his earpiece, "I get it Zack. I get it. Tell me where you are."

"Black Beacon, my ass," Zack said derisively. "If you don't get your story out, all this is for nothing. You know that don't you? We're standing down here in the Pedway and no one's the wiser. This is just one big disaster. No one has published your Communiqué. No one can understand your point and you can't explain it. Trust me, I know. Marketing's my game. I make a living making people believe."

"The world will know," K.P. stammered.

Zack spied the stores around him. "Yeah, sure. You ever eat at McDonald's like this one? Do you realize how much they spend to get their message out?"

"Zack, we got it. The Pedway McDonalds. We're on the way. Keep him talking," Harrison pleaded.

"I'm going to change the world. Your rules no longer apply. My way now," K.P. sputtered.

Zack felt nauseous and dizzy, a deadly combination of fatigue, adrenaline and Amanita. "Yeah, your way. People die because of your way." He felt his tongue getting thicker.

"I'm through talking to you. You're just one more capitalist pig." Beacon stepped forward and shoved Zack aside. "Amanita will take care of you."

Zack fell hard to the tile floor and looked up to see Beacon and the two youngsters step over him. The last thing he remembered was a swirling darkness.

C H A P T E R   31

▼

CHICAGO, NOVEMBER 7, 2001: 10:00 A.M.

The glare stung his eyes. A viscid, sticky coating fused to his eyelids making blinking difficult. He decided to turn his head, but his body did not respond as he expected—stiffer, slower, more awkward.

"Hey, he's awake. He's awake!" Lynne leaned against the bed rails and pushed the call button over and over. She hovered over him. "Zack, Zack, can you hear me?"

"Yahg," was all he could manage. His mouth and throat were parched and raspy. He tried unsuccessfully to swallow. "Where?"

She brushed her hand against his cheek. "Take it easy, OK? You're in the hospital. You scared the hell out of us."

"Hospital?" That explained the irritating plastic tube in his nose, but he had no memory of going to a hospital. He struggled to get oriented. He found himself in a narrow bed encased by rails, tethered to a complex of machines with wires and plastic hoses. Behind him, a metronome-like bleeping kept pace with a throbbing in his temple. "Why?"

"How much do you remember?" Lynne asked.

He was confused. "About?" His dry throat and a gluey tongue constrained his words.

"The demonstration. You followed Beacon. Remember?"

"A little. Water?"

By then the nurse had arrived. "Can he have some water?" Lynne asked.

"Yeah, a tiny bit. But take it easy. Remember he hasn't swallowed anything for a long time. It will take his system time to adjust."

"But the Doctor said that if Zack came out of the coma, he expected him to recover, right?"

The nurse nodded. "Just take it slow, that's all."

Lynne put a half full glass of water under Zack's chin and placed the end of a bent straw in the corner of his mouth. He sucked on it weakly. He dribbled more liquid than he swallowed. Even so, the tepid fluid soothed his throat and he wanted more.

"Easy, easy. Just a little at first," Lynne said.

By then the nurse was busy checking his blood pressure and his eyes. She seemed pleased as she scribbled something on the chart, smiled and said, "Things are looking up. I'll be back in a few minutes."

"Why?" Zack asked.

"Why are you here?" Lynne asked. "Well, because you lapsed into a coma from the poison after you cornered Beacon and his two thugs in the Pedway."

Slowly, things were starting to come back. "What happened?"

"Funny you should ask," she said with a broad, bright smile. She held up a two week old copy of the *Tribune* she had saved. The bold headline read:

Human Error Takes Lights Out
Blackout Spreads Across U.S.

"Water?" Zack asked.

"OK, just a little more." She placed the straw back into his mouth. He dribbled some more and she dabbed it away. "Here's the story. Beacon fired off the program and then disappeared. You followed him and confronted him, and kept him talking while you secretly clued Harrison in on your location. Do you remember, now?"

Zack nodded, but the headline still bothered him. He pointed to the newspaper.

"OK. I'm getting to that," she said.

"Why..."

She didn't wait for him to finish the question. "Why didn't the whole grid burn up? Because we outsmarted him, that's why."

Zack was more confused now. He wanted to sit up and hear what had happened. He reached for the bed control, but Lynne had anticipated his wish and was already raising it. She also fluffed the pillow under his head and adjusted his blanket, tucking it around him.

"How's that?" she asked. Without waiting, she continued. "OK, do you recall that I said I had a brainstorm that I wanted to try? Well, it worked. I'll give you the short version now, and I'll explain all the gory details later. I gambled that

Beacon never modified the cascade program, because he learned how to launch it exactly the way Marly set it up. He didn't want to take a chance that the program wouldn't function. If you remember, the way the cascade program works is by overloading key transformers until they fail, which in turn creates huge power surges that cause more transformers to fail and so on. Marly had pre-set the sequence. I had been trying to get into Beacon's computer to change the program so that it wouldn't work. Then, it dawned on me. All, I had to do is find out what sequence Marly had pre-set. I modified her program and used it to switch-out the second-level transformers downstream from those Marly had selected. With those transformers offline, they couldn't be overloaded and burn up. That stopped the cascade. I had to work fast though, because all four of the big grids were affected. Of course, switching off those big transformers caused huge blackouts and that's what the papers reported."

Zack was beginning to get the picture. "What about that 'Human Error' stuff?"

"That's something the FBI and the Homeland Defense guys cooked up in order to avoid a panic. They didn't want to publicize Beacon's scheme because of copycats. They're afraid others will try something similar. So, they concocted a story about a controller in a power plant in the Midwest. They made me swear not to talk to anyone except you and Harrison 'cause the two of you already knew."

"What happened after the blackout?"

"As far as the grid, nothing, at least nothing permanent. The power was interrupted for big chunks of the country but only for a short time. As soon as I was sure the threat was over, I reversed the switches and put the transformers back online. There were some outages caused by all that switching but the utilities had everyone back up before the end of the day. You know, when I think about it, I can't figure out why it took me so long. It was really a pretty simple solution."

Zack wasn't surprised it was Lynne who ultimately found the way to defeat Beacon. He had watched her labor over that keyboard, combining determination and expertise, hour after hour. He lay back against the pillow, reached for her hand and held it. He felt something he'd never experienced before, a deep connection he prized more than sex, or money, or job recognition—the values that had previously been his life's measures.

"How long have you been here?" he asked.

"You mean today?" she answered. "Only a few hours."

"Today?"

"Yeah, well, you've been out of it for almost two weeks."

"And, you've been here…?" He left the question hanging heavy for her response.

"I came every day praying you'd wake up," she answered, wiping her free hand across her eyes. "I was so worried."

He kissed her hand and held it tighter.

"The doctors said you had a fifty-fifty chance. I had to be here."

Abruptly, he remembered that Lynne also had stage three symptoms. "What about you? Your symptoms?"

"Bad, but not as bad as yours. The doctors think it's because I didn't eat as much of that spicy stuff with the mushrooms. Anyway, after I switched out the transformers, I'd done everything I could do, so I called 911 and they rushed me here. They kept me for a few days, but I'm OK now."

Zack was relieved, but then panicked. "What about Katie? Who's taking care of Katie?"

"Don't worry. Your neighbor Terry and I have been sharing doggy duties. Katie's fine, but she misses you, terribly."

"How much longer do I have to stay?" he asked.

"You'll have to ask the doctors that one. The good news is that you've got the best medical care anywhere. That's the reason for the fancy room."

Zack in his look around hadn't noticed that he was in a "single" and a nicely appointed one at that. "I don't get it?" he replied.

"When the FBI realized the service you had done by exposing Beacon, they couldn't tell the world about it, but they did push some buttons. Heck, you're getting the same treatment a congressman would get. Pretty decent, huh?"

"But you're the one who stopped him," Zack protested.

"Zack, I was just the techie. You were the General. If you hadn't forced Harrison and me to keep going, Lord knows where we'd be right now."

"Did I just hear my name in vain?" Rob Harrison said, sticking his head in the door. "I heard you were coming around. Good news travels fast."

"Hey," Zack said. "What's new in the cop business?"

"Well, I've got good news and bad news." A crafty smile appeared under the Detective's flat nose and half glasses.

"OK, OK. What's the good news?"

"The good news first, huh? OK, a secret grand jury is expected to indict Kevin Forsythe, a.k.a. Black Beacon, on one charge of first-degree murder, three counts of attempted murder and whatever terrorism offenses the FBI wants to pull together."

"And the bad news?" Zack asked.

"The bastard got away from us. We nailed his two butt boys, but unfortunately, they're no help. They're both dumber than paving stones. The FBI is hot after Beacon's ass, but so far nothing. What's got the Feds spooked, is how Beacon kind of floated in under the radar. They've been zooming around the country chasing down Middle Eastern types and along comes this asshole, a plain ol' American nut. I have a shitty feeling we haven't seen the end of that son of a bitch."

"I hope you guys get him. Hell, pull in some of those favors," he teased Harrison.

"Wait, there's more good news," Harrison smiled.

"What?"

"The Zack Dreyben case file is officially closed." Harrison's smile widened. "To mark this occasion I have something for you." He reached into a plastic bag and pulled out a red logo cap. "This is an Ohio State Coach's Cap. It's legit, the real deal, direct from Columbus. You da' man!"

Message received, Zack nodded in Harrison's direction. Neither man had more to say.

Lynne shook Harrison's hand, then hugged him. She turned back to Zack. "I think you need some incentive to get back on your feet," and leaned over the bed and kissed him sensuously. "Maybe that will do it."

"Yeah, well, that will do it!" he responded, still holding her hand. "Actually, all I want is life back to normal. I've had enough. Hey, like I said, I'm just a simple marketing guy."

0-595-29953-9